AS DEAD
as it gets

AS DEAD
as it gets

A BAD GIRLS
DON'T DIE NOVEL

....

katie alender

HYPERION
NEW YORK

For my parents

Text copyright © 2012 by Katie Alender

Printed in the United States of America

First Hyperion paperback edition, 2013

10 9 8 7 6 5 4 3 2

V475-2873-0-13189

Designed by Marci Senders

ISBN 978-1-4231-3778-8
Library of Congress Control Number for Hardcover Edition: 2011039240

Visit www.un-requiredreading.com

SUSTAINABLE FORESTRY INITIATIVE
Certified Chain of Custody
Promoting Sustainable Forestry
www.sfiprogram.org
SFI-01054
The SFI label applies to the text stock

Acknowledgments

Thank you to my husband, who inspires, supports, and challenges me.

Thank you to Matthew Elblonk, who gets right to the edge of "I told you so" but doesn't ever say it, and the rest of the excellent folks at DeFiore and Company.

Thank you to Abby Ranger, Stephanie Lurie, Laura Schreiber, Hallie Patterson, Marci Senders, Ann Dye, Dina Sherman, and all of the wonderful people doing their collective thing at Hyperion, for your constant and much-appreciated support.

Thank you to my whole entire ginormous family; I love you dearly (all nine hundred of you).

Thank you to my friends, who are like a second ginormous family; I love you guys, too (but I'll mostly only say so behind your backs).

And thank you, thank you, thank you to the people who have made it possible for me to continue to follow and live this dream: readers, bloggers, fellow authors, librarians, teachers, booksellers, fans and followers, and parents who teach their children to love reading.

I literally couldn't do it without you . . . and I mean the real kind of literally, not the fake kind.

THE BAD NEWS IS, ghosts are everywhere.

They're in your kitchen, your garage, your school cafeteria. They sit dumbly through your pool parties and your fights with parents and make-out sessions with your boyfriend. They hover in the background while you watch scary movies with your friends. You scream when the bad guy in the mask jumps out, but all the while, two feet away from you, a horrible spirit is breathing ectoplasm down your neck.

The good news—for you—is that you'll never know it.

Even if you're careless enough to tempt them with your stupid games, spinning around in a dark bathroom, chanting the name of a ghost who would just love to show up and rip your head off your body—and I mean literally pop that nice, round cantaloupe head right off your skinny neck—you'll probably never, in your entire life, so much as see a ghost.

But I do.

I see them all the time.

The first one I ever saw was at a funeral—appropriate, right? Funerals aren't exactly awesome to begin with. But they get way less fun when the ghost of the dead girl decides to show up and try to knock you into her open grave. This makes everyone at the funeral think you're crazy, on top of the fact that they all secretly suspect you're the one who killed her in the first place.

You spend a day or two wondering if you really saw what you think you saw, and you suspect that the people who think you're crazy might actually be on to something. Then you start noticing things—*weird* things that seem to appear and disappear in your peripheral vision—odd, smudgy shapes. Gradually, you realize the weird things are only in photos and on TV, and one day you wake up and realize the shapes and smudges have form, and they're not just shapes and smudges—

They're dead people.

At this point, you pretty much know you're crazy.

That's how it happened for me, anyway.

For instance, in a snapshot that used to hang over my desk, among the "say cheese" grinning faces is also an old dead woman with oozing sores on her face. Living in the local TV news studio is a man with a railway spike through his chest. And in most of the photographed step-by-step lab instructions in my science book, there's a pair of petite twin girls with sunken cheeks and hollow-looking eyes, who always have their arms wrapped around each other's waists. The ghosts in the images are just like regular people—perfectly still, unmoving, caught in a fraction of a moment of their undead lives.

Have you ever tried to go a day without looking at a photograph or seeing a television? My whole existence has become one extraordinarily un-fun game of spot-the-spirits. But school portraits, the latest issue of *Cosmo*, the evening news—those don't mean a thing. Because at the end of the day, the pictures I *really* care about are the ones I take with my own camera.

Since I was twelve years old, photography has been like a part of me—the best part. When everything else in my life was going wrong, I could retreat into my own little universe and see the world as I wanted to see it.

And now I don't even want to go near my camera. I don't want to look at my photos.

Because they're full of dead people.

So here I am. Life spectacularly in ruins, but nowhere to run. No place to hide. From the stares, the whispers, the suspicion . . . the ghosts . . . and worst of all . . .

From my own thoughts.

2

JARED MOVED LIKE A HUNTER, light on his feet—branches and leaves barely crackled beneath him. And he was always looking, listening, waiting for the right moment to soundlessly lift his camera and shoot.

Watching him work was like a tiny window into my old life.

"So I said, yes, I'd be glad to respect a substitute teacher, providing she had at least a *partial* understanding of the scientific method. And then—" His gaze traveled up over my head. He raised his camera and flashed off a quick sequence of photos as a shadow swept over the trail.

A moment later, he turned the camera to show me the viewfinder. "An owl. What's it doing out during the day? Something must have disturbed its nest."

My basic rule is: I don't look at pictures if I don't have to. But I figured it was a safe enough bet that there weren't any ghosts hovering above us in midair, so I took the bait and scrolled through Jared's images. They were perfect: the owl's belly was striped in vivid black-and-white lines, and its wings were outstretched, the feathers at their edges spread like fingers.

"I love these," I said.

I realized I was still holding on to the camera, and therefore still holding on to Jared, who had the strap looped around his neck. He didn't seem to mind being so close, but I gently handed him the camera and took a step back.

He gave me a quick smile. I turned away.

It was a blindingly bleak day. The sky was thick with clouds, and the weekend's cold snap had scared off the nature preserve's usual contingent of casual hikers. We'd been following the trail for an hour and passed only two joggers. It was the second day of winter, and the high that day hovered under forty degrees. I was bundled up three layers deep, but Jared just wore a thin jacket over his usual hipster-chic uniform: jeans and a flannel shirt with polished brown shoes.

"Did you get in trouble?" I asked.

He blinked, not remembering what we'd been talking about. "Oh . . . I got sent to the headmaster's office."

"That sucks."

"Nah." He shrugged. "Father Lopez gets it. He just told me to be nice."

I was only half listening. I was still thinking about

the owl—the way its wings cut into the gray winter sky. The way you could see its knobby feet tucked up against its body. Cold, miserable envy consumed me.

You might wonder why a person who's afraid to even look at a photograph would go out specifically to take them. But my afternoons with Jared weren't really about pictures. They were about hanging out with someone who knew me—but not *too* well. Who was interested in me—but not *too* interested. He was kind of the only person I could bear to be around. Besides, he was the only non–blood relative who ever asked me to do anything.

Even if I didn't want to take photos, I still needed the air and the distance from my suffocating home and my suffocating (though well-meaning) family. I always brought my camera, because I was afraid that if I didn't, Jared would think I was weird and stop inviting me to go with him. So it was basically a prop. My entrance fee. I rarely took pictures, but I got pretty good at faking it—taking just enough to avoid suspicion.

But thinking about the swooping arc of the owl's flight made me reckless. I raised the camera to my eye, and Jared fell silent and wandered away, as if he knew this was something I needed to do by myself.

First, I aimed my lens at the sky, toward the spindly, bald branches of the trees. I liked how they seemed to grow from the bottom of the frame like blades of grass.

I lowered the shot slightly and took another exposure. Then I let it fall a little lower and took another. I kept checking for the first hint of a ghost, but there was nothing. Relief washed over me, and I fell into a rhythm as natural to me as breathing—*click*, move, *click*, move. Jared was a few feet away, and we were like two dancers onstage—always aware of each other, but focused on our own work first.

Gradually, I forgot to worry about ghosts.

Then, as we rounded a bend in the trail, I scrolled back through the frames and glanced down at the display screen.

There was a person in my photos.

It took my brain a moment to catch up and process the sight of him: a little boy in a faded winter jacket, dark blond hair combed neatly across his forehead. He couldn't have been more than three or four years old. The knees of his light brown pants were muddy, like he'd fallen. He was looking off the path into the distance.

In the next picture, he stared at the lens through angelically big blue eyes, like a young Carter Blume—who was kind of the last person on the planet I needed to be thinking about at that moment.

In the third photo, he was gone.

"Um . . ." I said, suddenly feeling totally off balance,

like one of my legs had shrunk six inches. I glanced at Jared to see if he'd noticed anything, but he was honing in on the gnarled trunk of an old tree.

I looked around again—and heard the sound of rustling leaves in the distance.

I can't *hear* the ghosts I see in pictures. I can only see them. So if I'd heard the boy walking—could he have been real? He certainly looked like a real boy. No oozing anything or deathly gray skin. Nothing seemed to be wrong with him—except that he was out in the wilderness all by himself.

"What's up?" Jared asked.

"I—I think I might have seen someone," I said. "A little kid."

Jared's eyebrows went up. "Out here? Alone?"

"Maybe." I gazed doubtfully down the path. "Do you think we should look for him?"

"Of course," he said, capping his lens and letting the camera hang around his neck. "Let's go."

I tried not to notice the sensation of his hand pressing gently on my lower back as we walked.

Jared and I had met when we were finalists in a photography competition back in September. Even after a few months of hanging out two or three times a week, we'd never come close to having any kind of romantic episode. The couple of times he'd dropped a hint, I'd replied with a carefully clueless response. And things never went further than that.

Which, honestly, was just the way I liked it. A rebound relationship was out of the question. Just the thought of being close to anyone but Carter made my whole body go numb.

We rounded a corner. Still no sign of the boy. My heart sank at the prospect of yet another crushing paranormal smackdown. If I'd been alone, I would have stopped.

But Jared was hurrying now, urging me along. "It's too cold for a little kid to be outside."

We walked so fast that I began to get hot under all of my layers, and my worn old thrift-store satchel-slash-purse banged against my side painfully. Jared kept searching the distance, as if the boy would pop into view at any moment. His unquestioning belief half convinced me that it had been a real live child I'd seen, not some ghostly apparition.

Call me foolish, but I felt like if I wanted it bad enough, he really would appear on the trail ahead of us.

Only he never did.

"Wait." I slowed down. "I think maybe I didn't see what I thought I saw."

Jared turned to me, his face flushed pink from exertion. "What does that mean? You *imagined* seeing a little kid?"

I shrugged. "Maybe it was a shadow."

"But I'm sure I heard something ahead. Didn't you?" He stood still. "Listen—there it is again."

And sure enough, I heard snapping twigs.

A surge of hope traveled through my chest. "Okay," I said.

But as we went around the next curve, we stopped.

Ahead on the path was an opossum. It saw us and scurried noisily away into the brush.

"Oh," Jared said.

Before he could say more, I lifted my camera and took two pictures. As I looked down at the readout, all the muscles in my body tensed.

There he was. Five feet away, staring up at us.

The little boy.

So he *was* a ghost.

Of course he was.

I veered to the outside edge of the path, well clear of the ghost, then swung around and clicked off a few more exposures. As I looked at them, the breath caught in my throat.

The back of the boy's head was caved in.

What did you expect?

"Alexis? Are you all right?" Jared stood on the other side of the boy. Then he walked straight forward, right through him.

I stiffened.

Jared pulled his jacket around himself tightly. "I just got cold. Did you feel that breeze?"

That's what happens when you pass through a ghost. I nodded and hugged myself, even though I was still sweaty after rushing up the trail.

"The sun's going down, I guess," he said.

I didn't want to stick around and talk about the weather. The only thing worse than seeing dead people in photos is *them* seeing *me* and getting in my face. I grabbed Jared's arm and pulled him along with me, away from the little boy.

After a hundred yards or so, I stopped and stuck my shaking hands into my pockets. "I was wrong," I whispered. "I'm sorry. I didn't mean to interrupt you when you were working."

"There's no need to apologize." Jared's voice was soft and urgent. "Alexis . . . I'm worried about you."

I was embarrassed and miserable and still freaked out by the sight of the boy's caved-in head. "I don't know—I'm sorry—"

Jared stood right in front of me, his brown eyes as gentle as a deer's, and put his hands on my shoulders. "It's okay. Calm down. It's okay."

Without meaning to, I burst into tears.

Ugh.

I never would have done this before, not in a million years—cried like a maniac in a public place, especially in front of someone else. It was as though, along with losing control over my pictures, I'd lost control over myself.

Jared pulled me close, let me rest my head against his shoulder, and stroked my hair with his cold, gloveless hands.

"Cry if you need to," he said. "It's all right."

A second later, I swallowed hard and backed away.

Jared's fingers remained lightly on my upper back. "Were you thinking about Lydia?"

He knew I'd been there when a girl from my school had died. And he knew that my whole life had changed because of that day. He assumed, as did the rest of the world—including my parents, sister, and guidance counselors—that all of my issues stemmed from the trauma of witnessing Lydia's death.

And, yeah, okay, I'm sure a lot of them did. But it went so much deeper than that.

You know that saying *Pride comes before a fall*? Well, for me, it wasn't just pride. It was . . . happiness. Security. Comfort. Contentment. I'd been so positive I knew what I was doing. How can you be that confident and still be wrong? And then, once you've realized how horribly wrong you were . . . how can you ever be confident again?

The fact is, you can't. You just spend your whole life waiting for the next piano to fall out of the sky and smash you.

"You lost someone." There was a gruff intimacy in Jared's voice. He brushed the hair away from my eyes. "And that hurts. A lot. But it's okay. You're going to be okay."

I sniffled and nodded, then looked up into his endlessly deep eyes. It was as if there were ten layers of Jared behind the one he showed the world. When he gazed at me like this, it was like a few of the layers had been peeled back, revealing some hidden, tender thing.

He seemed to be holding his breath. He tucked my hair behind my ear . . . and then his fingers continued along my jawline, lightly lifting my chin.

There was a sudden heaviness in the air between us—that moment where things get fuzzy and the universe takes over.

Then we were kissing.

It was unlike any kiss I'd ever experienced. When Carter and I were a couple, it was all about the happy. Kissing was an extension of that, a celebration. A little party between us, amplifying our naive joy, our faith that the world was delighted to give us just what we wanted.

Between Jared and me, I felt a different kind of

amplification, an ache inside my chest. It was like a fight for survival—two people coming together because they need to be touching to keep from fading out of existence. It was as if we were trading sad secrets. . . .

And I *totally* didn't want it to stop.

Then I realized what I was doing and jerked out of the kiss, holding my hands up like a robbery victim.

"My *God*." Jared jumped back and stared at me, horrified. "Alexis, I'm *so sorry*. I didn't mean to—I mean, you were sad, and I—I shouldn't have. . . ."

I took a dizzy step away, unable to tear my eyes away from his. Should I tell him not to blame himself? Could I do that without somehow implying that the kiss was a good thing?

All right, yeah, it was *good*—but that didn't make it a good *thing*.

"I should go," I managed to say. "We've been gone for a long time. My parents will worry."

He was watching me, still in shock. Then he collected himself. "Of course," he said, straightening his already-straight jacket. And just like that, the moment was gone.

To my utter surprise, I felt a pang of regret.

I mean, it wasn't like I hadn't kissed back.

The gray afternoon sky was sliding headlong into a purple twilight. The low sun shone through a tangle of bare branches in a spot of brilliant white. For the first time all day, Jared looked cold. And tired.

And lonesome.

"Come on," I said, reaching out to untwist his camera strap. "You're going to freeze to death out here."

His mouth quirked up in an almost-smile. His dark brown hair—as long as the Sacred Heart Academy dress code would let him wear it—hung down over his forehead. His cheekbones were chiseled, as if he'd been sculpted from marble. He looked like an aristocrat. And his lips had a slight natural downturn, which made his smiles feel like something you had to earn.

"You're right," he said. "It's getting late."

We walked in silence, eventually reaching the thick wood stumps that marked the edge of the parking lot, which held only three cars—his Jeep, my mom's gray sedan (which I'd borrowed), and a little blue hatchback.

Near the blue car, in the dim light, I saw a small scuffle, and then a girl cried out, "No, Spike, come back! Sit! Stay!"

A little black dog came tearing across the parking lot toward us, dragging its leash behind it.

"Please stop him!" the girl called.

In one motion, Jared whipped the camera off his neck and handed it to me. Then he took off after the dog.

The girl came up to me, huffing and puffing. I

recognized her right away—it was Kendra Charnow, a girl I knew from school. As soon as she saw me, she came to an awkward stop. "Alexis!?" she said. "Um—which way did they go?"

I pointed back down the path, and we both started running. But just around the bend, we found Jared, leading the dog by its leash.

"Thank you!" Kendra scooped the dog off the ground and kissed its tiny snout. "He's a rescue, and they told us he was a runner, but I didn't know . . ."

Then she got a good look at Jared.

Not being his girlfriend, I could watch her behavior objectively, like a scientist taking notes in the field. And it was always the same when girls noticed him.

Kendra's shoulders went back, her stomach magically sucked itself in, and she fluffed the red ponytail sticking out from underneath her beige baseball cap. Then she tilted her head in that *See how cute I am?* way.

"I don't think we've met," she said to Jared. "I'm—"

"Glad to help with your dog," Jared said. "I'm really sorry, we'd better get going. It must be close to freezing by now."

Maybe it was the pull of my old Sunshine Club etiquette instincts, but I felt obligated to introduce them. "Jared, this is Kendra. She goes to Surrey."

Kendra gave him a smooth smile. "I'm a friend of Alexis's sister."

Right. Not a friend of mine.

"Nice to meet you, Kendra," Jared said, putting his hand on my elbow almost protectively. "Have a good night."

"Good night," she said.

And that was that. Jared walked me to the door of my mother's car and waited while I seat-belted my camera into the passenger seat.

I looked up at him, struck slightly dumb by the way the pale gold light of the sunset lit up one side of his face like a Renaissance painting, touching off the edges of his hair with a thin halo of fire. And then, on the shadow side, his skin was as cool blue and smooth as ice.

He looked like a half-man, half-god.

And he wouldn't even blink at another girl.

What was *wrong* with me?

"Take a picture," he said, a smile spreading slowly across his lips. "It'll last longer."

I smiled back. That had been one of the first things I'd ever said to him.

If I were a girl who knew what she wanted—a girl who knew the difference between what she could have and what she couldn't have—a girl who was able to let go of the past and move on—I would get out of the car, grab Jared, and smother him with kisses.

But I'm not that girl.

"'Night," I said. *You will make someone so insanely happy,* I thought.

He smiled. "'Night. Call me when you have some time."

"I will," I said.

And I would. Next time I was lonely, or feeling sorry for myself, or just needed to look at a face besides my mother's, father's, or sister's, I would call him—and he would come.

As I texted Mom to tell her I was on my way home, I kept an eye on Jared climbing into his Jeep.

SEE YOU SOON <3 U, Mom replied.

I dropped my phone into the cup holder and switched on the radio, watching Jared turn left on to the quiet highway and disappear down the narrow strip of road.

Something is seriously the matter with you, Alexis.

I'm not a complete idiot. I know I'm not special enough to play hard-to-get and hold the attention of someone like him for any amount of time under normal circumstances. Jared had his own baggage. It wasn't just me who needed him—he needed me, too.

He'd never said what it was that haunted him, but I suspected it might have had something to do with the fact that he and his father lived alone. He'd never so much as mentioned his mother—and of course I didn't ask for an explanation. The whole basis of our friendship was that we didn't press the subject—*any* subject.

We were like a pair of travelers who wandered together because it was an infinitesimal bit easier than wandering alone.

Pearl-size drops of rain began to splash against the windshield, so I flicked on the wipers and made sure the headlights were shining. The road was empty in both directions, but I used my right-turn signal anyway, just in case Mom had spies out in the middle of nowhere.

The public-radio announcer droned on in a comfortingly bland voice about last-minute gift buying.

I put my foot on the gas, and just as I started to apply pressure—

The radio cut out.

There was a split second of silence; then a roar of static filled the car. It was so loud it seemed to be coming from inside my head, vibrating through my body like a scream. I took my hand off the wheel to smack the power button. But the sound didn't go away.

My ears hurt all the way down to the corners of my jaw.

While I was focused on the radio, the car lurched violently to the left and went into a spin.

I tried to remember what I'd been told about spinning out of control—don't slam the brake, right? Steer in the direction you want to go?

But what if the direction I wanted to go was *behind* me?

A bright white light flooded the car, like the headlights of a semi bearing down from fifteen feet away.

I braced for impact. The seconds seemed to stretch endlessly. . . .

But the impact never came.

When one too many beats had passed, I glanced to my right and saw, as fast as a subliminal message flashing on a screen, a figure sitting in the front seat next to me: a girl—though it was too bright for me to see anything but her outline. As soon as I started to comprehend what I was seeing, she blinked away.

And the white light—what I had thought was headlights—blinked away with her.

After a millisecond of shock, I turned my attention to my spinning car.

The steering wheel was stuck, canted hard to the left. Hitting the brake didn't help. The tires slid across the wet asphalt. A burning-rubber smell filled the air.

In a final effort, I grabbed the parking brake and yanked on it with all my strength. The engine roared in protest, and the car skidded off the road, jolting over the deep grass on the shoulder.

I tried slamming on the brake again.

This time it worked. The tires straightened out, and the car bumped to a stop about five feet from a drainage canal.

The static from the radio died with a jagged shriek.

I put the car in park, then collapsed forward and rested my head on the steering wheel, trying to catch my breath.

Anyone else would have thought there was something wrong with the car—but I knew better. Because when I looked down at the passenger seat, I saw, resting on the upholstery . . .

A single yellow rose.

Just like the ones at Lydia Small's funeral.

3

I DIDN'T KILL LYDIA.

Yes, I was there when she died, but that's totally not the same thing.

Just try telling *her* that.

She clearly blamed me, and she showed up every couple of weeks to make sure I knew it. Up to now, she'd just been annoying—taunting me, threatening to hurt me . . . which might have been scary if she hadn't been such an obviously weak ghost. The most she'd been able to do was knock a textbook off my desk in class, after twenty minutes of trying.

But this—an actual attempt on my life—was new.

And it pissed me off.

I unfastened my seat belt and threw the door open, launching myself out into the rain. "Nice, Lydia!" I said, turning in a circle. "Trying to kill me? I guess you're going to have to try harder next time!"

Cold rivulets of water streamed down my face. And I

realized I was crying again, which just made me angrier. I wanted to kick something. So I kicked at the wet grass and almost lost my balance.

Perfect—to slide down the bank and land in the canal would have been the absolute icing on this ghastly cake of a day.

"Come on!" I yelled. "If you want me, I'm right here! *Come and freaking get me, Lydia!*"

I was on high alert, adrenaline pumping, ready for a fight. How a ghost and a human could fight, I don't know. I guess I figured the force of my fury alone might bruise her a little.

I waited for her to show up, in all her ghostly glory, as she usually did—barely five feet tall, with long, straight black hair, wearing the clothes she died in: a torn, bloodstained, red cocktail dress and no shoes. Determined to wreck my day—if not my entire life. Slightly see-through and eternally whiny.

But she didn't come. And as my adrenaline high faded to a post-adrenaline low, I began to feel not only sort of sheepish and humiliated, but also very cold and wet.

Adding to the splendor of the scene, Kendra had pulled her car up and rolled down her window. She looked more inconvenienced than concerned. "Alexis? Um . . . are you okay?"

Had she heard me yelling Lydia's name?

"Yeah," I said. "There was just . . . a squirrel crossing the road."

Her eyes went wide. "Did you hit it?"

I could hear the whispers already: *Alexis Warren ran over a squirrel—on purpose!* "The squirrel is fine," I said. "Thanks, though."

I waved her off and got back in the car, shaking with anger and a fresh dose of mortification. As I was putting my seat belt back on, my phone rang, startling me.

It was Jared. "Hey. I forgot to wish you a Merry Christmas."

"Oh, yeah," I said. "Merry Christmas."

"All right, well . . . be careful. The roads are kind of slick."

So I noticed. "I will, thanks. You, too."

Then we hung up.

Feeling even emptier than before, I did a three-point turn and headed home.

Lydia appeared as I was making the left into Silver Sage Acres, the master-planned community of town houses where my family moved after our old house burned down. (Two murderous ghosts ago—old news.)

She faded into view in the passenger seat, her filthy, bloody ghost feet resting on the dashboard. "Come and get me?" she asked. "Is that some kind of joke?"

Seeing ghosts in pictures? Totally my fault, and I'm the first person to admit it. (Never to another human being, of course. Just to myself.) I'm the one who re-took the oath to the evil spirit Aralt when Lydia splashed noxious chemicals in my eyes. I thought I could beat the system—take the oath, then read another spell—one that would release him from my body again. But that was before I knew that Lydia was planning to destroy Aralt's book—his dwelling—so she could have him to herself forever.

My eyes absorbed a healthy dose of supernatural hoodoo, and I got stuck with the consequences. Totally, totally my bad.

At least it only resulted in my being able to *see* most ghosts. Not hear their despairing, wormy-mouthed, pleading whispers.

But Lydia? I straight-up refuse to take the blame for Lydia. She got selfish at the end and died in pain and in fear, which usually produces a ghost. In this case, it produced a ghost that walks and talks and annoys me just like Lydia did when she was a real live girl. Same attitude, just deader.

When she came into view, I tensed, tightening my grip on the wheel.

But she didn't try anything. I pulled Mom's car into the garage and hesitated before grabbing my camera—it would mean reaching right through Lydia's semi-opaque body. I decided to come back for it later and headed for the door to the hallway, which was always unlocked.

Lydia passed through the car door and stood in my path, both feet planted on the floor. She—and most of the other undead spirits I'd seen—preferred to move like a living person, walking and standing on the ground. Some of them float, but only when they're too angry or distracted to think about it.

She tossed her hair and sniffed. "What makes you think I'm at your beck and call?"

I almost walked right through her, but my nerve faltered at the last second. I hated the way it felt, like jumping into a freezing swimming pool—or being pushed in. Lydia hated it, too—which almost made it worthwhile.

But not quite.

"Move," I said.

She came a half step closer. "Since when do I take orders from murderers?"

See what I mean? Passing the blame much? As if I'd *forced* her to start the Sunshine Club and fall madly in love with an evil spirit. As if it had been *my* idea for him to devour her life force. I'd tried to talk her out of it. I'd even tried to save her—and, rather pathetically, *kept* trying, way after the point where she was savable. But there's no way to convey that to an angry ghost.

They just don't listen.

"I get it, okay?" I said. "You hate me. You tried to kill me, and it didn't work. But take comfort in the fact that you *definitely* ended my day on a low note, and move along, please. See you in a few weeks."

Her eyebrows went up.

When she didn't move, I held my breath and charged forward. The frigid rush of blood in my veins left me light-headed, with Lydia's outraged yelp resonating in my ears.

What happened next took me by complete surprise.

A second blast of cold hit me from behind, and then Lydia was in front of me again.

The double dose was like a hundred full-body ice-cream headaches. I doubled over in pain, wondering if it was possible to die of ghost-induced hypothermia. My fingers were so frozen I couldn't feel them. I stumbled, put my hands out, and sank to the floor before I could lose my balance and fall.

After a minute, the feeling of imminent freezing-to-death passed, and I looked up at Lydia. She stood on the step by the door that led into the house. The effort of passing through me had left her a little hunched over and slightly more see-through than usual. And when she spoke, her voice was weaker.

"I'll leave you alone," she rasped, "when I *feel* like it."

She disappeared through the door, and I heard the light *ka-chunk* of the lock turning.

I got up a moment later, my legs like tree stumps being stuck with a million pins. The circulation gradually came back as I made my way to the door. I knocked a few times before giving up. My parents were probably in the kitchen with the TV on, so I went around to the front of the town house.

My little sister, Kasey, pulled the door open just as I was about to turn the key in the dead bolt. Her hand tightened on the doorframe when she saw me, soaked and shivering like a half-drowned rat. She, on the other hand, practically glowed, her long hair draped over her shoulder like a gold silk scarf.

Once upon a time, I'd been worried about Kasey fitting in and making friends, but that had proved to be yet another shining example of my general cluelessness about how the world works.

My sister was A-list. She'd growth-spurted over the fall, and now she was almost as tall as me. Her hair was long and caramel blond, just wavy enough to make every hairstyle look effortlessly natural. She had an innate sense of what to wear, what to say, when to laugh, how to stand, and how to tell jokes so everyone in the room would strain to hear the punch line. On top of that, she was smart. Way smarter than me.

It would have been completely insufferable, except she was so *nice*.

Even the niceness would probably have been insufferable if I hadn't been so relieved that she wasn't a total outcast.

One per family was plenty.

Most important to me, she'd been through hard times with ghosts just like I had—but she had moved past those times. She was free from worrying about evil spirits and power centers. Free to be normal and happy.

She was safe.

And I intended to make sure that she stayed that way.

"I got caught in the rain," I said, before she could ask.

From the kitchen wafted the mixed scent of simmering spaghetti sauce and fresh-baked sugar cookies. "Get any good pictures?" Dad called.

Someone was chopping something. The *thunk* of the knife on the cutting board stopped as they waited for my answer.

"Not really," I called, careful to hover in the shadows. "I'm getting a little bored with photography, to be honest. I might cut back."

Kasey's eyes widened almost imperceptibly, but she didn't say anything. I walked past her toward my bedroom, trying to stay steady on my trembling legs.

* * *

The ridiculous thing was, I knew *exactly* how to stop Lydia.

All I had to do was get up the courage to go to her house and find her power center—whatever object was holding her to this world—and destroy it, and I'd be free. Free of her, and (though I only let myself hope for this in my most desperate and pitiful of moments) maybe even free of the ghosts that haunted my photos. Who was to say the two problems weren't related?

The trouble was, when I contemplated facing Mr. and Mrs. Small, my hands began to sweat and my mind went all wobbly. Their daughter's death had basically ruined their not-so-great-to-begin-with lives. Under the weight of their desolate gazes, there was no way I'd be able to play it cool enough to concentrate on finding something that had been precious to Lydia—much less obliterating it.

The whole situation was like an itch I couldn't bear to scratch.

Lydia believed I was a murderer. The kids at school never came out and said anything, but I could see in their eyes that they suspected me, too. After all, when Lydia went running after me, she was totally alive. Five minutes later, we were alone in a fiery beauty salon together, and Lydia was dead. So her parents *had* to wonder.

And maybe what scared me most was that underneath all of my denial and nightmares and anger . . . some part of me might figure out it actually *was* my fault.

Here's a hint of how my life used to be: all I had wanted from the day I turned sixteen was a car. I begged, I cajoled, I bargained. Amazing how when you have a cute boyfriend and a popular best friend and everything in your life is just one peppy, perky little party, something like a car can seem really, really crucial. After everything went down with Aralt, I finally forgot about cars. I forgot to care about them, forgot to nag Mom and Dad about them.

So of course I got one for Christmas.

It was an act of profound sympathy on the part of my parents, I guess, because God knows my behavior and grades thus far in my junior year hadn't exactly been car-for-Christmas-worthy. I'd even gone back to my old habit of skipping classes on a fairly regular basis. But Mom and Dad were insanely excited, giggly and pink-cheeked. I tried to give them a little pink-faced giggling right back, but I think they saw through it.

I could tell Kasey did.

The car was six years old and ugly: brown, rounded off at the corners like a bubble or an egg or something—with a big splotch on the backseat that I'd just as soon never find out the cause of, thank you very much. But it was a car. It had windows and locks and seats and a gas pedal—and it was *mine*.

I fell in love immediately.

Grandma was off windsurfing in Australia with her women's club for the holidays, so it was just the four of us—Mom, Dad, Kasey, and me. We finished opening presents in about ten minutes and ate our traditional holiday breakfast of scrambled eggs and a giant pile of artery-clogging bacon. I took my trying-too-hard parents on a drive around the neighborhood.

Then the house fell back into deathly silence.

Kasey retreated to her bedroom to talk to her boyfriend, Keaton Perry (could someone please tell me how on earth my little sister was old enough to have a boyfriend? And a *senior,* no less?), and I went to the living room and turned on the TV. The local news was playing, and the anchors were decked out in cheesy holiday sweaters. They were joking and jolly, talking about Santa Claus as if he really existed, that thing adults do to humor the kids who are mostly just humoring adults.

Then they turned serious.

"A Christmas tragedy," the female anchor said, frowning. "Surrey police are investigating the disappearance of sixteen-year-old Kendra Charnow, whose parents reported yesterday that their daughter apparently left the house in the middle of the night. The Surrey High School junior's wallet and winter coat were both left behind, and footprints found in the mud outside her window seem to suggest that she left the house barefoot."

"What?" Kasey appeared from her bedroom and plunked down onto the sofa. "Kendra?"

The cameras turned from the front of the Charnows' house to show the side yard, which was cordoned off with bright yellow crime-scene tape. A bunch of neighbors milled around as busy-looking police officers walked from the house to the street and back again.

Mom sat next to me. "You're kidding me . . . and on Christmas."

I was watching a woman in the background who had to be Kendra's mother. She had short reddish hair and dark circles under her eyes, and leaned heavily on the arm of the man next to her.

Then they cut to footage of Kendra's bedroom. There was crime-scene tape blocking the doorway, but they showed her unmade bed, her open window, and her dresser.

"Wait." I grabbed the remote and skipped back to the shot of the bedroom. The end of the news camera's pan settled on the surface of Kendra's dresser. What you were supposed to notice was that her purse was still there, with her wallet sitting next to it.

I felt like I'd been punched in the stomach.

Because what I noticed was the single yellow rose.

4

COULD LYDIA REALLY BE BEHIND THIS? Did she hate me so much that she was going after not just me but random people I knew, too?

And then it hit me: Kendra had been in the Sunshine Club.

Yet another girl who'd survived when Lydia died.

Maybe it *wasn't* just me Lydia was coming after—maybe she was planning to hunt all of us down, one at a time.

Unless someone stopped her.

Well, it won't be me. The thought was like a command from my subconscious. I was done playing with ghosts. Done thinking I knew how to fight them.

But who else would—who else could?—if I didn't? I was the only person who could even see Lydia.

It's still not my problem.

Only . . . the longer I thought about it, the more it kind of *looked* like my problem.

"Police are searching the densely wooded areas nearby—both the Pelham Nature Preserve and Sage Canyon are within a mile of the Charnow home," the reporter said. "Unfortunately, though, rescuers have told us that it could take days to canvas the area—and last night's rain washed away a lot of important information."

Pelham? That was the nature preserve where Jared and I had been. Where we'd run into Kendra the day before her parents reported her missing.

They cut to an overhead shot of the area, taken from a news helicopter.

In the upper right corner of the screen, among the trees, was a bright splotch of white. At first I thought there was something wrong with the TV, but when the camera moved, the position of the white light moved, too. So, its source was actually there in the forest.

"What *is* that?" I asked.

"What's what, honey?" Mom asked.

It was a small, glowing spot of light—like someone was aiming a really powerful flashlight directly at the screen.

I'd never seen anything like it before . . . except for the brilliant white light in my car. Which came immediately before Lydia's yellow rose showed up.

Because of my "special" relationship with Lydia, I could see, hear, and interact with her in ways that

I couldn't with other ghosts. So it was possible that she could appear as a bright glow in photos—and on TV—when regular ghosts didn't. I didn't actually have any idea—I'd never gone out of my way to photograph her.

The helicopter spun to reveal the thin line of the highway. The light glowed on, about halfway between the main hiking trail and the road.

"What?" Kasey asked. "What are you looking for? Did you see something?"

The camera panned a little farther to reveal a billboard bearing the logo of a car dealership.

"I thought I did, but I didn't," I said, getting up off the couch and going to my room.

A few minutes later, I came back to the kitchen and found both of my parents huddled protectively near Kasey, who was on the phone with one of her dozens of friends.

"What's up?" Dad asked.

I held up my car keys. "I think I'll go for a little drive."

Kasey gave me a worried look. "Don't you want to talk to anybody? Did you call Megan?"

"Why would I call Megan?" I asked, leaning against the doorway.

"She knows Kendra. She was in the—"

"Kase," I said. "Trust me. Megan's not waiting for my call."

My parents looked stricken.

"It's fine. Don't look at me like that," I said. "I'll be home in a while."

"Where will you go?" Dad asked.

"Just . . . out," I said, leaving before they had a chance to ask me not to.

As I drove past the entrance to the nature preserve, I saw that the lot was choked with police cars and news vans. So I kept going, about a half-mile farther, until I came to an abandoned diner. I parked my car behind the building and backtracked on foot toward the billboard I'd seen on the news, staying close to the trees until I was directly below the sign. Then I plunged straight into the woods, my phone in my hand to keep track of my location.

I stepped over exposed roots and low, rough brush, dividing my concentration between not falling and looking for Kendra. The cold cut right through my sweater and bit into my skin. Added to that were the chills I got when I took the time to wonder what Lydia could do to someone who couldn't see her, someone she caught off guard.

Kendra might already be dead.

I kept my eye out for Lydia, but I also had my camera strapped around my neck. Every once in a while I'd take a volley of photos and search them for any sign of the bright light.

Nothing.

Finally I came to a small, rocky cliff and paused, unable to go farther without climbing down. I lifted the camera and fired off a few shots.

Bingo.

The photo showed the white light directly in front of me, glaringly bright.

"Lydia?" I called.

My only answer was the distant chopping of helicopter blades.

Silent night, I thought.

"Boo." Lydia had materialized a few feet away from me, eyebrow cocked.

At the sound of her voice, I hurried away from the edge of the cliff.

"Merry Christmas, Alexis," she sneered. "Get lots of presents? I'll bet you did. I'll bet it was *super awesome.* So tell me: did you stop for a single *minute* and think about me or my family? I'll bet anything you didn't. You're completely wrapped up in yourself, as usual. And I'm just a rotting corpse in the ground."

But I did. Before I fell asleep last night, I thought about

your mother sitting alone in the darkness, and it made me cry.
Sometimes it feels like all I do is cry.

"I *wish* you were just a rotting corpse." I put my hands on my hips. "Where is she?"

"Who?"

"Kendra," I said.

She gave me a flat stare. "What am I, a bloodhound?"

Then she vanished.

I sighed and walked back toward the cliff, turning around and carefully edging my way down, scraping the bejeezus out of my hands and balancing precariously on wobbly rocks and slick piles of gravel.

When I reached the bottom, I started to go to the right.

Lydia appeared in my path. "She's actually behind you," she said, tossing her hair. "Better hurry. She looks dead."

Then she gave me a nasty glare and disappeared again.

Just as Lydia had said, Kendra was about thirty feet away. She lay on the rocks, her eyes closed and her leg canted at a sickening angle; she must have fallen and broken it.

For a second, I really did think she was dead.

I lifted her wrist and felt a faint pulse, but when I gently patted her cheek, her eyes remained tightly shut.

I pulled out my phone and prepared to dial 911.

I was trying to look up my GPS coordinates when a filthy hand lifted off the ground and rested on my arm.

"Alexis . . . ?"

"Kendra!" I said. "Are you okay?"

"I need water." Her eyes fluttered from the effort of opening, and her mouth made a futile swallowing motion. "Please."

I had a bottle in my backpack. I pulled the cap off and tipped it toward her cracked lips. "Just sip," I said. "There's plenty. Don't try to drink too much at once."

She took a couple of small swallows, then stared up at me. "I'm tired."

"Don't worry. You're safe. I'm going to call the police," I said. "They'll come save you."

She nodded stiffly, but I could tell by the glimmer in her eyes that she was still afraid.

"What happened? Why did you come out here? Was it—" I cut myself off before I could say *Lydia*.

"I was . . . trying to get away from something." Her eyes grew hazier, more distant. "I was . . . trying to get away from . . ."

"From what?" I wanted to coax the name out of her. I didn't want to say it myself, because if I was wrong—

Kendra's eyes suddenly went wide with fright. "From *you*, Alexis."

I blinked.

Trying to get away from *me?*

Then, before I knew what was happening, Kendra's eyes rolled back in her head, and she was unconscious again.

I grabbed my phone, about to call for help. But suddenly I wondered how this would look. The police might believe I'd just gone out to hike, and take pictures . . . but would my parents?

Would Kasey?

Not a chance.

I backed a few steps away, trying not to slip on the mossy rocks. And a thread of fear wove up through my heart, like a snake being charmed.

I couldn't face the police. I couldn't spend another day trying to avoid my parents' searching gazes, lying my way through the explanation everyone would demand.

Someone would save Kendra, I would make sure of that—but I didn't plan to be there when it happened.

If I weren't me (oh, to be some average girl living in an average place with average problems! The magic of it!), if I were some other person looking in on me and my messed-up life, I think the obvious questions would be— why did I bother trying to keep so many secrets?

And why didn't I ask for help?

Like Carter said after the whole Sunshine Club disaster—why didn't I turn to him, or my parents, or anyone? After all, there's strength in numbers, right?

It's more complicated than that.

This isn't my first rodeo. I've dealt with ghosts before. And when you're dealing with murderous spirits, more isn't merrier. It's not like Scooby-Doo. The amount of people you have on your side doesn't matter. You can't physically fight a ghost, so there's no point in having an army of friends standing at the ready.

That just means there are more people who potentially could get hurt.

So I could go to my parents, yeah. But would they try to help me figure out what was going on? Would they help me get to the core of the situation?

No. They'd call Agent Hasan, the government agent who'd come in twice now to clean up our supernatural messes, and then they'd have Kasey and me packed into the car and on the road to some no-name town in North Dakota before lunch.

But that wouldn't work.

I've learned something in my months spent inadvertently spying on ghosts: if you notice them, they notice you. If you're aware of a ghost, it becomes aware of you.

And when a ghost is aware of you, you're that much more likely to have ghost trouble. The kind you can't

drive away from. The kind that ends in pain and misery
. . . or death.

Especially when the ghost hates you as much as
Lydia hated me.

That night, while my family was sitting down to a fes-
tive Christmas dinner of delivered pizza, the local news
report ran an update on the rescue effort. Kendra had
been located and taken by helicopter to a nearby hospital.
She hadn't been able to say anything because she was in
a coma.

Her whereabouts had been called in by an anonymous tipster from an old pay phone at an abandoned
diner near the woods.

"It's awfully strange," my mother said. "But I'm so
relieved they found her."

I was relieved, too—

Relieved that they found her, relieved that she was
alive . . .

And relieved that she couldn't talk.

5

I'M PRETTY SURE TAGGING ALONG with your little sister to her popular-people New Year's Eve party dumps you off the deep end of the loser scale, but there I was, anyway.

I tried to hold my head high as I followed Kasey through the immense front door of the equally immense Laird house. She was immediately swarmed by a pack of chattering girls who pulled her in the direction of the fittingly enormous couch. Dear devoted Keaton, spotting her from across the room, cut short his conversation and made a beeline for her.

I commandeered a chair in the corner next to the snack table, set down my unfashionable, un-party-appropriate bag, and went into *Alexis Doesn't Want to Be Here* mode, talking to people only when they talked to me, nursing a cup of punch, and watching my fingers slowly grow oranger and oranger from all the cheese puffs I couldn't seem to stop eating.

A shadow fell over me, and I looked up. The first

thing I saw was the hair—dark brown, just past shoulder length. Then the skin, perfectly gold, even in winter. Then the eyes, dark and knowing—and maybe a little bit tired.

"Megan," I said.

My best friend, whom I'd seen maybe four times since October, did a double take when she saw me. She took a halting step back, which made me notice how she still limped on her left knee.

The knee I'd destroyed.

"Wow—your hair," she said. "I didn't recognize you."

I tried to smile. It didn't really work.

"When did you do that?" she asked. "What does it *mean?*"

I reached up and touched it self-consciously. Megan, who'd never given my pink hair a second glance, seemed utterly horrified by my white hair. She was looking at me like I'd announced I had a bomb strapped to my chest or something.

"It doesn't really mean anything," I said. "Mom took me to the salon a couple of weeks ago, and I told the lady to stop when it looked like this."

Megan pursed her lips, almost in disapproval.

"I just sort of . . . liked it." I knew how lame that sounded. The truth was, the white hair looked blank and empty, which felt like a good reflection of my life at the moment. Going back to my pink hair would have felt like putting on a costume.

But I couldn't say that to Megan. Not when she was looking at me almost like a stranger.

"So, uh . . . what have you been up to? Did you get my texts?"

She glanced around, as if people would be watching us. But no one was. "Yeah, sorry. I've been busy."

"How's your new school?"

"It's not new," she said. "I've been there for two months."

Yeah, but she'd never returned my calls when I wanted to ask her about it. So it was new to me. Jared went there, too, which meant I knew a little about Sacred Heart Academy itself. But he was a senior and she was a junior; they didn't have any classes together. Therefore I knew absolutely nothing about how Megan was doing.

And she wasn't talking, so apparently that wasn't going to change.

"I got a car for Christmas," I said, grasping now, trying to provoke some kind of response.

It didn't work. Megan's eyes flickered to meet mine briefly, then flickered away. She gazed at the wall over my head, at the floor, at the front hallway—everywhere but at me.

"Great," she said.

She didn't even care what kind it was.

"Megan." My voice was thin and strained and so pathetic that I hated myself. "What's going on? Did I do something wrong?"

Her nostrils flared. "No, of course not."

"Then why won't you—"

"I can't believe Carter and Zoe are together," she said, studying her bracelet. "It's so weird."

I had to make a conscious effort not to squeeze my cup until it collapsed. *"What?"*

Finally, she looked directly at me. "He and Zoe Perry are kind of a thing now. It happened a week or two ago, I guess. . . . You didn't know?"

"No," I said. "I didn't know." I took a sharp breath in and leaned back away from the table. Even though part of me had expected it to happen eventually, I hadn't known it would feel like this—like being punched in the soul.

"Sorry," Megan said. "I just figured you'd been to some of the parties and—"

"I don't go to a lot of parties," I said.

"But . . . you have a new boyfriend, right?" she asked. "That guy from my school?"

"Jared," I said. "He's not my boyfriend."

Her lips pressed tightly together, and she looked around for an escape. "I'm sorry, Alexis. Truly. But I . . . I have to go. Maybe we'll run into each other later."

I nodded and forced a painful half smile, feeling the

47

muscles in my jaw pull tight as she walked away.

Then, as if on cue, I glanced up at the door and saw them enter together: Carter and Zoe, her hand clenched around his. I was inordinately relieved that at least he'd cut his blond hair short, so she couldn't reach up and touch his soft blond curls the way I'd always done.

A few short months ago, Zoe had been a shining, golden girl—all sweetness and smiles. Needless to say, that was *before* she took the oath and joined the Sunshine Club.

She'd come through the experience a little less sunny than most of the members, to put it mildly. For starters, she'd cut her long blond hair and dyed it dark magenta. And she'd ditched the preppy clothes—or rather, thrashed them. Everything she wore was like a torn, wrinkled, ripped version of its former self.

With a jolt that felt like a zillion watts of electricity, Carter's eyes met mine, and he snatched his hand out of Zoe's. It felt like he'd done it for me, to protect me from having to see them together.

Part of me was grateful, but part of me—a much bigger part—felt like the knife, once it had pierced the surface of my heart, might as well go all the way through.

I checked the time on my phone. Eight thirty—still three and a half hours till midnight. I stared at the numbers for a moment and then sat back.

Megan seemed to be slinking around the edges of the party, staying as far from me as she could, and Kasey was planted in the center of a group of kids, a glittery gold party hat stuck on her head, and her eyes squinting shut as she laughed at something. I watched her, aware of how relieved it made me to see her having fun, being goofy. It was everything I wanted for her.

So I relaxed—minutely.

A figure came and stood in front of me, *almost* obscuring my view of my sister.

I sat up straight.

"Yawn," Lydia said. With a flat smile, she swept her hand across the surface of the table. It passed through most of the dishes but caught on my punch cup, which clattered to the floor, spilling bright red liquid all over the pale floor tiles.

The room fell silent, and everyone looked at me.

"Whoops," Lydia said.

A few seconds later, Pepper Laird came over with a roll of paper towels. The captain of the cheerleading squad kneeling to clean up my mess. I imagined it wouldn't be long before Kasey's invitations didn't automatically include me anymore.

"Sorry," I said, trying to help clean up, but more concerned with keeping an eye on Lydia.

"Sorry," Lydia mimicked. "Still kissing up to the

cheerleaders. *Oh, Pepper, please forgive me.* You make me *sick*."

She disappeared, and I looked around frantically. There were easily a dozen former Sunshine Club members here. I didn't want any of them to end up comatose like Kendra.

"No big deal," Pepper said, but I could tell she was annoyed. She stood up, her hands full of sopping-wet napkins.

This whole night was a mistake. I grabbed my bag. "I'd better go. Thanks for letting me come. Sorry about the mess."

Pepper had to get to the trash can before she got dripped on, so she couldn't protest even if she'd wanted to, which, frankly, I don't think she did. I got up and headed for the door, with Lydia walking backward in front of me.

"Leaving so soon?" She drew up all of her energy and bumped into a kid who was perched on a barstool. He grunted in surprise as he almost fell off, then steadied himself and shot me an irritated look.

"Pardon me," I said. I turned around to look for Kasey. I had to tell her I was leaving, but I couldn't risk going back through the crowd.

As I got to the front hall, the guest bathroom door opened and Megan came out. "You're leaving?"

"Yes," I said. "I have to go. Um . . . could you do me a favor and tell my sister?"

Megan's forehead wrinkled. "Why don't *you* tell her?"

"Megan's looking well," Lydia said. "Too bad she wasn't the one who died. Then you might be the tiniest bit sorry."

As she said that, she swung her arm at Megan's forehead. I flinched as it went through and came out the other side.

"Oh, no . . . not another migraine." Megan winced and rubbed her temple. "So listen. There's this thing I've been doing at school—on Tuesday afternoons—it's like a club. . . ."

I listened, trying to keep an eye out for Lydia.

"And I was thinking, if you want to come with me sometime, maybe . . ."

"Yes," I said. "What time? Where?"

She half laughed. "Don't you even want to know what it is?"

"No. I don't care."

For a moment she looked as if she regretted mentioning it at all. "Tuesday, four forty-five, at the Sacred Heart Community Hall. The entrance is on Poplar Street."

"Great," I said, glancing around.

Oh, jeez. Lydia was studying the giant tropical aquarium in the dining room.

My mere presence put every living creature around me in danger, regardless of species. I felt like a ticking time bomb. "I have to go," I said. "Never mind about Kasey—I'll just text her."

"I can tell her if you need me to," Megan said. I heard a razor-thin edge of judgment in her voice.

"No, don't worry," I said. "Bye."

But as I reached the front door, I heard my sister shout my name. She was pushing through the crowd to get to me.

"You're leaving?" Kasey asked. "What happened?"

I looked around before I stopped. Lydia was gone.

"Nothing," I said. "Do you think maybe Keaton could drive you home? Otherwise I'll come back and get you at one o'clock."

"What?" Immediately, she was suspicious. "Where are you going, Lexi?"

"Nowhere. Away."

"Why?" She pursed her lips, clearly not looking to take any of my nonsense.

"Because you're a coward and a freak, that's why," Lydia said, popping out behind me.

"I just . . ." I gestured around the room, which seemed overpoweringly jammed with bodies. "There are too many people here."

My sister followed me all the way out to my car,

52

exhaling loudly through her nose to convey how annoyed she was. I pulled my gray hoodie over the shirt she'd made me wear—black and gauzy, with ruffles around the neck—and slipped into the driver's seat.

"When is this going to end?" she asked, her voice breaking. "When are you going to let it go?"

"I don't know what you're talking about," I said. "Now get back inside. It's about to rain."

Kasey stared at me, on the verge of protesting. Then she stormed back up the front walk.

I watched her go, thinking, *You have no idea how lucky you are.*

The Sunshine Club ended up being an evil cult designed to feed on its members' free will and life energy, but it started out as a scheme to become beautiful and popular. And maybe the craziest thing was—it had actually worked, kind of. Sure, the paranormal perks were gone, but the charm, the poise—all of the things that grew better with practice—that stuff stuck.

As for the club's evil supernatural roots, for the most part the other girls had managed to convince themselves and everyone around them that the whole thing was just a mild case of mass hysteria. The longer they told themselves that, the more they believed it. And why not? Let's be realistic—the alternative was crazy.

A few of us didn't make it out unscathed—me, Zoe,

Megan, Lydia. And poor Emily Rosen was being home-schooled and treated for PTSD. But for the lucky ones, that magic too-good-to-be-true popularity pill wasn't actually too good to be true. It was just . . . true.

Of course, all that could change. Their perfect lives could end in death and destruction if I didn't find a way to stop Lydia.

I kicked off my ballet flats and pressed my bare foot against the brake pedal, relishing the feel of its hard rubber ridges beneath my toes.

"Oh, snap. Did I wreck your party?" Lydia materialized in the passenger seat. "Is Alexis scared? Is she running home with her tail between her legs?"

"Shut up," I said, on edge but relieved that she'd followed me instead of staying inside.

She made a pouty face. "Waaaaah. Lexi wants to be alone. Lexi hates herself. Well, join the club. I hate you, too."

I turned the key and buckled my seat belt.

Lydia made an irritated noise and faded out of sight.

Until she'd attacked me—and then Kendra—I'd thought she wasn't a very powerful ghost. But now I had to be constantly on guard. Because apparently it's not hard for a weak ghost to get strong—

And dangerous.

I DROVE AWAY FROM THE LAIRDS' upscale neighborhood toward the empty highways that led out of town, stretching the speed limit in my rush to get away from civilization.

On the seat next to me, my phone lit up with a text message. The word MOM flashed onscreen. I figured I'd better reply before I ended up grounded, so I pulled onto the shoulder.

K SAID YOU LEFT PARTY ARE YOU COMING HOME?

NOT YET, I texted. GETTING COFFEE.

A second later, her reply came through.

:-/

"What's wrong?" Lydia asked, fading in. "Tired? Dejected? Suicidal? Don't let me stop you if you had any, you know, *plans*."

I took a deep breath, shut off the engine, and stared out the window. I was surrounded by farmland, no cars or houses in sight.

What Lydia had done to Kendra erased any doubt in my mind that she needed to be eliminated. But even a week after Kendra had been found, something still kept me from going to Lydia's house and facing her parents. I kept coming up with excuses—places to go, rooms of the house that needed scrubbing, distant school projects that needed urgent attention.

The girls from the Sunshine Club were in danger, and I couldn't bring myself to do anything about it. But the only reason Lydia had any power over me was that I gave it to her. All wrapped up with a pretty bow.

"Lydia." I steeled myself and tried to sound assertive. "I'm only going to have this conversation with you once. This has to stop."

"Or what?" she sneered.

"Well, let's see. I got rid of the hundred-year-old evil ghost that possessed my sister and tried to kill our dad. I got rid of Aralt in a room full of twenty-two people who wanted to kill me. So, no offense—but I think I could take you."

She tossed her hair. "What are you saying?"

"I'm saying, leave me—and all the other girls— alone, and I'll leave your power center alone."

Her mocking smile disappeared.

To a ghost, a power center isn't something you joke about. They're automatically driven to protect it, to prolong their existence—whether they have something worth existing for or not.

Kind of like the rest of us, I guess.

Lydia glared at me, arms crossed. "You wouldn't dare. Don't forget, you're already responsible for my death. That would be like killing me twice."

Her words sent a spike of dread up my spine, but I was determined not to let her sense it. "*Please* believe me," I said, "when I say it would be my absolute pleasure."

She pouted. "Lighten up! I was just having *fun*."

I wondered what part of putting Kendra into a coma or almost steering me into a murky canal seemed fun to her. I reached for my key. "Forget it," I said. "I'll just go to your house and do it right now."

"No!"

"Then *leave*," I said. "You have *five seconds*. Leave all of us alone. Forever."

She gave me a disgusted look. "You are extremely oversensitive, Alexis."

"One," I said. "Two—"

She disappeared.

A magnificent silence filled the car.

I closed my eyes and soaked it in for a minute before I reached down to start the ignition. The engine made a sound like it was going to turn over—but then it whined and died out.

"No," I said. "Come on. Not tonight."

I tried again. Nothing.

The first drop of rain thumped like a drumbeat on the roof of the car. Then another, and another. Soon it was pouring.

I couldn't call my parents. I didn't have a boyfriend. My best friend seemed reluctant to even acknowledge my existence. I was stranded.

Then I remembered that there was one person who might care—who might come if I called him.

I stood out in the sheeting rain and flagged Jared down— which may not have been necessary, considering the only thing besides me and my car was miles of farmland, furrowed in deep rows, with a low, dense winter carpet of clover. He parked his Jeep nose-to-nose with my car and got out, wearing a yellow poncho. He hurried over and offered me an umbrella.

"What's the use?" I yelled over the storm. "I'm already soaked!"

We opened our hoods and he hooked up a pair of jumper cables between the cars. When he turned his car on, I tried mine again. This time the engine rumbled and came to life.

Jared disconnected everything, neatly rolling the cables and stowing them in his trunk. Then he came back over and watched me close my hood.

"Thanks a lot," I yelled. "I didn't know who else to call. "

"Anytime," he yelled back.

There was a pause.

"What are you doing so far out of town, anyway?" he yelled.

I shrugged and yelled, "Nothing, really. So . . . I'll call you this week or something?"

He hesitated, then pulled me into a loose, tentative hug and backed away, giving me a little wave as he walked to his car.

I sat in my driver's seat, soaking my upholstery but absolutely powerless to do anything about it. According to the clock, it was nine fifteen. The cold began to seep through my clothes and chill my skin.

My cell phone rang. Jared. With shivering fingers, I flipped it open.

"Hi," I said. "Thanks again."

"No problem," he said. The rain still roared in the background, but at least we didn't have to shout to hear each other. "So . . . I was just wondering if you wanted to come over and have some hot chocolate or something. Dad's out of town, and I just didn't feel like going to any parties tonight."

I knew he didn't mean *Dad's out of town, wink wink*. Mr. Elkins was hardly ever home even when he was in town. That didn't automatically equal debauchery.

"Well . . . thanks." For a moment, I was tempted. I really did like spending time with Jared. But then my loner instincts kicked in, and before I could stop myself, I was saying, "But I think I'll just go home."

"All right," he said. "Make sure you get into some dry clothes."

I said I would, and we hung up. Then I wrapped my hands around my steering wheel and stared out at the road, determined not to think about the note of hurt I'd heard in his voice.

I tried to cheer myself up by remembering that I didn't have to go *straight* home—I could go get coffee, like I'd told Mom.

But the rain came down in torrents, and suddenly I realized that I wasn't remotely interested in sitting in a coffee shop, having everyone stare at me in my soaking-wet clothes, wondering why I was alone on a major party holiday. Only slightly less awful was the prospect of facing my parents and having to explain why I'd left the party early.

But where else would I go?

I was about to give up and start for home when I heard a sound—a convulsive, high-pitched sound. Was it . . . crying?

A woman crying? Or maybe a girl? It was hard to

be sure, with the wind and rain and my rumbling engine.

I used my hand to clear a circle in the fogged-up window, and stared out at the field.

I didn't see anyone, but the sound wasn't in my imagination, that much I was sure of—it was so distinct that I could hear each individual sob.

A voice in my head said, *Get out of here.*

But there was some part of me that needed to defy the voice—or at least second-guess it. As much as I hated Lydia, what I hated slightly more was the idea of being so fearful of her that I let it change me into a person I didn't want to be.

And I didn't want to be a person who ignores a cry for help.

My body ached with dread at the thought of what—or whom—I'd find . . . but I got out of the car.

Standing in the rain again, I could hear the crying as clearly as if the girl were ten feet away.

I pocketed my phone and walked closer to the crumbling soil at the edge of the field, looking out across the clover.

She was obviously, like, *right there.*

"Hello?" I said.

It wasn't a terribly dark night; rather than blocking out the moonlight, the clouds diffused it into an allover glow, with a few stars twinkling through the clear spots.

If somebody were moving around out there, I'd have seen her already. Which meant she wasn't moving. She was hurt.

I took a step out into the dirt. "Hello? Who's there?"

The crying stopped, as if the girl hadn't known anyone could hear her.

"Are you okay?" I called. "Where are you?"

The answer was a pitiful sob.

"Are you hurt?" Three more steps in. I stayed aware of the clear path waiting behind me. "Tell me where you are! I'll come help you!"

Silence again.

What if it wasn't really a person crying? What if it was Lydia trying to get me to wander out into the darkness? Maybe this was how she'd lured Kendra out of her house in the middle of the night. Looking at the situation objectively, it didn't make sense at all that there would be a real person out there. Would they find my car the next morning with a yellow rose on the dashboard?

I took a few more strides forward, blinded by the cold raindrops and my fresh disgust. "We had a *deal*! I guess now that you've let your end go, I can—"

I was about to turn and leave. But a fresh burst of sobs hit my ears, and I forced myself to stop and reconsider.

There had been plenty of situations in my life that

didn't make sense—objectively. Just because I didn't know who was out there didn't mean it wasn't a real person.

If she dies . . . whoever she is . . . it will be your fault.

Again

So I kept going. I went cautiously, slowly. Ten feet. Another ten.

By this time, I was a fair distance from the road, and there was no sign of an injured girl—except for the crying. She still cried, and she *still* sounded like she was ten feet away. But I'd called out to her multiple times, and she hadn't said so much as "Help."

If I could hear her, surely *she* could hear *me.*

And surely . . . she would have said something . . .

If she was a real person.

Forget this.

I stopped and made an abrupt about-face. But as I started back in the direction of the road, I heard the crying again—

Now it was in front of me.

Whatever was out here . . . it wasn't a girl. Not a human girl, anyway.

"Stop it, Lydia!" I yelled. "Go away! Leave me alone!"

The wailing ended abruptly, like it was a recording and somebody had switched it off.

Just keep going. You're almost there—

A laugh. A brilliant, sparkling, musical laugh.

So close it sounded like the person was right next to me.

As a flash of lightning lit up the night, I flinched and hunched over, waiting for the clap of thunder. A moment later, I realized that it had never come.

That wasn't lightning.

It was the white light.

I turned and ran blindly, managing to go about four feet before tripping over the cutoff stubble of whatever had last been harvested from the field. I went flying and landed flat on my stomach, my face splashing into the wet green leaves, but I scrambled up and started running again.

Almost immediately, something clotheslined me, hitting me hard in the throat. The explosive shock of pain buckled my knees and left me doubled over and gasping.

The laughter came again, only now it seemed to be surrounding me, coming from every side. I gagged against the pain and tried to catch my breath, managing to suck in a shallow stream of air as I struggled to get to my feet.

But I'd only taken a few steps when the whole world started spinning like a merry-go-round with me at the center. I tried to take another step, but I couldn't seem to keep myself from walking in a spiral over the mad obstacle course of the uneven ground. Every turn I made to correct my path went too far in the other direction. I lost my footing and dropped to the muddy ground, trying to find stability on my hands and knees.

Still, the world looped around me. And when I looked up at the patchy clouds, the rain seemed to be falling in circles. The stars wobbled, swelling and contracting, as the sky itself moved in waves overhead.

The laughter never stopped. It didn't sound brilliant and sparkling anymore—it was hard and glinting and cruel.

Finally, I gave up trying to move and clung to the ground. But even then I seemed to slip forward, like I was falling downhill—or being dragged. My chin scraped against a rough, broken root as my hands groped through the delicate clover for something solid to hold on to, but they only grabbed clumps of muddy earth.

Wherever Lydia was trying to take me, I didn't want to go.

I curled into a ball and covered my face with my arms.

I give up.

And then, as suddenly as it had started, the laughter stopped.

For a minute I lay there curled into a ball, hearing raindrops padding on the soft green leaves around me.

Then I sat up, on the alert for the slightest hint of Lydia's demonic laughter, ready to throw myself back down to the ground.

I glanced up. The clouds were at rest in the sky overhead. The rain came down in soft sheets instead of spirals.

So I started back for the road on my shaky legs. Once I got some momentum, I upgraded to a slow jog, navigating the slick terrain as fast as I dared.

My car was just a short walk up the sloping hill. I stumbled the few remaining feet to the grass and fell to my knees, somehow feeling safe now that I was off the soil. But even though I knew the attack was over, I was too frightened to look back out at the field.

The car was still running, thank God. I got in and checked the clock.

Five minutes. I'd only been out there for five minutes.

A racking cough forced its way out of my lungs, and the effort made my throat feel like someone had lit it on fire.

In the rearview mirror I could see blood mixing with rainwater on my forehead, where something had scraped the skin at my hairline and turned my white hair pink. A red line crossed my throat, and a bright pink semicircle decorated my jaw. I was pretty sure they'd both be revolting purple-and-black bruises before long.

I couldn't go home like this.

7

THE SOUND OF THE DOORBELL echoing inside the house almost made me dash back to my car. But just as my nerve totally abandoned me, the porch light came on, illuminating me like an actor on a stage. And it was too late.

Jared stood at the open door, a big confused smile on his face. The edges of his dark hair were still damp from where the rain had crept under the hood of his poncho. His wide brown eyes settled on me.

Then came the pause I'd been dreading.

Then: *"Alexis?"*

I was too cold to speak, so I stood there dripping all over the welcome mat, pretty sure the blood from my forehead had tinted my entire face pink.

Jared grabbed me by the arms, and his fingertips squeezed a sore spot on my shoulder, making me flinch. He let go like I'd tried to bite him.

"What happened?" he asked. "Who did this to you?"

I opened my mouth to answer, but it felt like there was a wad of cotton blocking my vocal cords.

"Should I call the police?" Jared asked. "Alexis? Why won't you answer me? Are you in shock?"

"No," I finally managed to say. "I'm sorry."

"Sorry? For what?" He looked out into the night as if something might be following me. "Come in—you're freezing."

"I can't, I'm all wet," I said.

He herded me inside, a protective hand on the back of my neck, and led me to the dining room, where he flipped on the light and pulled out a chair. "Sit."

A minute later he was back with a washcloth, a roll of bandages, and a bowl of water.

"Now," he said, "tell me what happened."

I stared at the gleaming surface of the table. "I can't."

But I did let him push back the hood of my sweatshirt and press the warm, wet washcloth against my hairline. "This cut needs stitches," he said.

"No."

"But it's going to leave a—"

"*No,*" I said again. And then, aware of how utterly childish and ungrateful I sounded, I softened my voice. "Thank you, but it's fine. It doesn't matter."

He sat back and gave me an incredulous look. Then

he went into the kitchen and turned on the faucet. I looked around the room, which was immaculate.

I hadn't known anyone could be as obsessively neat as my father and I, until I came to the Elkins house, which hardly even looked like anyone was living in it. At worst, you'd spy a clean dish or two in the drying rack, not yet put away. Pretty impressive for a single dad and a teenage son. Especially since Jared didn't have the look of a neat freak. He was slightly scruffy; his unkempt dark eyebrows made him look incredibly serious even when he was joking. (To be honest, sometimes it was hard to tell when he *was* joking.)

Jared came back and went to work on my face. He put a bandage over the cut on my forehead and gently dabbed at my cheek. "Was it a car accident?"

"No," I said.

"No, I didn't think so." He traced his finger in a short line under the smaller cut.

The simple chandelier over the dinner table was the only pocket of light in the house. Even the kitchen was dark. I felt oddly like Jared and I were the only two people in a hundred-mile radius.

He sat back and neatly folded the bloody washcloth. "People don't do this, you know."

"I know."

"You think there's something you can't tell me."

"Jared," I said. "It's bad."

"Whatever it is . . ." His voice died out. "Alexis . . . you . . . you lost someone. I know that."

I took a sharp breath. I don't know if you could say I "lost" Lydia. I'd never *had* her to begin with—I mean, we weren't friends, or anything. I just happened to be there when she died a horrible, scary, painful death. And now she was out to destroy me.

It would probably be more accurate to say I'd lost myself. But how lame is *that*?

"What I mean to say is, you're not the only one who—" He shifted in his chair. "I mean, I feel connected to you because . . . I know what it's like."

I stared at him, wondering whether he'd gotten his deep brown eyes from his mother.

He got up and walked out of the room.

I studied the crisp, white crown molding and waited for him to return. But he didn't.

I got up and went into the kitchen. Empty. The blank silence pressed in on my ears as I walked through the kitchen into the living room, which looked like a page from a furniture catalog. But he wasn't there.

Where did he go?

"Jared?" I pulled my hoodie tighter around my body and tucked my hands into the sleeves. I briefly considered leaving. I even started backing toward the foyer. But something stopped me.

Running out—just as unexpectedly as I'd run in—wouldn't accomplish anything. It wouldn't solve the current awkwardness—it would just set me up for double the awkwardness in the future. And possibly cost me the only friend I had left.

Not only that, but it wouldn't be fair to Jared. He didn't deserve to be treated that way.

Behind me, the refrigerator began to hum, startling me and setting my nerves on a knife-blade edge.

"Jared." In the darkness, my voice sounded like the woof of a frightened dog.

Fair or not, I turned and took another slow step toward the front door.

Behind me, there was a soft sound—a rustle, like someone had crossed the hardwood floor in socks.

I spun around. The room was empty.

A pair of windows overlooked the backyard, which was still buffeted by torrential rain. Lightning struck nearby—and in the brief instant of light, I saw a figure silhouetted against the windows—right up next to them, like it was watching me.

Then the house was dark again.

And again, no thunder.

I was past taking Lydia's powers for granted. My breath forced itself out in a gasp, and I turned to run, colliding with Jared.

"Whoa, whoa." He switched on a lamp that sat on a side table. "What are you doing?"

"I saw—" I looked back toward the window. "I mean, I thought . . ."

There was another flash of lightning, a real one. This time all I saw was the yard. No eerie figure looking in.

You're imagining things, I told myself. *You're seeing what you expect to see.* There *was* a tall shrub that waved and swayed under the falling rain.

See? That's all it was. A shrub.

Not Lydia.

He glanced at the window, then held out a bundle of fabric. "I brought you some dry clothes."

"Thank you. That's sweet, but I can't wear those home."

He cocked his head to one side. "You don't have to leave yet, do you? Put them on for now."

I hesitated, then took the clothes and headed toward the bathroom, where I had a chance to look at my injuries in the light.

The bruise on my jaw was a well-defined purple line, but I could probably cover it with makeup. The line across my throat could be hidden with scarves or turtlenecks. The gash on my forehead would be under my bangs. And the cut on my cheek was really just a glorified scratch—I could say I'd petted an unfriendly cat or something.

It wasn't great, but it was manageable.

Jared had given me a pair of plaid flannel pajama pants, a T-shirt, and a baggy sweatshirt. The idea of changing out of my wet jeans into warm, comfortable clothes for a little while was too delicious to pass up. After I was dressed, I balled up my own clothes and carried them back out to the living room.

Jared was sitting on the arm of the sofa, staring into the yard. He jumped up when I came into the room. "I'll take those," he said, gesturing to the bundle under my arm. "If I put them in the dryer, you should be able to wear them home."

"I should probably shake them out," I said. "They're covered in dirt. I should have thought about that before I came into the house."

"I'll take care of it."

"I can go outside and—"

His brown eyes flashed with hurt. "Alexis, *please.*"

So I handed my clothes over. He went past me to a door in the hallway, and his footsteps thumped down a flight of stairs. A minute later, I heard the *whoosh* and tumbling of the clothes dryer.

He came back, closed the door behind him, and sat down on the chair next to the couch. I faced the yard. He faced the wall. We studiously avoided looking at each other, and for a long time, neither of us spoke.

Finally I found my voice and said, "Thank you."

"*No.*"

I looked up in surprise.

Jared raked his fingers through his hair. "No. You don't *do* that! You don't show up here looking like you got jumped in an alley and refuse to tell me anything and then *thank* me. I don't want your thanks."

I didn't have any fight left in me. Besides, he was right. I drew in a breath.

"Stop." He held up a hand. "I don't want an apology, either. I just want . . ."

I knew what he wanted—the truth. But that wasn't an option.

"I just want to know you're okay."

Oh.

He stared at me, at all my bruises and cuts. "I'm trying *so hard* to understand what's going on. Just tell me, please . . . are you okay? Are you really okay?"

"Yes," I said. And I was, in the way he meant.

Beyond that, who could say?

He sighed. The air settled around us.

"I'll leave if you want me to," I said. It was more of a question.

"You think I want you to leave? *God*, Alexis." Jared shook his head and looked at me. "Just hang on for a minute, all right?"

He disappeared, and I heard the sound of liquid pouring into a glass. Then drinking and the clatter of the glass being set on the counter.

A second later, he came in, rubbing the back of his neck, and sat down. The room filled with silence again. We didn't talk, because we had nothing to say. I laid my head on my arm and closed my eyes.

I heard movement, and I felt Jared's weight press on the sofa cushion next to mine.

I leaned into him and felt his arms wrap around me. It was a friendly gesture, although I could feel the tension in his muscles.

"Jared?" I said, looking up at him.

"What?"

I felt the weight of my unspoken apology like an overfilled water balloon. But he didn't want to hear it, and I wasn't in a position to impose. So instead I said, "What happened tonight . . ."

How could I explain it?

Suddenly, my whole life seemed like a never-ending succession of things I couldn't explain.

And in that moment, it hit me:

Enough. Enough secrets. Enough of living this way.

It was time to conquer my fear—and take care of Lydia for good.

I stared up into his eyes. "I can't tell you what

it was, but it's not going to happen again."

"Well . . ." He looked around helplessly. "Good, I guess. Because seeing you like this—I mean, I thought somebody had attacked you."

"No," I said.

"I'm serious, Alexis. I saw you standing there, and I wanted to *kill* whoever did this to you." His whispery voice held the smoky scent of whatever he'd drunk in the kitchen. His eyes were soft and deep and brown, like the saddest puppy in the world. His jaw was tight with worry. Under my arm, his was solid and unmoving. He was like a suit of armor around me.

Nothing could get past him.

"I wish you could trust me," he said, his lips brushing against my hair.

I sat there, in shock from the heat of his breath, wrapped in warm flannel and soft cotton and strong arms.

And in that moment, it all seemed so pointless. All of the lonely, empty nights. Isolating myself at school and at home. Always holding Jared at arm's length—and why? Because I thought Carter might take me back?

Even if he weren't dating Zoe, he would never come back to me. *"Do you even know how to trust?"* he'd asked me the day of Lydia's funeral—our last day. The day he'd broken up with me.

Everything I'd been doing for the past two and a half

months was about being afraid. It wasn't living. It was just . . . hiding. Hiding from ghosts. From my family. From people at school. From the reality that Carter had moved on and left me behind.

From Jared.

Suddenly, desperately, I needed to stop hiding. I needed to do something real and new and meaningful.

"Jared . . ." I said.

He turned to me, perfectly attentive and gentle. "Yes?"

The small cuckoo clock on the dustless mantel began to tweet.

Midnight.

"Happy new year," I whispered.

Then I kissed him.

Our kiss was like a stormy night—the end of something and the beginning of something else—hungry, almost frantic. After a minute, I pulled back, and we stared at each other, my heart pounding all the way up to my ears.

Tears fought to escape my eyes. I pushed my fingers through Jared's hair and turned my face into his chest. For a few minutes, I let myself be tangled up against him, listening to the distant buzz of the dryer as it finished tumbling my clothes, trying to comprehend what I'd just done.

What I'd started.

Jared didn't speak or move. After a minute, our breathing aligned. I must have drifted off, because the next thing I heard was Jared's voice.

"Alexis." His whisper was quiet and intimately close to my ear. "What time do you need to get home?"

"One," I said.

"Okay. It's only twelve thirty."

"Good," I said, sleepily turning toward him.

"I'm so glad you came here tonight." His hand absently stroked my hair. "I've been . . . I don't think 'hoping' is the right word. But I've been . . . waiting."

"Really?" I said, even though I knew it.

"You don't have to be sad or scared anymore." He pulled me closer. "You're safe with me."

I could have said, *That's nice* or *You're sweet* or some other generic thing.

But then he leaned down and started a line of light kisses across the back of my neck, and I didn't have to say anything at all.

The next morning, I lay in my bed, staring at the ceiling.

I'd slept in Jared's T-shirt. It was warm and soft against my skin.

Yeah, so he wasn't Carter. But he was decent and kind, and there was something else about him—some secret undercurrent of intensity that I couldn't imagine Carter ever having.

Jared had walked me to my car the night before. "You're not going to wake up in the morning and regret this, are you?" he'd asked, leaning down and resting his elbows on the window ledge.

"No," I said. "Are you?"

His eyes crinkled. "Are you *kidding* me?" Then he'd kissed me in a way that made me believe him. Thinking about it, nestled under my comforter, I felt myself starting to smile.

A few minutes later I got up and went to the bathroom, where I carefully covered the bruise on my chin and combed my hair over the cut on my forehead. Then I went out to the kitchen, where Mom was making pancakes.

"Happy new year," she said, giving me a hug. "Let's make it a good one, okay?"

"Sure," I said, pouring a glass of orange juice.

"Do you have any resolutions?"

I took a swig of juice and thought of what I'd promised myself I would do that day. "Just one."

8

I DROVE SLOWLY THROUGH the west part of Surrey, my stomach doing unhappy backflips. At first I wasn't sure I'd remember where to turn off the main road. But when I passed a mini-mall with a burned-out, boarded-up beauty salon in the middle, the odd twinge in my abdomen turned into a spasm.

Who was I trying to fool? Like I'd ever forget this route as long as I lived.

A few more turns led me to Lydia's house. What had been a mild air of homeownerly neglect back in October had matured to a very real sense of impending collapse by January. The garage door was dented like someone had driven right into it. One of the porch steps was missing altogether, and flies swarmed over the mountain of trash bags just outside the front door.

I remembered that the doorbell didn't work, and knocked gently. I counted to fifty-Mississippi, but just as I was about to leave, the door opened a few inches to reveal a haggard face defined by sharp gray shadows.

"Mrs. Small?" I asked.

She stared dead-eyed at me, as if I hadn't spoken at all.

"I'm . . . I was a friend of Lydia's," I said.

The door opened, and Mrs. Small backed away to let me inside. She wore a long nightgown, tattered at the hem, with a knee-length robe over it. The ties of the robe fell limply down to the floor.

The house was dark—all of the shades were pulled down. And the smell of cigarettes, beer, and rotting food hung heavily in the air.

I took a shaky breath and forced myself to speak. "I'm really sorry about Lydia."

That got her attention—kind of. But her eyes couldn't seem to focus on me.

"I was wondering if . . ." Even though I'd made up this story and rehearsed it a dozen times, I could hardly spit out the words. "She borrowed something from me and I wanted to get it back . . . to remember her by."

It sounded weird and false to me, but Lydia's mother just pointed at the stairs.

"Thank you," I said, leaving her behind.

There were three doors at the top of the stairs, all closed. I went through the one with the Dead Kennedys poster on it.

Lydia's bedroom was much cleaner than the rest of the house. Her closet door was open, revealing a perfect line of shoes and rows of neat skirts, shirts, and dresses. No sign of the ripped jeans or baggy black Goth clothes she wore during the brief period when we'd been friends freshman year. Naturally, she would have thrown them all away. They were useless to a Sunshine Club girl.

Her jewelry was laid out in a grid on the dresser, and a hook on the wall held three purses—black, brown, and red.

Two hangers were tossed sloppily on the bed, and I realized that they must have been the hangers from which her mother pulled the clothes Lydia was buried in—a gray silk skirt and black angora turtleneck.

I closed my eyes for a moment.

No matter how awful Lydia had been at the end (*very,* by the way—let's be clear on that), I couldn't forget what Carter said at the funeral: *She was just sad.*

Thing is, she wasn't "just sad" anymore—or she wouldn't be trying to kill people.

I began to inspect the room, though I was having a hard time figuring out what might be her power center. I had absolutely no idea where to start. What would I do, destroy every last thing in the room?

I was on the verge of utter hopelessness when the door opened behind me and Mrs. Small came in, looking around in bewilderment. It was like someone had dropped her off outside and she'd wandered in to ask for directions.

Until last year, she'd owned one of those hair salons where they valet park your car and give you champagne while they do your hair, but it had gone out of business when people stopped paying two hundred dollars for a haircut. Now she was a faded version of her former self. Her hair looked like it hadn't been brushed in about a week, and the gray roots crept over the top of her head like a river overflowing its banks.

"What are you looking for?" she asked.

"It's, um, a shirt," I said. "But I don't see it, so I'll—"

"She got rid of a lot of things before she died." Mrs. Small's voice sounded strained. "She might have let someone else have it, or . . . I don't mean to say she would throw something of yours away—"

"No, I understand," I said. "Now that I think about it, I probably told her it was okay to lend it to someone else. It's all right. I should get going."

It felt like my lungs were compressed, and no breath I could take was deep enough to fill them.

No matter how determined I was to get rid of Lydia's ghost, bursting into this place, which was filled with sadness that was a direct consequence of my own actions, was too much for me. This whole thing had been a serious strategic misfire. I was treading behind enemy lines without a single weapon. It was time to retreat.

But Mrs. Small sat on the edge of the mattress and looked up at me. "Are you one of the girls from her little club?"

I didn't know whether to confirm or deny. I gave up and nodded.

"I was glad she found so many nice friends." Mrs. Small's fingers toyed with the hem of her robe. "I'd been worried about her. But she started hanging out with all those girls—all you girls—and she got so . . . pretty. She looked happy. So I stayed out of her way. But now I wonder if I should have . . . I don't know."

I started to feel like I was suffocating. I almost excused myself, but now that Mrs. Small had begun talking, the words poured out of her mouth.

"The doctors said there was no way we could have known. You can't predict an aneurysm. But don't you think a mother should be able to tell there's something wrong with her baby?" She reached out, grabbed one of the hangers, and brought it down hard against her leg. "I wasn't paying attention. I can't even remember the last time I told her I loved her. If I could just go back and have one more minute—"

So she didn't blame me. . . .

She blamed herself.

Tears bit at the edges of my eyes. "I should really get going."

"They remember her, don't they?" she asked. "The other girls? They think about her?"

"I do." At last I could speak the truth. "I think about her all the time."

To be honest, I didn't know if the Sunshine Club girls thought about Lydia or not. You certainly never heard her name mentioned in casual conversation. Maybe I *was* the only person who ever thought about her. How depressing would *that* be?

"I just like to think people aren't forgetting." Mrs. Small refused to stop staring up at me, her tired eyes wide and pleading.

"I'm sure they're planning some kind of memorial," I said. "In the yearbook or something."

There was the tiniest glimmer of hope in her eyes. "Yes, they might be . . . that would mean so much to her."

"Yes," I choked. As if Lydia cared in the least about the yearbook. "I'm sure."

"Could you—" She looked afraid to speak, but steeled herself and kept talking. "Could you ask and see if they are? Could you tell them how much it would mean?"

What? As in, actually go to the yearbook office and make an official request to memorialize the girl who was actively trying to destroy my life?

No freaking way.

But then I saw how Mrs. Small looked like an actual living human being for the first time since I'd come into the house, and I couldn't help myself. "Yeah, okay."

"I'd offer to pay for something, but money's a little scarce."

"No," I said. "Don't worry. I'm sure it's free."

"Thank you," she said, getting up and going to the dresser. "I'm so grateful that she had such nice friends . . . at the end."

She turned to me, her fingers lightly petting some tiny object. When she saw me looking at it, she held out her hand and dropped something small and cool into my palm: a delicate gold chain with a little glass bird charm, black with a red head.

"It was her favorite piece," her mother said. "A gift from my mother for Lydia's ninth birthday. It's a wood-pecker. It means you have a guardian."

Her favorite piece.

Her power center. The key to getting rid of her once and for all.

Mrs. Small's fingers hovered in the air near mine, like she was eager to grab the necklace back.

"You know . . ." I said, "I could take a photo of this and . . . put it in the yearbook."

I pictured myself taking it into the garage and smashing it to bits with a hammer.

Her hand trembled.

"It would be really nice, I think," I said. "I think Lydia would have liked it."

Welcome aboard, Alexis. This train goes straight to hell.

Mrs. Small's mouth was open, and she looked at the bird one last time before reaching over and closing my fingers around it. "All right. Just . . . please . . . be careful with it. Promise me."

I felt the cool glass on my skin, and I thought of what Lydia had done to Kendra. And to me.

"I promise," I lied.

I really *did* intend to take pictures of it before I destroyed it.

But I didn't get the chance.

When I got home and retreated to my room, after sneaking the hammer from the toolbox in the garage and setting a protective layer of cardboard on my desk, I dug down into my bag for the charm. But it wasn't there.

Instead, there was a hole in the corner of the bag where a seam had come apart.

I retraced my steps to my car, and then I drove all the way back to Lydia's house and retraced my steps there. I looked at every square inch of space within ten feet of where I'd walked, not even caring if Mrs. Small looked outside and saw me.

But the bird was gone.

9

SCHOOL STARTED UP AGAIN on a Wednesday. I took a deep breath as I got out of my car. New year, hopeful new outlook. (Or at least slightly less terrible outlook.)

The 700 wing was the newest building in the school. It had wide, spacious hallways with skylights and classrooms with air-conditioning that actually functioned. The only reason to stray this far from the center of campus before school was to be part of an advanced science lab or some sort of extracurricular organization, so all the kids I passed moved with purpose, like they had somewhere to be.

Halfway down the hall was a door marked PUBLICATIONS. A printed sign hung beneath that with the name of the yearbook: THE WINGSPAN.

I pushed the door open and walked into a large room that was painted nonregulation dark blue, with a row of computers along the far wall and bookshelves along the near one. About a third of the floor space was taken up with matching file cabinets, and next to those were a conference table and a small, untidy cluster of desks. Five or six kids sat on the desks, staring up at a giant whiteboard on the side wall. The whiteboard was covered in printed pages that seemed to represent an early draft of a yearbook.

A girl was talking. She had short curly hair, thin wire-frame glasses, and dark olive skin. Her baggy sweatshirt read HARVARD.

"It doesn't make sense to try to divide clubs up by grade level. There are only six that determine their membership that way." She pointed to a sheet with a list of club names on it. "We're going to list them either alphabetically or grouped according to the type of activity. Actually . . . both. Alphabetically by activity."

One of the boys opened his mouth to reply.

"Forget it, Chad," she said. "That's my final answer."

They all scattered, with no one taking any particular notice of me. I hung back, not knowing whom to approach.

Finally, the curly-haired girl glanced over at me. "You look lost."

"I'm looking for . . ." I consulted the note the office secretary had written for me. "Elliot Quilimaco? Is he here?"

"Hmm . . . someone's looking for Elliot. . . . Is *he*

here?" She put her hands on her hips and looked around the room, speaking in a loud voice. "You know, the *boy* in charge of the yearbook, because of course no mere *female* could ever be a yearbook editor. Has anyone seen Elliot, the exalted *male*?"

Nobody looked up. But the boy she'd called Chad, a burly guy with spiky dirty-blond hair, said, "Did you skip your meds today?"

She ignored him and turned back to me. "*I* am Elliot Quilimaco."

"Sorry." Couldn't she have just said so? I mean, it *is* a boy's name.

"Bless my stars!" she said, eyes widening in horror. "A girl named Elliot! Stop the presses!"

"Wait, really?" asked a boy a few feet away. He was hovering over a humming machine.

Elliot rolled her eyes. "That's not a *press*, Kevin. It's a laser printer."

If I hadn't already been saturated with regret about my promise to Mrs. Small, this would definitely have tipped me over the edge.

"What brings you to our humble corner of the school, Alexis?" she asked. "I thought you spent your time in the courtyard with the important people."

She knew who I was?

She tapped her foot, waiting for my answer.

"Um," I said. "I have a favor to ask."

"I'm listening."

I lowered my voice, not that anyone in the room seemed to be paying attention to us. "I was wondering if it would be possible to have some sort of memorial in the yearbook for Lydia Small—I mean, if you weren't already planning something."

Elliot's alert, questioning expression didn't change at all. "No, sorry, I don't think so. Have a nice day."

She started to turn away.

"Wait!" I said. "Are you kidding? You know she died, right?"

Elliot shrugged. "Even if I didn't, which I did, the request for a memorial would have been a pretty good clue."

"And . . ." I decided to change tactics. "It would really mean a lot to . . . people."

"Oh, I *see*." She blew air out of her nostrils. "Well, that doesn't actually change anything."

"Come on, seriously?"

Elliot put her hands back on her hips and leaned ever so slightly forward. "All right. Let's move this along. Here's the part where you say, 'What did she ever do to you?'"

"Um, no," I said. "That's probably not a good question to ask about Lydia."

"You're right," she said, moving closer. "Because I'll tell you what your little friend did to me. Last year—I don't know if you know this, but I doubt it, because obviously you've never deigned to notice me before—my older sister was a senior. And she was diagnosed with cancer, so she had to miss the last two months of school."

My hands were suddenly slick with sweat. I didn't see what this had to do with Lydia. Had Elliot's sister died and not gotten a yearbook memorial? Why did everything end with death and misery?

"She's in remission now, thank God," Elliot said a little more gently, probably after seeing my face. "But anyway, her greatest wish was to have her senior yearbook signed by all of her friends and teachers. So I brought it to school, carried it around for a week, made sure everyone wrote in it. And the stuff people wrote? *Epic*, Alexis. Poems, song lyrics, quotes—so much amazing material."

A vague sense of dread began to churn in my stomach.

"So on the last day of school, Lydia Small—who I kind of knew in junior high—comes up to me and asks if she can write something for Dale—yes, my sister also has a boy's name."

Lord, here it comes.

"She signed it, I said thanks, took it home and gave it to my sister. It was a huge surprise—Dale was so happy, we were crying . . . and she opened it up and started to read, and it was, like, better than I *ever* imagined."

92

She was telling the story with such relish that I couldn't bear to interrupt her, even though I knew I didn't want to hear how it ended.

"And then she gets to some random page . . . and stops smiling." Elliot's face turned from rapturous to deadly serious. "And the next page after that, she's frowning. And so on, until she's in tears, and she gets up and *throws the yearbook in the trash*. Because Lydia Small took a bright red Sharpie and wrote on, I don't know, I never actually counted—fifteen pages? Stuff like, 'Sorry you had to miss school because of the chlamydia,' 'Hope those crabs clear up before bathing suit season!'"

Now Elliot's eyes were bright and cold and diamond-hard, and everyone in the room was staring at us.

"So, yeah," she said. "Forgive me if I don't want to devote a two-page spread to your little friend who didn't give a flying—"

"Language, Quilimaco," said a voice from the corner. A teacher was sitting with his feet up on a desk, reading a magazine.

"A flying *foot*," Elliot said primly, "about what could have ended up being my sister's dying wish."

The words were out of my mouth before I could stop them. "She's not my friend. I couldn't stand her, for the record."

Elliot shifted her weight and looked at me with

blank curiosity. "Then why are you here?"

"I promised her mother I'd ask. But whatever." I turned to go.

Elliot heaved a mighty put-upon sigh. "Okay, fine."

"Wait, really?" To be honest, if I'd been in her shoes, I don't think anything could have changed my mind.

"Yes," Elliot said. "Mostly because you didn't try to go over my head and ask Mr. Janicke about it."

I glanced at the teacher, whose shirt was covered in doughnut crumbs. He gave me a wave. "I have no authority here," he said. "Carry on."

"Thank you *so much*," I said.

She turned and looked at the board. "We'll probably put it after the junior class photos. Just try to have it finished by Valentine's Day, because, no offense, it's probably going to need some tweaking."

"Wait—have it finished? Me?"

"Yes, you. Who else? We're understaffed. Here, let me give you the specs." She reached for a pad of paper. "We'll need a PSD with all the layers, and include the files of any exotic fonts you use. Eight by ten and a half, three hundred DPI, and obviously nothing with a copyright, please."

I stared at her, not even sure where to start. "Um . . . what's a PSD?"

"It's"—she blinked, momentarily stunned by my

ignorance—"a Photoshop document. This isn't going to work, is it?"

"Please," I said. "Isn't there any way someone who knows about that stuff can do it?"

Elliot scanned the room. "Of course there's a way. Chad, want to do this memorial page? Make it glorious."

Chad turned to us and shrugged, then went back to his work.

"He looks like a hoodlum, but he's brilliant with graphics," Elliot said.

"Thank you. Again." I still couldn't believe she'd changed her mind.

Her eyes were lit up, like she was enjoying this. "So. Chad does your layout, you do something for us."

"But . . . I don't know how to do any of this."

"You know how to take pictures."

True.

"Here's the deal. *We* devote two pages to making Lydia Small look like a dearly missed pillar of the school community, and *you* take on some photography work. Chad's pictures suck, anyway."

Without taking his eyes off the monitor, Chad held up his middle finger in our direction.

I was about to say no . . . and then I remembered Mrs. Small.

"Fine," I said.

"Great," Elliot said, looking pleased. "Perfect, in fact."

"What am I going to be shooting?"

"Nothing too exciting," she said, turning to walk back to her desk. "Clubs, teams, Student Council stuff."

I followed her. "Um, I can't do that."

"Okay." She sat and stuck the end of a pen in her mouth. "Then I can't do your special project."

"You don't understand," I said.

"I'll bet I do," she said, not even looking up. "You used to go out with Carter Blume. And now he's dating Zoe Perry. And they're both on Student Council. But somehow, you're going to rise above all that and take really good pictures of them."

I glanced at the teacher, hoping he would speak up.

"No authority," he said.

I turned back to Elliot.

"Deal?" she asked. "Or no deal?"

I looked at the ceiling, thinking of the bird necklace Lydia's mother was never going to get back.

"Deal," I said, turning and walking toward the door with as much dignity as I could muster.

"Our weekly meetings are Thursdays at two thirty-five!" she called. "Don't be late!"

10

SUDDENLY, MY LIFE WAS awash with meetings. On Thursday, I went to my first *Wingspan* staff meeting. And the following Tuesday, I drove across town to Sacred Heart Academy to join Megan's new club, whatever it was.

I was ten minutes early, but the school day was well over, and the spacious, tree-covered campus was mostly deserted. A few kids wandered by my car, spectacularly preppy in their private-school uniforms, all plaid and blazers and kneesocks.

Me? I was in a blue-and-white-striped sweater with a hole in the shoulder and an unraveling hem, ripped jeans, and a ratty pair of Converse.

After a few minutes of people-watching, I got out of my car and found the community room, but I didn't go inside. Considering I didn't know what I was getting into, I wasn't eager to jump in alone.

Megan arrived a few minutes later, limping up the

wheelchair ramp, holding her books to her chest with one hand and keeping the other one suspended over the railing. She gave me a small smile and waved with the tips of the fingers that were wrapped around her books.

"Hi," I said, hugging her. But she didn't hug back; the most you could really say was that she let herself be hugged.

"Hey," she said.

"Can I get your books for you?"

"No, I'm okay." She turned to me, shifting them in her arm. Her mouth was turned down in a slight frown. "I wish you would have let me tell you what this meeting is. I wanted you to know what you were getting into."

"I told you, I don't care," I said. "How bad could it be?"

"Yo." A man in wrinkled khaki pants and a worn dark-blue polo shirt shuffled up the aisle between our rows of folding chairs. "What's the word, young'uns?"

An uneven chorus of hellos echoed back to him as he took his place behind a podium at the front of the room.

"New face today—groovy," he said, smiling at me. "Welcome, welcome, *welcome* to the Brighter Path family. I'm Brother Ben, and I hope that you'll find all the support you need here. Never be afraid to speak up or ask for help."

I pressed my spine against the vinyl padding of my chair and averted my eyes from Brother Ben's by looking around the room. About half of the kids in attendance wore Sacred Heart uniforms, and the rest were dressed pretty much like me.

"First of all, thanks for coming." Ben seemed like he was in his early forties, but his hair was blond and as fine as a baby's, and his round face dwarfed his tiny, too-close blue eyes. "I know it's not always easy to make a change, and I'm not kidding myself—we're swimming upstream here. This culture wants you to believe that the easy way out is down a very dark and dangerous path. But we're here to support each other on the *brighter* path."

The way out of what? Was this some kind of twelve-step meeting? Maybe Megan had started drinking or doing drugs and wanted me here for support. I glanced at her, but she was staring straight ahead.

"I'm going to pass around the box." He pulled out a shoe box with a clamshell top. "If you have anything you'd like to turn in, please drop it inside. Remember, no one is judging you. We're all here to help each other get stronger."

His eyes found mine.

"Think of the box as a safe," he said. "Anything you might own or acquire—any books or trinkets or just anything, really, you can put in there and it will disappear."

Books about drugs? Alcohol trinkets? Like . . . a bottle opener or something?

He handed it to one of the kids and looked around. "Now, would anyone like to speak?"

A mousy girl stood up and went to the front of the room, her head bowed so low that her chin practically touched her chest.

"I'm Savannah," she said.

I waited for everyone to say, *"Hi, Savannah!"* like they do at addiction meetings on TV and in movies.

They didn't.

She braced her hands against the podium. "This Saturday was a hundred days since my last experience with the occult."

The *occult*?

I stared at Megan, who glanced at me, swallowed hard, and then pointedly looked back toward the front of the room.

Brother Ben was applauding Savannah's hundred days with a thick, moist-handed clap, and a few other people halfheartedly joined in.

Savannah turned bright pink. "Yeah, thanks . . . So my mom and dad took me out to dinner to celebrate. But they didn't know that the nail place next to our favorite restaurant closed and got replaced by a palm reader."

"Uh-oh," Ben said, shaking his head. "That is *not* good."

Before I could stop myself, I started to laugh. I managed to turn it into a fake cough, which still attracted the attention of every single person in the room.

"You okay back there?" Ben asked.

I nodded and looked up at Savannah, vowing to keep better control of myself.

"My dad got totally stressed out, and we ended up fighting, even though I said I didn't even care. But we had to leave, and when I got home, I was super depressed, and I . . . I really, really wanted to look at my tarot cards."

You could have heard a pin drop.

"But I didn't," she said, letting out a huge breath. She reached into her pocket and pulled out a plastic bag filled with gray powder. "Dad helped me burn them, and I brought the ashes for the box."

I turned to Megan. "Seriously?" I whispered.

She didn't look at me. Brother Ben started clapping again.

This time, Megan joined in.

I sat back, self-conscious.

Next, some junior high kid talked about how he finally realized his friends are Satanists and he had to stop hanging out with them and listening to their rock band rehearsals.

I started to feel twitchy.

Look, don't get me wrong. In the grand scheme of things, I'm right there with Brother Ben.

The occult, the dark side, the netherworld—I believe in them. I've lived them. I believe—no, I *know*, through direct, horrible experience—that they're dangerous. And I think, one hundred and fifty percent, that people should leave them alone.

But sue me: after going toe-to-toe *twice* with ghosts who wanted me dead, the idea of a garage full of twelve-year-old quote-unquote devil worshippers striking terror in my heart just seemed a little ridiculous.

"Anybody else?" Ben asked, looking straight at me.

Um, no. I leaned back and tried to smile in a convincingly apologetic manner.

But to my utter shock, Megan said, "Okay," and went up to the podium. "Hi . . . I'm Megan."

I watched her, powerless to stop the frown line from spreading across my forehead. Knowing she saw it.

"As a lot of you know, I've had some trouble," she said. "The thing I struggle with is, I'm more than willing to leave behind the bad stuff, but what about the . . . good?"

I pressed my fingertips into my jeans so hard the skin turned white.

Megan's mother had been a ghost—a good one. Good ghosts are rare, but there are a few out there. In the end, she'd helped save us all—Megan, me, my entire family, and the dozens of people Kasey would have killed if the evil spirit living in her doll hadn't been stopped.

How could anyone ask a daughter to turn her back on the memory of her own mother? And how could Megan even *begin* to think that was a good idea? If it had just been the two of us hanging out, like in the old days, I would have told her right to her face to get real—that remembering her mother could never be a bad thing.

But that's not how things worked at Brighter Path.

Ben sighed and ran a hand through his hair, leaving it sticking up at weird angles. "If something isn't of this world," he said, a patronizing twinge of regret in his voice, "then it's of the *other* world. And if something is of the other world . . ."

From the audience, a half dozen unenthusiastic voices finished: *"Then it's not for us."*

Megan looked anxious to explain. "But—"

"You can leave a door open for your 'friends,'" Ben said, air-quoting with his fingers. "But the truth is, *anybody* can come in through that open door. And how do you know these friends are who they say they are, anyway? It's the nature of those who aren't of this world to deceive us and betray us."

"Right," Megan said, so quietly I could barely hear her.

As Ben patted her shoulder, I wanted to bat his hand away.

Then, like he could sense my anger, he looked right at me. "What about you, Alexis? Would you like to share today?"

Yeah, I'd love to. I'd share how narrow-minded he was and how stupid and unfair this whole new insulated life of Megan's was. I'd share a few choice words that had popped into my head when Ben air-quoted about her mom, and I'd share where he could stick his box of contraband mood rings.

"No," I said, shaking my head. "I don't think that's going to happen."

I could tell that Megan, who had come back to her seat, was watching me. But when I turned to look at her, I found that she was actually *glaring* at me.

"All right," Ben said mildly. "You share when you're ready."

"*As if,*" I whispered under my breath.

Suddenly, Megan grabbed my sleeve and pulled me to my feet. With everyone's eyes on us, she dragged me down the aisle and out the door.

As soon as we were outside, I took a huge breath. "Please tell me this is a joke."

"*See?*" Her voice was tight. "*This* is exactly why I was afraid to invite you."

"What?" For a moment, I didn't even understand what she was trying to say. Then it sank in. "What do you mean?"

"I'm trying to give it a chance, okay?"

"But *why?* Is it your grandmother?" Mrs. Wiley was used to getting whatever she wanted. And used to being obeyed. Had she ordered Megan to do this? "If she's asking you to pretend nothing happened, she's *wrong.*"

"*Don't,*" Megan said, her voice like ice. "*Don't* talk badly about my grandmother. She's the only family I have."

She'd never spoken to me so sharply before. It felt like being slapped. I looked down at the crack-covered sidewalk.

"It's not her, Alexis. It's *me.* It's my choice." Megan finally looked at me, on the verge of tears. "Maybe you don't get it, but I want to get better. And I can't do that if I feel like you're judging me the whole time."

"I'm not judging *you!*" I protested. "I'm judging . . ."

I was judging what she wanted for herself.

She gazed off into the distance. "This was a huge mistake."

"Megan." I hardly trusted myself not to cry. "You're my best friend. Just tell me what to do. Tell me what you want."

"I want to be normal," Megan said, her voice rigid.

"Come back inside if you can understand that. But if you can't—if you're going to be like this—then don't."

I spoke before I had time to think about what I was saying. "I'm sorry. I'll try. I'll really try."

After all, weren't we after the same thing? Didn't I wish I could leave ghosts behind and be normal again? But there was "normal," and then there was . . . this.

I hushed my traitorous inner voice and watched Megan for any sign of a reaction.

Finally she gave me a small, sad smile. "Okay, then."

I followed her back inside, feeling like a hostage. Brother Ben's curious eyes were all over us. And when the kid who was speaking sat down, Ben looked directly at me. "Anyone else?"

Megan sat with her hands folded in her lap, watching the podium expectantly.

I stood up.

When I got to the front of the room, I was surprised to find that my heart was pounding like a drum. "My name is Alexis." My voice trembled. "I've had some . . . issues."

The whole room was silent. Everyone was listening raptly.

I swallowed the lump in my throat. "My problem is that . . . even though I want a normal life, I can't . . . get away from certain things. I'm not looking for them. The things—they come to me."

Ben's baby-blue eyes pounced on me. "Alexis, what I'm sensing in you is a lack of commitment."

I was about to protest, but I saw the look on Megan's face and stopped myself.

"Only *you* can take responsibility for the things you do and the forces you let into your life. Have you ever heard the phrase 'garbage in, garbage out'?"

I nodded dumbly.

"Well, it sounds like you're letting plenty of garbage in."

I stared down at the wood surface of the podium. Someone had taped an index card to it that read DO NOT LEAN ON ME. I WILL COLLAPSE!

"So instead of saying, 'Trouble finds me, it's not my fault,' ask yourself, 'What am I doing to invite this garbage into my life? How can I improve *myself* and be stronger?'" He took a step toward me, and I had to fight not to flinch. "Do you have any ideas?"

It took a moment for me to realize he actually wanted me to come up with something. And I would totally have fed him a line of BS, except I couldn't even think of one.

"Nope," I said, feeling my cheeks redden. "Fresh out of ideas, I guess."

"Maybe you could start," Ben said gently, "by admitting that you're not strong enough."

I glanced up in surprise.

"Alexis, you are a weak person," he said. "We all are. And you've got to accept your weakness or you'll never be free."

Well, he did kind of have a point. This *had* all started because I'd had a moment of utter spinelessness. If I hadn't been so terrified of being blind, I wouldn't have taken the oath to Aralt again. And maybe I could have focused on finding some other way to stop Lydia, instead of just thinking about myself and my own well-being.

"Try saying it," Ben coaxed. "Admit it."

Accept your weakness. And suddenly I *felt* weak. I felt helpless. After all, wasn't my whole life proof that there was something fundamentally wrong with me?

"I'm . . ." The letters on the index card blurred, and I found myself leaning on the podium, my breath catching in my chest, desperate not to cry in front of a room full of people. "I'm . . . weak?"

Ben started applauding. Most of the kids slapped their hands together once or twice out of obligation.

And Megan sat forward in her seat, clapping like her life depended on it.

11

ASHLEEN PULLED THE DOOR OPEN, and the thudding beat of music spilled out around her. Her face lit up. "Hi, you guys!"

Being addressed as "you guys" or "you two" instead of "Alexis" was something I was getting pretty used to. It had been almost a month since Jared and I started showing up at parties together, and people at school had stopped thinking of me as single. *I* even stopped thinking of me as single.

"Hey," I said, trying (but failing) to match her enthusiasm.

"Come in, come in," Ashleen said, moving out of the way so Jared and I could pass. "It's cold tonight, isn't it? I think the hedgehog's going to say six more weeks of winter tomorrow."

Jared coughed to cover his laugh. I could only shake my head and smile. "I don't know," I managed to say.

"Coats in the dining room, people and food in the

game room," she said. "The pizzas just got here."

Jared realized he'd left his phone in the car, so I waited for him while Ashleen straightened out the welcome mat and stood up.

"Jared's really nice," she said, looking after him wistfully. "You're soooo lucky."

"Yeah," I said.

"Does he have any friends?" She lowered her voice and patted her dark wavy hair. "Single ones?"

Every unattached girl, I was learning, wanted what I had—a boy whose eyes always traced her movements in a crowd, who would leave any conversation to stand silently at her side. And most of them seemed to think I was covered in magical boyfriend dust that would rub off on them if they talked to me.

Yeah, seeing Carter and Zoe together was still a shock, every single time.

But at least I could turn to Jared and lose myself in his presence—let him nuzzle my neck, talk quietly into my ear, wrap his arms around my waist and rest his head on my shoulder. We were one of *those* couples—the kind that are always irritatingly wrapped up in each other. Who never have much to say to anyone else.

Life was good. I'd wanted to be average, and that was what I got. My grades were better. I slept more. I saw Megan every week—even if I did have to sit through

Brighter Path meetings to earn the privilege. Instead of worrying about Kasey and me making pacts with the devil, my parents were starting to worry that Jared and I were getting too serious too fast. I'd done some shoots for the yearbook, and I went to the weekly meetings. I wasn't sure if any of the other staffers liked me, but I enjoyed being part of it—part of something bigger than myself.

And best of all by far: in four weeks, there had been no sign of Lydia. No shadows in my car, no disembodied laughter, no yellow roses, no more missing girls. I concluded that I must have dropped the glass bird in the street, where it had been pulverized by a passing car or the blessed, oblivious crunch of a mailman's boot.

My days had a slow, steady rhythm. They still had good parts and bad parts, but there were no *insanely* bad parts, which was a huge improvement over my recent past.

I'd be lying if I didn't say that, in some ways—in a lot of ways—it was like finding myself washed ashore after spending five months lost at sea.

But sometimes when I lay in bed at night, or happened to catch a glimpse of a picture in a magazine or on a wall, and saw a dead woman staring pleadingly from her spot next to a nail polish model, or a burned face in the middle of a family photo taken at somebody's vacation house, I felt a stab of . . .

What was it?

Fear? Dread? The suspicion that I was just fooling myself and it could never last?

All of the above?

The party spilled out of the game room onto the back patio, where a group of kids were huddled around the fire pit. Over the course of the night, I caught a few glimpses of short blond hair and forced myself to ignore the subsequent soul-crunching pang. At one point, I looked up to see Carter watching Jared and me. Did his soul crunch? Did he feel the same pang?

He didn't *act* like he felt it. As always, he was near Zoe, with a hand on her shoulder. I watched his fingers drift across her skin in a way that threatened to hollow me out.

So I leaned deeper into the crook of Jared's arm. He pulled me closer and touched his lips to the side of my face, then went on talking to some random kid about a video game. I saw a girl across the room gazing at us with undisguised envy, and reminded myself how lucky I was.

Jared's hand slipped around my body, just under my ribs. "Ready to go?" he asked, in a voice only I could hear.

I nodded. We'd only been there for two hours, but we were never the first to arrive—or the last to leave.

"Bye, guys," he said to the whole room, giving a wave. People waved back, and we started for the dining room, where our coats were slung over a chair.

I stopped in the kitchen and put my hand on Jared's

chest. "Hang on," I said. "I need to find Ashleen. She wanted to borrow my Spanish notes from yesterday, and I need her e-mail address."

Jared took a deep, impatient breath. "Does it have to be now?"

"It'll only take thirty seconds."

"We already said good-bye."

"Yeah, but—"

"I know those girls, Alexis. You go back to say one thing, and fifteen minutes later you'll still be talking about some idiotic reality show."

I opened my mouth to protest, but then I looked up at Jared's face.

"Please," he said. "I'm just not in the mood to be here right now."

"All right," I said.

"Let me help you with your coat," he said, standing behind me to slide it over my arms.

I heard the sound of a throat being cleared, and looked up to see Carter at the door to the dining room, watching us.

How long had he been there? How much had he heard?

Even though I knew Jared had seen him, he took a second to straighten the collar of my coat, like I was a little girl, before seeming to notice Carter and asking, "What's up?"

They'd crossed paths at several parties, but they'd

never been formally introduced. And I got the distinct feeling tonight wasn't the night to do it.

Jared put his arm around my waist and shepherded me out, not waiting for Carter's reply.

It bugged me in a way I couldn't quite put my finger on. As we made our way down the sidewalk, I thought about saying something, but glanced over at Jared and saw that his expression hadn't softened.

Whatever, I thought. Not like Carter and I had anything to say to each other anyway.

The car was silent except for the sounds of other cars passing by—*whoosh, whoosh, whoosh.* Jared's fingers drummed noiselessly on the steering wheel.

"Is everything okay?" I asked.

He glanced at me. "If it weren't, don't you think I'd tell you?"

"Sure," I said.

He took his right hand off the wheel and rested it gently on my knee. A few more quiet minutes passed.

"So," he said suddenly, "these parties."

"What about them?"

"To be honest, I'm not sure how many more I can take." He was smiling, but his smile was tight, forced. "You don't really like them, do you?"

"*Them?* You mean the kids or the parties?"

He shrugged. "Either?"

"The kids are fine," I said. "The parties are . . . okay. Good pizza, right?"

He didn't laugh.

I sighed.

"You're just so different from those people." He glanced at me. "They're not like you at all."

No they're not. They're all decent people who haven't messed up their lives.

"It's so shallow, you know?"

"I don't know," I said. "I think people just like to have fun at parties. How are the kids from your school?"

"Not like that."

"Kasey's not shallow. Her boyfriend's not shallow." Another name rose to the tip of my tongue, but I swallowed it. Carter might not be shallow, but that wasn't what Jared was looking to hear.

"Two people out of fifty?" he asked.

"Never mind, then," I said. "We don't have to go to every party. We don't have to go to any of them, for all I care."

He was silent again, and I wondered what I'd said wrong.

"Look," I said, trying to sound reasonable. "I thought you had a good time, but if you don't, I—"

"No," Jared said. "Forget it. You're right. I'm wrong."

I sighed and sat back. "I don't have to be right. I just don't think they're that bad."

He slowed for a yellow light and glanced over at me. "It's not about the shallowness, okay? It's about you."

"What does that mean?"

He shook his head. "I just get the feeling that we're—that *you're* being . . . watched."

The hairs pricked up at the back of my neck. I always felt like I was being watched.

"Or—not *watched*, exactly."

I gazed out the windshield at the headlights of the cars opposite us. They began to blur into halos. My voice turned brittle. "Then what," I said, "exactly?"

He sighed. "Judged."

I turned my face toward the window. I didn't want Jared to see how hard it was for me to hold back the tears that had sprung to my eyes. "Why do you say that?"

"It bothers me, Alexis. The way they look at you. It's like you're some kind of . . ."

Murderer?

He didn't finish the sentence. He just went on. "You're too good to be treated that way. So why do you hang around with them?"

"I don't know," I said. "I guess because . . . I don't know."

But I had a pretty good idea, actually.

Because I'm weak.

12

AFTER JARED DROPPED ME OFF, I said good night to my parents and went straight to bed. In spite of my weariness, I didn't go right to sleep. I lay under the covers, staring up at the ceiling, thinking about what he'd said.

I felt hotly embarrassed. If Jared, who hardly knew them, had picked up on their judgment, then it must have been completely obvious to everyone but me. When I showed up to a party, did everybody think, *Oh, here she is again*? Did they all think I was just a freak, trying to wedge myself into their normal social order?

Did Carter think that?

Was I the only person who couldn't see how little they wanted me around?

My cheeks tingled with shame. My eyes burned with tears. I curled up into a ball and shut my eyes as tightly as I could.

Finally, I fell asleep.

* * *

It was the weirdest dream—almost like being awake.

I was drawn out of bed so delicately that I didn't even remember getting out from under the covers. I just found myself standing in front of the mirror. The room was dark, and I couldn't see myself clearly, but I could tell that I wore some kind of fancy dress, like you'd wear to a dance or a tea party. The fabric was light and flimsy. The room was cold, and my bare feet felt like ice.

I tried to stare into the reflection of my own eyes, but I couldn't focus on them.

I felt restless, as if I had somewhere to go, somewhere to be—but I couldn't figure out where.

A wave of helpless loneliness washed through me, and then I burst into tears. I was crying for something . . . for someone. It was the most desolate emotion I'd ever felt—like half of me had been ripped away.

From behind me—from some dark corner of the room—came a soft sound: *vzzzzzzzzzz.* The sound grew louder until I took my eyes off the mirror and swung around to look for its source.

That's when I snapped out of the dream to find that I really was standing in front of the mirror. The dress was gone, but the sense of unendurable solitude still coated me like a terrible second skin.

I crept back under the covers, convinced that no one

would ever again really care about me, or believe in me, or want me around.

On the nightstand, my phone chirped. The screen lit up with a text message.

Can't sleep, Jared wrote. *Thinking about you.*

I grabbed the phone like it was a life preserver, and dialed Jared's cell so quickly that my fingers tripped over themselves.

He picked up on the first ring. "Hi."

I swallowed back tears of relief.

"Is this a booty call? Because . . . I don't know what you've heard, but I'm not that kind of guy." His voice, low and gentle, filled the emptiness in my heart like honey in a bowl.

We talked quietly for a while and finally got to the point where we were both dozing off, so we hung up.

I slept like a baby.

That Tuesday, the landline rang at six forty-five in the morning. A few seconds later, there was a knock at my door, and Mom came in holding the phone.

"Alexis," she said. "It's for you."

"What? Really?" I sat up, stifled a yawn, and took the phone. "Hello?"

"Alexis, this is Laurel Evans."

I couldn't place the name.

"Ashleen's mother."

"Oh," I said. "Hi."

"Sorry if I woke you up. I'm calling everyone who came to her party Saturday. I need to know if you know of anyone she might have wanted to meet or talk to or—"

"I'm sorry?" I motioned for Mom to flip my light on. Kasey had come to the door, too. "I don't understand."

"Ashleen is missing," she said. "We think she may have run away."

"Run away?" I repeated. "Why?"

"She's been having some problems with her step-father." Mrs. Evans sighed. "I thought maybe someone would know if there was a place she'd go . . . maybe with a boy?"

"No—I don't know anything," I said, feeling dazed. "I'm sorry. I hope you find her soon."

I stared at the phone for a second until my mother reached down and took it.

"Laurel? It's Claire again. I don't even know what to say. I'm sure she'll be fine. Have you called the police?" Mom shook her head. "Well, that's shocking. But it has to be a good sign, right? They would know. I'm sure she'll turn up. You know how teenagers are. . . ."

Mom glanced up at Kasey and me. I got the feeling she might have said more about *how teenagers are* if we hadn't been in the room. "Maybe," she said into the phone. "That sounds highly likely. . . . All right, I'll let you go. And if you need any phone numbers, call here. Kasey and Alexis may have them."

My sister sank onto the bed next to me.

"We'll be thinking about you. Keep us posted." Mom hung up the phone, then looked down at us, hugging herself. "The police won't investigate yet, because they think she ran away. But she didn't take her wallet. It's just like . . ."

She didn't have to finish her sentence. It was just like Kendra.

"The police won't do anything?" Kasey said. "Even after Kendra practically died?"

"She's not dead," I snapped. "She's doing much better."

Mom sighed. "Don't forget, there were no indications that what happened to Kendra was any kind of foul play. She just got lost."

"Barefoot?" Kasey asked. "In the middle of the night?"

Mom shrugged. "Kase, we haven't seen the police report, so we don't know what happened. But there's no point in getting paranoid. It sounds like Ashleen ran away with a boy. Would you guys know anything about that?"

"No; why do you say that—about the boy?" I asked. If Ashleen had a secret boyfriend, she wouldn't have been so yearny over Jared.

Mom's chest rose and fell in a sigh. "Because there was a rose on the ground just outside her bedroom—a yellow rose."

I spun away to hide my reaction from my mother and sister.

So the bird necklace either hadn't been destroyed . . . or it wasn't Lydia's power center.

She was still out there. She hadn't been stopped.

Which meant my normal life was pretty much over.

But Ashleen hadn't even been in the Sunshine Club. Had she and Lydia even known each other? Maybe Lydia had tried to recruit her at some point and Ashleen had said no. Or maybe she said yes and just didn't have a chance to join.

Or could there be some other random reason? And now Lydia was just going to carry out revenge against *anyone* who got on her bad side? God knows *that* wasn't hard to do. There was no rhyme or reason to this, no common link—it seemed she was just going to go around luring people into the woods and try to kill them.

Unless someone stopped her. And who else would—who else could—except me?

I spent the whole school day in a haze, knowing that the clock was ticking and the odds of Ashleen being found alive were decreasing by the minute.

I'm weak. It had become almost a mantra, and I had a headful of anecdotal evidence to back it up. If I went out looking for Lydia, she could kill me. How on earth could I possibly win?

What *right* did I have to fight her?

But then, walking down the hall toward lunch, seeing a poster on the wall for the silent auction being held to help with Kendra's medical bills, it struck me:

What right did I have to fight Lydia . . . ?

That was the wrong question.

What right did I have *not* to fight her—even if I knew I'd lose?

But I still needed a plan.

By the time the final bell rang, I'd exhausted all of my mental energy trying to come up with a way to stop her. And I still had nothing, no magical ghost-fighting scheme.

Then, when I least expected it, I got the next best thing:

A lucky break.

13

SAVANNAH, SAVANNAH, SAVANNAH.

She'd backslid with a vengeance since her virtuous tarot card–burning days. For three weeks in a row, she'd come to Brighter Path with new stories of her paranormal adventures and new trinkets for the box.

As Savannah walked to the podium that day, Megan leaned toward me conspiratorially and whispered, "I'm starting to question her commitment."

In the old days, that would have been a joke. And I would have had to pinch myself to keep from laughing and getting into trouble. But Megan was deadly serious, which made it about as funny as a funeral.

"Hello. Savannah, again," she said, tossing her long ponytail and practically grinning. "Um . . . this week it was a Ouija board, levitating—"

"Levitating?" Ben repeated, aghast.

"Well, we tried. And we made a chanting circle, and we found this book of charms and tried some of them."

She held up a small blue paperback and shrugged. "None of it worked. I think it's because my cousin wasn't pure of intention, but—"

Savannah's voice blurred in my mind as I stared at the paperback, grateful for once that Megan always wanted us to sit right up front so I could see the title of the book: *Charms for Containment of Hostile Spirits.*

But more important, I could read the author's name: WALTER SAWAMURA.

Walter Sawamura was the real deal. He'd written the book that helped me save my sister from the evil ghost that lived in our old house.

"Thank you, no need to go into detail," Ben said hastily. He got up and held out the box, and Savannah piled her latest contraband—including the book—into it.

I was starting to think she might have a real problem, the kind of thing Brother Ben couldn't fix. She was like a snorkeler throwing pork chops around in shark-infested waters. Eventually, some evil spirit was going to take a chomp out of her. I was even tempted to talk to her outside of Brighter Path.

One problem at a time, Alexis.

For the rest of the meeting I focused on thinking of a way to get to that book. I was so distracted that I didn't even listen to Megan's weekly testimony, and when she came back and sat next to me with that shiny hopeful look in her eyes, I didn't have the energy to seem apologetic.

"Not this week," I said.

She sighed and gave me a tiny smile. "Maybe next time."

Yeah, sure. Not likely.

After Brother Ben delivered his closing "Choose the Brighter Path!" pep talk and said good-bye for the day, Megan gathered her things and looked at me expectantly.

"Um, hang on," I said. "Wait for me outside, okay? I need to talk to Ben."

Her eyes burned with curiosity, but she headed for the door.

Ben was packing up his plastic crate. He wasn't even looking at the contraband box, which was unattended on a chair in the first row of seats. If I were slightly braver, I would have just opened it, grabbed what I wanted, and run out.

But I cleared my throat, and he stood up and turned to face me. "Lex! What's up?"

I tried to look uncomfortable. It wasn't much of a stretch. "I sort of have something to turn in. I couldn't do it, you know, in front of . . ."

I was going to say *everyone,* but Ben said, "Megan?"

"Um, right."

He clasped his hands in front of his stomach. "Do you want to talk about it?"

"No," I said. "Not really."

His tiny eyes gave me a long appraising look. "This makes me feel a lot of hope for you, Alexis. I think you should be really proud of yourself."

"Thank you," I said.

"May I see it?" he asked.

Um. I hadn't actually planned to produce an item. I was just going to pretend I had one and filch the book of charms. But I gave him a brave smile and dug around in my bag until I felt my fingers close around the first remotely suitable object—a Sharpie.

Ben's expression was understandably confused when I held up a permanent marker.

"I've been, um, using this," I said, "to create pictures. Of symbols and signs . . . and stuff."

He nodded slowly.

"It's more kind of . . . what it *represents?*" I said.

"Of course," he said. "Well, that's very conscientious of you. Why don't you go ahead and put it in the box?"

I smiled and turned away from him, blocking his view of the box with my body. I dropped the pen in with exaggerated loudness. But there was no way to slip the book out without his noticing.

"Good girl!" he said. "Now, want to help me carry this stuff out to my car?"

"Of course," I said, picking up the box.

He lifted the crate and led the way. I followed a few feet behind, finally summoning the burst of daring I needed to open the cover of the box and remove the book, sliding it into my bag.

And then we were outside, where Megan was waiting on a bench, smiling bigger than she'd smiled at me in a long time.

Universe, 9 bazillion. Alexis, 1.

Then there was the question of how to actually *find* Ashleen. I turned on the local news as soon as I got home, hoping they would show a view from a helicopter. But Ashleen's coverage was lighter than Kendra's had been. They had a quick update about her—apparently the police had finally decided to get involved—and put her picture in a little on-screen graphic, but they didn't go into much detail about the investigation.

The only way I'd get any information was to go after it myself. I grabbed my car keys and hurried out to my car before I could lose my nerve.

I stopped at the grocery store, bought a small vase of flowers, and drove across town to the Evanses' house. Someone was home—there were cars in the driveway, so I walked up the front path and rang the doorbell.

Mrs. Evans pulled the door open. She looked at me vacantly for a moment, then blinked in recognition. One of the advantages of having white hair—people tend to remember meeting you. "Alexis?"

I held up the flowers. "Um, I brought you these."

I'd intended to use the flowers as a reason to go there. What I hadn't thought about was the fact that they made it seem like I thought Ashleen was dead. But from the way Mrs. Evans stared down at them, I realized my mistake.

"They're to cheer you up," I said stupidly, and she reached out and took the vase. She stepped back into the house, probably not intending to invite me in, but I followed her anyway.

We went all the way to the kitchen, where two boys, one older than me, one younger—both of whom looked like Ashleen—were moping at the table. They raised their heads when we came in, then slumped again.

"I wanted you to know how sorry I am," I said, and Mrs. Evans startled and turned around, not expecting to see me behind her. "I'm sure she's all right."

Her eyes widened. "Do you know something? Something you want to tell me?"

"No," I said. "Sorry. I'm just worried, and I thought coming here might . . ."

How to jump into the topic of where she might have gone?

Mrs. Evans went hazy again. But one of the boys

at the table, the older one, looked at me.

"Did Ashleen like to hike?" I asked. "I'm just thinking if she had, you know, wilderness skills . . ."

The boy raised his eyebrows. "She didn't hike. She rode horses. And she had plenty of survivalist experience. She did this ride last summer—one of those 'live off the land' things. She was gone for two weeks." His voice swelled with pride.

"That's great," I said. "Where did she ride around here?"

"Mostly the trails over at Wyndham Forest," the boy said. He leaned forward, his interest waning. "But they've searched it already."

The younger boy looked up at me suddenly, his eyes burning. "Do you know how hard it is to find someone who doesn't want to be found?"

"Shh," the older boy said, putting a hand on his brother's shoulder. "That forest ranger didn't know what he was talking about."

Then the younger boy started crying, and the older one glanced up at me.

"Thanks for coming by," he said. "And thanks for the flowers."

It's time for you to go, he didn't say.

"You're welcome," I said, grateful for the opportunity to leave.

An expedition to a deep dark forest in the middle of the night wasn't exactly my first choice, but there was no other way to get out the door without concocting an elaborate web of lies for my parents. So I passed the rest of the afternoon thumbing through the book of charms and marking the ones I hoped would be useful. I had a lot of faith in Walter Sawamura, so when the paragraph on the back of the book claimed it would help "send the lingering spirits of the dead onward to a state of permanent transitional resting," especially since he promised "a minimum of trouble and danger to the executor of the spells," I believed him. His work had saved a whole town full of women from my sister's evil doll.

After my parents and sister went to bed, I slipped on a pair of jeans, a hoodie, and my Converse. I took a piece of chalk from the chalkboard that hung over my desk and dropped it into my pocket. Then I grabbed my coat, car keys, and wallet, and slipped silently out the front door.

It was weird. You'd think it would have felt like more of an event—giving up everything I'd spent a month trying to build for myself, jumping back into the fight.

But instead, it felt more like I was starting a really hard project for school—something I didn't want to do but didn't have a choice about.

As much as I hated the idea of having anything to do

with ghosts, I couldn't just sit back and let Lydia rampage around Surrey, hurting people. Until I found a way to stop her permanently, I might just have to stop her on a case-by-case basis.

Unless she stopped me first, of course.

As my headlights swept over the empty roads, I thought, *So much for normal.*

14

I PULLED DOWN A DIRT ACCESS road and parked on the shoulder. In the highly unlikely event that someone came by, I'd just say I'd been driving home and got lost. That wouldn't explain why I was wandering around in the forest, but if I combined it with a simpering helpless-teenager face, I was positive it would do the trick.

Logistically speaking, I felt pretty confident about the whole operation. The rain had let up, and the moon was full and round, bathing the night with blue light so bright that even under the canopy of the trees I could see the reddish-brown color of the pine needles on the ground. I had my phone with me, and approximately every fifty feet I checked to make sure the GPS signal worked so I could find my way back to my car. In case that failed, I also marked my trail, putting slashes of chalk on tree trunks to indicate which direction I should go to find the previous tree.

In other words, getting lost in the woods—not an option.

And I wasn't exactly *scared* of encountering Lydia— for all the awful things she'd done, she still had yet to really hurt me. I still thought of her as Lydia first, ghost second—more pest than danger. I couldn't help it, even though I knew it would be smarter to see her as a real threat.

But my faith in the book of charms was nearly absolute. I had it tucked between my two sweatshirts, because just seeing it might even be enough to scare her off. I'd bookmarked "For Temporary Immobilization of Spirits" and "To Send Spirits to a State of Rest," and I wanted her to stick around long enough for me to read one and dispatch her to the next plane. Lydia in a state of rest—someplace far, far away from me—sounded pretty heavenly, if you'll excuse the pun.

An hour later, I was freezing through all of my layers and beginning to lose hope. My camera was slung around my neck, and I'd been taking pictures every twenty feet or so—trying to stay alert in case Lydia decided to drop a tree branch on my head (or the whole tree).

I'd seen one ghost so far—a Native American girl about my age, with a bullet hole in her shoulder and a healthy splotch of blood on her animal-skin cape. She was intent on some kind of hunt, and she didn't even look up at the flash of the camera.

I kept moving.

The sound of every footstep, no matter how lightly I tried to tread, seemed magnified in the air around me. And the harder I concentrated, the longer I walked, the louder my breathing got. It became a complex little routine—walk, pause, chalk a tree, take picture, look at picture; repeat.

As the minutes continued to tick by, I wondered if I'd made a mistake. Luckily, not the terrifying kind of mistake I usually ended up stumbling into—more of a tactical error. Just because this was a place Ashleen knew didn't mean I'd find her here. And if she wasn't out here, what good would it do for me to be stomping around in the wilderness in the middle of the night? Like her brother said—they'd searched these woods already.

Two and a half hours in, there was no sign of Ashleen, the white light, or Lydia herself. If it hadn't been for the fact that I was an ice cube on legs, I would have fallen asleep on my feet. A growing sense of futility began to overwhelm me. I gave myself five more pictures before I would call it a night and go home.

The next picture, nothing.

Or maybe just three more.

The next picture, nothing.

This will be the last one.

But in this picture—

Not nothing. Something up ahead, disappearing around a tree. I zoomed in on it.

The heel of a bare foot, mid-stride.

I hurried to that tree and took another volley of photographs, then started scanning them. Nothing, nothing, nothing, nothing—

Ashleen. And she wasn't lying on the ground, comatose. She was standing up, walking around.

I looked up. "Ashleen!" I called. "Ashleen! It's Alexis!"

There was no answer. I sped up to a trot, as fast as I dared go on unfamiliar terrain.

"Hello? Ashleen? Are you out here?"

I went about fifty feet before stopping to take more pictures. If I could find the bright white light that I'd seen when I found Kendra, I'd know Lydia was nearby and I could force her to lead me to Ashleen. I took one last exposure and looked down at the screen.

"Oh," I said, taking an unsteady step backward.

Ashleen was standing in front of me.

But only in the picture.

It was like I was suddenly two people: myself, stunned, mentally and emotionally; and also a version of myself who was vividly aware that there was a ticking clock counting down the seconds until I completely and utterly lost the ability to think or act rationally.

Ashleen, a girl I knew well enough to call a friend—a girl whose party I'd been to a few days earlier—was dead.

I'd never seen the ghost of a person I knew before—I mean, besides Lydia. But Lydia was no friend to me.

I wandered away and sat on a fallen log, squeezing my eyes shut to hold back the tears. I couldn't let my emotions take over. I couldn't let myself think about Ashleen's mother or brothers—or my mother—or anyone at school or how they would react. Not out here in the middle of the woods. Not when I was a sitting duck for Lydia to attack.

"Stop it," I said out loud. "Stop it. Get a hold of yourself."

For a moment I sat among the soft sounds of the February night. There were no birds singing, no insects creaking—only the rustling of the pine trees around me.

I sighed and looked at the picture again.

Ashleen stood a few feet away from me, staring right at the camera. She was barefoot, wearing a light purple dress made of gauzy layers of fabric. The top was detailed, ruffly, and feminine. But the bottom of the dress just kind of . . . disappeared. I mean, looking at it,

you couldn't really say, "That's the bottom of the dress."
It just dissolved into the air.

I stared at it, with a sense déjà vu, until it hit me:
it was the dress from the dream I'd had the night of
Ashleen's party.

I looked around, suddenly in a panic, thinking that
not only had Lydia just crossed over from bad ghost to
evil ghost, but that there was a distinct possibility she
could invade my subconscious mind, too. But even if
she could plant dreams in my head, why would she use a
purple dress? As far as I could remember, I'd never seen
Lydia wearing a dress like that one. What could it mean?

I looked back down at the picture and studied
Ashleen's confused expression. Sometimes ghosts don't
understand what's happened to them—they don't even
know they're dead. So they just wander, thinking they're
in a dream.

But it wasn't the look on her face—or even the
dress—that bothered me the most.

No, the *really* bizarre thing was that, in her left
hand, Ashleen held a bouquet of yellow roses.

In all my pictures of ghosts, I'd never seen one actually carrying something that wasn't part of what they
wore when they died. For example, one day I'd taken a
picture of a woman downtown—she wore a long black
Edwardian-era dress and walked hunched over, with her

hands out in front of her. The whole effect was startling and horrible, almost demonic, like she was prowling around, ready to strike out at someone.

Then, after watching her pass countless living people without even noticing them, I realized what she was doing: pushing a baby carriage. Only, the baby carriage didn't exist in her ghostly plane. Have you ever heard the saying, *You can't take it with you*? Well, it's true. Unless you're wearing it, you can't.

So why—and how—was Ashleen's ghost holding roses?

There was something else in the last picture. I glanced at the photograph and noticed, over her shoulder, a bright white spot of light, barely shining through the trees.

My heart raced. I raised my camera, removed the lens cap, and flashed off a few more exposures.

Ashleen had begun to wander away, but the light was still there. It was getting closer, in fact.

"I'm sorry, Ashleen," I said into the night air. But I wasn't focused on her any longer. I had to get rid of Lydia before she could do this to anyone else.

"Lydia!" I called, in the direction of the light. "Stop being a coward and show yourself!"

I reached for the charm book and opened it to one of the pages I'd bookmarked. My hands shook as I looked over the spell. Should I immobilize her first and then send her away? Or just send her away? The immobilization spell was much shorter. I had a better chance of actually finishing it.

I began to read it aloud.

"Excuse me." Lydia's voice interrupted me. "What are you doing?"

I raised my voice and kept reading.

Lydia slapped the book from my hands.

As I knelt to pick it up, she got right in my face. "I asked you a question. Why are you out here in the middle of the night?"

"I know what you did," I said. The bookmarks had fallen out of the book, so I flipped through the pages. I found the "move to a transitional state" first and held the book in an iron grip.

Lydia looked over my shoulder. "What does that mean? A transitional state? Permanently? Do you know what that sounds like?"

"It sounds awesome," I said, starting to read.

"No," Lydia said, having the gall to act appalled. "It sounds like limbo. Like a gray void. You would put me in a gray void forever?" She tried to knock the book out of my hands again, but her fingers passed right through it.

She was weak right now. I stopped reading and

looked at her, unable to pass up the opportunity to tell her off.

"You made the choice," I said. "You're the one who killed Ashleen."

Her eyes went wide. "Who's Ashleen?"

"Give me a break."

"No, seriously. Who's Ashleen?" She looked around. "Is there a killer out here?"

Oh. My. God. "You're already dead, Lydia," I said. "And if you didn't kill her, who did? And why does she have your yellow roses?"

"What yellow roses?" she asked. She was beginning to sound scared. "Alexis, I don't *want* to go to a transitional plane forever. I didn't kill anybody—"

Biggest, fattest "whatever" in the history of humanity.

I glanced down at the page and opened my mouth to read the spell, determined not to let her distract me again.

And then—

The laugh.

It swirled in circles just like it had in the empty field—a tornado of malevolent energy, with me at its center. I felt it pulse against my skin like the wings of a thousand evil butterflies.

And in one motion, the book was ripped from my hands.

It exploded into dust in midair.

I shrieked, unable to stop myself, and covered my

ears with my palms. Then, in a panic, I turned to run, my camera bouncing against my side. I felt a crunch and the rough jolt of a tree trunk against my hip, and changed directions.

Still, the laughter followed me, wrapping around me as tightly as a spider binding its prey.

If only I could find my way out of the woods—back to my car—

But my mind flailed like a bird with a broken wing. There was no way I would be able to focus enough to find the trees I'd marked. I'd be driven deeper and deeper into the woods—and if I didn't freeze to death or fall off a cliff, I'd be driven mad by the laughter.

Suddenly, my mad scrambling carried me through a pocket of freezing air.

As I tumbled out the other side, the laughter disappeared.

I plopped to the ground, my breath as loud in my ears as a passing train, and looked up to see Lydia standing a few feet away.

She pursed her lips and stared down at me.

"Why . . . ?" I had to stop speaking to suck more air into my lungs. "*Why*, Lydia?"

I couldn't contain my tears anymore, and I started to sob.

It was the ultimate display of weakness, and I

expected Lydia to try to hurt me, to torment me, to chase me farther into the woods.

But she didn't.

A few minutes passed, and Lydia didn't go away. She didn't speak, either.

She just stood there, looking at me.

Finally, I got to my feet, my legs unsteady beneath me. "I'll leave you alone. I won't try to send you to the void. I swear to God. Just stop hurting people. Please, Lydia."

Without speaking, she turned to walk away. Her body grew fainter and fainter.

"Please!" I cried, too exhausted for pride. "I'll get down on my knees and beg you, if that's what you want. Or take me—kill me—do whatever you want to me, but . . ."

She was gone.

I pulled my phone out of my pocket and groaned. The crunch I'd felt when I hit the tree had been the face of my phone cracking.

I drew in a breath of cold air, burning my throat and lungs.

I was totally lost, with no way to get back to my car.

Life's not fair—I get it—but this was ridiculous.

And then there was a sudden sharp *snap!* and I looked up just in time to see a huge branch about to fall right where I was standing. I rushed out of the way, swinging around another tree trunk, full-on bear-hugging it like a frightened toddler hugging her mother's leg.

After the massive branch crashed to the ground, and the dust and leaves settled, I took a step back . . . and saw the chalk slash on the bark of the tree in front of me.

I would have broken down in relief, except there was no part of me whole enough to break down. So I just followed the chalk mark to the next marked tree, and gradually made my way back to the car, surrounded by the miserable silence of the forest.

15

"HEY, HONEY, YOU'RE GOING to be late for school," my father said, sticking his head into my bedroom the next morning.

I squeezed my eyes shut tighter and pulled the blankets up to my chin.

"It's already seven fifteen, you know."

He was waiting for an answer, so I croaked one out. "It's a four-minute drive."

"But don't you have all sorts of elaborate beauty rituals?"

"No." I burrowed down into my pillow. "That's Kasey."

"What's me?" my sister's voice piped up. "Lexi, you're going to be late."

I turned away from them to look out the window.

"Never mind," Kasey sighed. I heard her walk away.

"Well, don't cut it too close," Dad said. He left too.

Could I really make myself get out of bed and go to

school—just walk around like a regular person having a regular day?

I felt a gentle hand on the back of my head. "Sweetheart, you overslept," Mom said.

I collected all of my strength and sat up.

"Oh, you're already dressed," she said. "Are you feeling okay?"

I muttered that I was, and Mom went to the kitchen. I swung my legs—stiff in the dirty jeans I'd been wearing for nearly twenty-four hours—over the side of the bed and sat there, staring at nothing.

The fact is, I wasn't "already" dressed. I was *still* dressed. And any paranoid parent worth his or her paranoid salt would have noticed that—and the scattered pieces of dirt on my pale beige carpet—especially *my* carpet, of all carpets, because I was a borderline OCD-level clean freak.

My parents hadn't noticed.

But apparently my sister had.

"What happened to your carpet?"

I swung around. "My shoes were muddy."

Kasey stood in the doorway, staring at the floor. "Why were your shoes muddy?"

"Because I stepped in some mud," I said.

"How's Jared?" she asked.

"He's great," I said. "How's the cradle-robber?"

She rolled her eyes and sniffed, but she didn't back

away in a huff like I'd been hoping she would. "Keaton is fine. He got accepted to Berkeley."

"No kidding," I said. "That's good. I mean, it's pretty close . . . if you guys are still together."

She shrugged and sort of swung on the doorframe a little. "I don't know. I'm too young to get that serious . . . don't you think?"

Kasey had just turned fifteen. I'd just turned sixteen when Carter and I started dating. And I didn't feel like we were too young to be serious. It just felt so right with him. I mean, until Aralt and the Sunshine Club came between us, I could see myself with Carter forever. Not that we'd have gotten married right out of high school or anything, but I just never pictured us breaking up, because I just couldn't imagine not wanting to be with him.

"I think it depends," I said. "I think if it's important to you to make it work, you'll make it work."

"Was it—" She cut herself off, and I knew she'd been about to ask about Carter—if it was important to me.

"Yeah, well," I said.

She gave me a sad smile.

"Anyway, it doesn't matter," I said. "I have Jared now."

Her sad smile turned into a little grimace.

That's when I noticed, out of the corner of my eye,

my cell phone. It sat on the nightstand with the shattered screen on display for everyone to see. Naturally, my life would be much easier if I could keep my sister from seeing it.

"I'd better get dressed for school," I said.

"You're already dressed." Her eyes narrowed. "Wait, did you sleep in your clothes?"

"Good-bye, Kasey," I said, getting up and moving toward the door.

She backed away. I gave the door a push and picked up my phone to get a better look at it.

But Kasey had peeked back in. "Holy cow, what happened?"

I stepped forward, tucking the phone behind my back. "Excuse me, have you ever heard of privacy?"

"Your phone—" She craned her neck to try to see. "It looks like—"

"It's fine," I said, slipping the phone into my pocket. "I cracked the screen yesterday. It still works, though."

I waited for her to ask me what I'd been doing that would crack the screen.

Stop, I thought. *Don't ask any more questions. Just go be normal. Be happy. One of us to has to come through this okay, and it's not going to be me. So stop asking questions.*

Her face fell. Her feelings were hurt. She looked like a little girl.

It's for your own good.

She didn't need to get messed up with ghosts again. She just needed to be a normal teenager.

"Sorry, Kase," I said, and shut the door.

By the end of the day I was so exhausted from my constant fear of saying the wrong thing that I didn't even want to go to Jared's house. I knew they'd find the body before long—maybe even that same night. So I went straight home and got into bed.

Luckily, Kasey was off with her friends, so at least I didn't have to justify my bedridden afternoon. I closed my eyes and let the misery sink down through my body. I could feel it going into my pores, through my skin, into the muscle and sinew, right into the core of my soul.

I was the only person in the world who knew Ashleen was dead.

How long would I have to carry that knowledge around with me while the police searched and Ashleen's family suffered?

Lydia's voice was clear and cold. "Warren, pity party of one, we have your table ready."

I opened my eyes and stared at the ceiling, afraid to move. But Lydia came and stood right above me. Her long ghost-hair hung down, almost touching my face. I fought the urge to try to brush it away.

"Listen to me," she said. "I didn't kill that Ashley chick. I didn't push Kendra off that cliff. And I *don't* want to be sent to the transitional plane."

"Go away," I whispered.

"I'm not going away until you apologize."

I sat up, not afraid anymore. I couldn't help it. Lydia was just too aggravating. "*Apologize?* For what?"

"For accusing me of murder," she said, sitting on my desk, right on top of my camera. "I'm not a murderer."

"You tried to kill the whole Sunshine Club," I said. "Or have you forgotten?"

Her jaw dropped. "That doesn't count! A, I was possessed, and B, it didn't work."

"So if you didn't kill Ashleen, why were you in the forest last night?" I asked. "Hmm? Just out for a hike?"

The thing was, I did believe her. Taking even a fraction of a moment to think about it, I realized that luring girls to a miserable demise in the woods was way too subtle for Lydia. If she wanted to kill people, she'd do it in the mall food court or something.

"I was there . . ." Her voice trailed off, like she really didn't know why, and then she reloaded. "I was there because I . . ." She was staring at the floor, as if trying to remember something that bothered her.

"And you were out there when Kendra was hurt,

too!" I said. "And you were in my car that day at the nature preserve—"

"No, I wasn't," she said. "That wasn't me. And yeah, I was there when you found Kendra—I mean, when *I* found her *for* you, you're welcome very much—but I'm not the one who hurt her."

"Honest to God?" I asked.

"I swear on my own grave," Lydia said.

I rolled my eyes.

"Excuse me, my grave is pretty important to me."

I leaned back against my pillows and covered my face with my hands, suddenly exhausted.

"I'm telling the truth," she said.

I opened my eyes. "I know. But if you didn't attack Kendra and Ashleen, then who did, Lydia?" A giant sigh forced its way out of my lungs. "And why are you always around?"

I would never have thought ghosts could blush, but Lydia was actually blushing. She pursed her lips and stared out the window. "I'm not telling you."

"Tell me," I said, "or I'll find another copy of that book, and it's off to never-never land you go."

She flounced and huffed and folded her arms and gave me the dirtiest look in the history of dirty looks.

"All right," I said, standing up. "I'm going to go check eBay."

"You won't send me to limbo?" she asked. "If I tell you? You promise?"

Technically, I'd promised the night before. Not that there was any reason to remind her of that.

"Fine. I promise." As much as I wanted Lydia to go away, I knew I had a really unique opportunity, and I had the presence of mind not to squander it. I'd met ghosts before, but always in battle. Never just in a regular conversation. "But . . . Lydia, ghosts aren't natural. You shouldn't even be here to begin with. Why wouldn't you want to move on? Isn't it lonely for you here?"

"I do want to move on," she said, swinging her legs through my desk chair. "I guess. But not to a transitional state—for all eternity. I mean, think about it, Alexis. No matter how much you hate me, do I deserve to be in a gray void for the rest of time?"

I sighed. And I really did think about it.

If Lydia didn't kill Ashleen—and if that wasn't her in my car . . .

Then, no, of course not. Yeah, she tried to kill the Sunshine Club—but to be fair, when I was possessed, I tried to kill my family in their sleep. If Kasey hadn't stopped me, I could easily have been a mass murderer.

I leaned my head forward and rested it in my hands. Of all the things I didn't need.

"Ha!" Lydia said. "I'm right, and you know it."

"Okay," I said. "If you *didn't* hurt Kendra or kill Ashleen, you don't deserve the gray void. Now tell me. Why are you always around when these things happen, if you're not causing them?"

"You know what?" She raised her chin haughtily. "I'm tired of your accusations. I'll see you later. If I feel like it."

And she disappeared.

When I heard my mother's car pull into the garage, I strained my ears to listen to her—the way she walked, the way she hung her keys on the hook—for any indication that she'd heard something about Ashleen. Overcome by my need to know if *she* knew, I stuck my head into the hallway.

Mom stood by the garage door, head down.

"Mom?" I asked.

She turned and looked at me, a magazine open in her hand. "Hi, honey. How was your day?" Her voice sounded normal—light, but with an undertone of tension. Still, nothing that hinted at an awareness of Ashleen's death.

"Fine," I said, going back into my room.

Later, I went out into the living room and turned on the TV, slumping in the corner of the couch with the remote in my hand.

Behind me I heard the front door open. Kasey's voice called, "See you tomorrow!" and the door closed.

"Hey," she said, leaning over the couch. "What's up? What are you watching?"

It was some lame Judge Somebody show where the judge works herself up into a lather trying to be funny while she messes with people's lives.

"Nothing," I said.

Kasey dumped her stuff behind the couch and came around to sit next to me. I moved my legs to make room for her, but I turned up the volume a little, too—just enough to hint that I wasn't in the mood for conversation. My sister caught the hint, so we watched the rest of the show in silence.

"If we ever end up suing each other over a rowboat," Kasey finally said, "just shoot me, okay?"

"You got it," I said.

The trumpety music that announced the start of the six o'clock news sounded, and suddenly I didn't want to know if there was any news about Ashleen. So I flipped to a show about misbehaving dogs and leaned back with my eyes closed.

A minute later, Mom came out into the kitchen. "What do you girls want for dinner?"

Before we could reply, her cell phone rang.

My whole body tensed. It was like the energy

in the room spiked before she even answered it.

"Hey, Jim. . . . What? No. What? Okay. Thanks. Bye." Her phone hit the counter with a clunk. Her voice was like a clear tube made of glass so thin it would shatter if you touched it. "Alexis . . . turn to the news."

My fingers were like stumps. I fumbled with the remote until Kasey took it from me and switched the channel.

A reporter stood on location at Ashleen's house, wearing her sad face. "Although police aren't releasing details about the location of the body, they did confirm that it *was* missing teen Ashleen Evans. Autopsy results will be available later this week, but an anonymous source inside the police department told us there doesn't appear to be any evidence of assault. The family has declined to speak to reporters, but they have released a statement asking for prayers and information that could lead to the arrest of whoever is responsible."

Mom's face was gray. She came up behind the couch and put a hand on Kasey's and my shoulders.

They went to a split screen with the reporter in the studio. "Have the police compared this to the Kendra Charnow case at all?"

The field reporter adjusted her earpiece. "No, Dana, not officially. But obviously that's something that we're hearing a lot of from neighbors."

Their chatter blurred together like squawking birds in my brain.

I searched the trees for a flash of Ashleen's ghost or the purple dress. But what I saw, right behind the reporter, was a blast of white light.

I sat up and leaned forward. It hovered by the trees, and then it slowly grew larger in the frame—coming closer to the woman with the microphone, who was interviewing a crying teenage boy.

"Alexis," Kasey said, and I turned to look at her, feeling my pulse pound against my ears. I thought she was going to accuse me of being involved or knowing something. But she was just looking for a shoulder to cry on. She wiped her eyes and leaned toward me, burying her face in my hoodie.

I put my arms around her, but I couldn't take my eyes off the newscast.

"They found the body?" Lydia had come back and was staring at the TV. Her voice was serious and utterly snarkless. "I saw it last night. It was pretty close to where you were standing."

"What was she wearing?" I asked.

Kasey sat up and looked at me, sniffling. "What? Why would you ask that?"

Lydia shrugged. "Regular clothes. Sweatpants . . . a shirt. Blue? I don't know. It was dark."

But *not* a purple dress?

I kept my eyes on Lydia, wanting to ask her more questions but unable to as long as Kasey was in earshot.

Suddenly, the room was filled with a brilliant white light—just for a moment. Then it was gone.

I glanced back at the TV. The white spot that had been drawing close to the reporter was gone.

"That—" I searched the edges of the room. "What—"

Kasey sniffled. "Huh?"

"What?" Lydia said.

"Nothing," I said, to both of them. "Never mind."

The field reporter was running out of things to say, but she kept talking, clearly desperate to remain the center of attention. "One of the search party members mentioned to me that they found a—a lens cap, like from a camera. Not like a small snapshot camera, but the bigger kind—"

An SLR.

"—about fifty feet from the location of the body. So that might be something the police are interested in, but it also might be unrelated."

I went stiff.

"Lexi?" Kasey asked. "Are you okay?"

"I'm fine," I said. "I'm just fine."

I sat in my car with the engine off, watching the rain

slide down the windshield. I wished I'd brought an extra sweatshirt, but I didn't want to go back inside and risk having Kasey ask me what I was doing.

Plus, being cold made it easy for me to lie to myself and believe that's why my hands were shaking—not because of what I was about to do.

I balanced the business card on my knee and picked up my phone.

AGENT F. HASAN, was all it said. And her phone number.

Agent Hasan was maybe the second scariest thing in my life besides ghosts. She worked for the government—though it was impossible to tell exactly which department she worked for—and she had a talent for showing up right when you needed her. When she'd come to clean up the Sunshine Club mess, she'd told my sister and me that she didn't give third chances.

So I might be burning a third chance I didn't have. But even I had to admit that it was time to get someone else involved.

Lydia walked through the passenger door and sat down, reclining so her feet went through the window. "Where are you off to?"

It was too late to hang up—the call was already going through.

"Nowhere," I said. "Go away."

Lydia peered at the business card. "Who's that?" she whispered.

"Hello, Alexis."

There was no mistaking Agent Hasan's voice. She always sounded slightly bored, like she couldn't believe she was wasting her time with you. It was, to put it mildly, insanely intimidating.

"Hi," I said. "How . . . how are you?"

"What's happening?"

"Um," I said. "I don't know if you've seen the news at all lately."

"With regard to what," she said, "specifically?"

"The girls," I said. "The ones who go out into the woods."

"Kendra Charnow and Ashleen Evans?"

Okay, so she had been watching the news. "Yeah . . . I was thinking that maybe you might want to find out more about that."

She waited a beat before speaking. "And why would you think so?"

"It just seems like maybe there's something weird going on." I glanced over at Lydia, who was leaning close to hear both sides of the conversation.

"Define *weird*."

"I don't know," I said. "Maybe . . . possibly . . . supernatural?"

"Hmm," she said, though she clearly knew all along that that's what I was getting at. "Why don't you tell me why you think so?"

"I don't know," I said. "I mean, I don't have a specific reason. But doesn't it seem worth . . . I don't know, looking into?"

"Alexis, let me clarify something for you."

"Okay." My voice had dropped to a rasp.

"If I think there are mice in my kitchen, eating my protein bars, I can install a camera and a motion sensor and look into the situation. You follow?"

"I think so," I said.

"Or I can set out some poison and mousetraps and take care of the situation. Understand?"

"I understand," I said.

"Poor mice," Lydia whispered.

"I don't *look into* things," Agent Hasan said. "I *take care* of things. Now, if you know something about Kendra and Ashleen, and you think we should talk, I would really appreciate it if you could say so right now."

"No!" I said. "No, I just wanted to bring it to your attention."

"All right, then," she said. "Because if you have any special reason to suspect paranormal activity, I need to know so that I can come over to Surrey and deal with it."

It hit me that it wasn't just the laughing white light that would be caught in Agent Hasan's mousetrap. It would be Lydia. And me.

Because having supernatural eyes made me a supernatural freak, too.

"I don't," I said. "I don't have a reason."

"Then we don't have anything else to talk about, do we?" she asked.

"Nope," I said. "Nothing. Thanks."

"You're welcome, Alexis."

I hung up and sat back, staring into the rain.

"Who is that woman?" Lydia asked. "She talks like a mafia hit man."

"Close enough," I said.

"What does she do?"

"She's the one who locked Kasey up for ten months," I said.

"Wow," Lydia said. "You'd end up in a padded room."

"And you'd end up in the gray void," I said. "And to her, it would be a job well done."

Lydia gave me a wary look and vanished.

16

IT MIGHT HAVE BEEN the last thing in the universe I felt like doing, but when the bell rang after school on the following Monday, I took my camera and reported to the *Wingspan* office for the Student Council shoot.

As I put my hand on the doorknob, everything hit me at once: dizziness, confusion, hope, misery—a veritable smoothie of conflicting emotions.

Just be professional, I told myself. I'd seen Carter. I'd talked to him. How bad could it be?

But when I walked into the studio I saw *exactly* how bad it could be.

Carter and the other three officers were standing together, talking about some student government issue, which would have been fine—if Zoe hadn't been hanging off of Carter's arm like an overprotective purple-haired poodle.

She glared at me, but I was distracted by Marley Chen, who came and stood next to me. Marley was the features editor—basically my partner on all things yearbook-related. She had long, straight black hair, and most of her clothes were vintage. She acted like an airheaded Valley girl, but having worked with her a few times, I knew she was the second smartest person (behind Elliot, of course—no one was as smart as Elliot) on the yearbook staff. Maybe I was deluding myself, but I felt like we were becoming almost friends.

"Hi, guys," she said to the Student Council officers. "Give us a minute to get set up, and then we'll start."

I went through to the adjoining classroom that the *Wingspan* staff used as a studio. Marley and Elliot came in while I was slipping my camera onto the tripod.

"Why is she here?" Marley whispered. "This is only for officers. She's just a class rep!"

"I don't get what he sees in her," Elliot said simply, pushing up the sleeves of her NYU hoodie.

I locked the camera in place.

"Not to mention," Marley said, "that it's completely juvenile to drag your girlfriend to a yearbook photo shoot."

"Agreed," Elliot said, casting a disdainful look toward the doorway.

"Um . . . thanks, guys." I was taken aback by this unexpected show of loyalty.

Marley sensed it. She shrugged. "You're part of the

Wingspan now, Alexis. We look out for our own."

Part of the *Wingspan*? Yeah, I'd done a couple of shoots, but . . . did they not know anything about me? More to the point, if they did know, would they still want me to be part of their group?

I had no idea how to respond. So I didn't. I said, "I think we're ready."

Elliot went back to the office and announced, "It's pretty tight in there. Why don't we just keep it to a minimum of people? Just Marley and whoever's turn it is?"

I leaned forward to check my aperture setting as Marley brought the first person in. "Here's Carter."

"Great," I said, not looking up. "Have a seat."

He sat, head turned toward the door.

"Look at Alexis, please," Marley said.

His piercing blue eyes found me through the viewfinder. "How's the camera?"

I tried to make my voice completely aloof. "Good."

Marley, bless her heart, tried to lighten the tension in the room. "It's a really nice one. It looks expensive."

"Um." I felt like my stomach had left my body. "Yeah, I'm not really sure how much it was."

"Fifteen hundred dollars," Carter said.

My breath caught in my throat. What was he trying to imply? That it was so expensive, he didn't think I should have kept it after we'd broken up? He could have it, for all I cared. I would have returned it to him in a heartbeat. But he'd never so much as hinted that he wanted it back.

Then I had a flash of angry shame. He'd basically *forced* me to take it one night when he was supernaturally crazy-obsessed with me. He'd had three months since then—plenty of time to ask for it *privately*. He knew my phone numbers. Was he doing this to humiliate me in front of Marley? To show her that I was a bad person?

But when I looked up at him, ready to come back with a reply, there was no expectation on his face. In fact, his expression was completely calm and composed as he said, "I'm glad you like it."

"Thanks," I said shortly. "I do."

I took a few test shots, then had him angle his shoulders away from me.

"Raise your chin?" I asked, clicking off a run of exposures.

I went on directing him, growing more relaxed with each frame. Why had I dreaded this? Carter was a mature almost-eighteen-year-old. He wouldn't make a scene. And I certainly wasn't going to.

After about five minutes, I stood up. "We got it," I said to Marley. "Next?"

Carter had started to stand when a voice spoke up from the doorway. "Wait just a minute, please!"

Zoe edged her way in toward Carter.

She turned to me, venom in her eyes and a smile on her lips. "Can you take some pictures of us . . . you know, as a couple? We have some from when we went to the winter dance together, but I'm sure *you* can take better ones."

"We're pretty busy," Marley said, in a strangled, high-pitched tone.

"It's fine, Mar," I said. "Sure. Why not?"

Carter didn't look thrilled about it, but Zoe sat and pulled him down next to her. I repositioned the shot and fired off a couple of frames.

"Thanks," Zoe said, dripping with artificial sweetness.

"Stop it," Carter said, under his breath.

I looked at him over the top of the camera. "You might as well smile," I said. "This is for posterity."

Next to him, Zoe's face bloomed into a blissful fake smile. With her short dark hair and pale skin in contrast to Carter's conservative style, she looked like an elf on a date with an accountant.

A cute accountant, piped up the voice in the back of my head.

Shut up, voice.

I glanced at them as I clicked the shutter, challenging myself to let the full meaning of their smiles sink into my heart.

They looked like the perfect couple.

And it hurt. A lot.

"That's probably enough," Marley said nervously.

I straightened up. "Marley's the boss. See you later. It's been real."

"I'm so sure," Zoe said. She gave me a sickening smirk, then took Carter by the hand and led him out of the studio.

He didn't look back.

I called Jared from the parking lot.

"Hey, stranger," he said.

"Are you busy?"

"Not if you need me."

I hesitated. *Need* seemed like a really powerful word—a powerful word containing a lot of powerlessness.

Then the sound of Carter's voice came rushing through my head, making me dizzy with loneliness. Tears stung at my eyes.

"I think . . . I do," I said.

Jared was on the porch before I had even put the car in park, and he was there opening my car door by the time I hit the emergency brake.

"Hey," he said, looking down at me. "You all right?"

I tried to smile. "Better now."

I leaned over to get my purse, and when I sat up, he was staring at me like I'd said something in a foreign language. But he just extended his hand and helped me out of the car.

"So what happened?" he asked, steering me up to the porch.

I sighed. "Rough day."

"I'm sorry."

"It's not your fault," I said.

"No, I know. Come on in." He held the door for me. "I'll make you some hot chocolate. Dad's working from home, but he's in his office."

Sitting on a comfy lounge chair a few minutes later, chasing marshmallows around my cup with the tips of my fingers, I tried to suppress the uneasy feeling inside me—the feeling that I was here for the wrong reasons.

It wasn't like we didn't enjoy each other's company. We never ran out of things to talk about. So what if it wasn't like when Carter and I were together? Jared wasn't like Carter, he'd never be like Carter, and honestly, I didn't even know if I wanted him to be. Because something had obviously gone horribly wrong with Carter . . . or I wouldn't be in Jared's living room, drinking Jared's hot chocolate.

He leaned back. "I'm glad you called, actually. I've had sort of a sucky day, too."

"Is everything okay?"

There was a hint of sadness on his face. "We had a meeting about graduation."

"Wow," I said. "In February?"

"Well, it's kind of a production at Sacred Heart," he said. "Lots of alumni, ceremonies, rituals—"

"Animal sacrifice?" I asked.

That won me a smile. "More like a bunch of old people carrying banners, students dancing around Maypoles . . . Attendance is required for the whole school. It's just a really big deal for us."

"So you're bummed about having to spend a whole day dancing around a Maypole?"

"No, it's not that," he said. "That's just the girls. It's more like . . . something is ending. Endings are always sad."

"Kind of," I said, though I'd begun to itch for not only the end of my junior year but for my graduation the next year, too, and the promise of leaving Surrey and all its ghosts behind me for good. I knew there would be other ghosts out there, but surely the air couldn't be this thick with them everywhere. Maybe I could move to Montana or something. A house in the country, a hundred miles from other people. Although, with my luck, I'd end up living in the middle of some old battlefield. "Or you could think of it as the beginning of something. Moving on. A fresh start."

He shrugged, his smile gone. "I don't need to move on. I don't really want a fresh start."

"I'm sorry," I said, reaching over and taking his hand.

He stared intently at my face for so long that I got shy. "You're sweet."

"I get called a lot of things," I said, "but *sweet* isn't usually one of them."

"Well, I see right through you, Alexis." He raised my hand to his mouth and kissed it.

I tried to ignore the thrill that coursed through my body—but I couldn't.

His eyes crinkled around the edges and he gave a gentle tug on my hand. I got out of the chair and went to sit on the sofa with him. His arms wrapped around my shoulders, but he didn't kiss me.

"Hey there," Mr. Elkins said, coming out of the hallway. He was in his mid-fifties—Jared called himself a "whoops baby"—and he always seemed surprised to see me. He was tall, with dark hair like Jared's, and a short beard.

I bolted upright, out of Jared's arms. "Hi, Mr. Elkins."

"Pete," he said. "Call me Pete."

Jared's father gave us an awkward smile and disappeared into the kitchen.

I looked at Jared and shook my head. He pulled me back close to his chest. "He doesn't mind," Jared said, and I didn't know if he meant his father didn't mind that we were snuggled up together on the couch, or being called by his first name.

I un-snuggled. Whether he minded or not, it felt too weird to be so cuddly in front of somebody's dad.

Mr. Elkins didn't seem any more comfortable with it than I did. "Well, good to see you," he said, coming back through with a cup of coffee in his hand and eyes averted.

"You too," I said.

"Jared?" he said, and Jared looked up at him. "Um . . . things good? You happy?"

"Dad." Jared said the word as a kind of laugh. "Go back to your office."

Mr. Elkins flushed a little. "All right. I'll do that. I—good to see you again—"

"Dad."

After all tongue-tied parents were safely stowed, I finished my hot chocolate and nestled back into Jared's arms, nearly dozing off. I lingered in that twilighty pre-sleep state, forgetting Carter and Zoe, forgetting Ashleen, forgetting the bright white light.

"I was just wondering. . . ." Jared's voice woke me up by sending delicious shivers down my spine. "Why's your camera in your car?"

The question stunned me for a millisecond, and I knew from the way I found myself scrambling for an answer that nothing I could say would be good enough.

Our cameras had been what brought us together; creating photos was Jared's greatest love, and when I said I wanted to cut back, he'd basically given it up to spend time with me, doing anything *but* photography. Now I'd been going behind his back and taking pictures—for almost a month. True, they were only for the yearbook, but I knew that didn't matter. It was the principle of the thing.

"I'm just . . . doing this stupid thing for school," I said. I could hear how inadequate it sounded.

"What stupid thing?" His voice was light, as if it weren't a big deal. But if that had been the case, he would have let it go.

"Taking some pictures for the yearbook. Nothing big."

He tensed. "What kind of pictures?"

"Um . . . posed portraits. Of the language clubs, sports teams . . ." I sat up and shook my head, trying to remember. "Student Council . . ."

Jared narrowed his eyes. "Huh. So by Student Council, you mean Carter?"

I know honesty is the best policy and all, but I was severely regretting that particular bit of honesty.

"Yeah," I said. "I mean, he was there. But it's not a big deal."

Jared choked out a laugh. "No, of course not. Why would it be a big deal? I mean, you were only together for five months. Why shouldn't you spend the afternoon with him?"

"It's not like that." My heart started to flutter. "I'm spending the afternoon with *you*. I spent maybe five minutes with Carter."

He was silent for a moment. I started to hope he would let the subject drop, but no such luck.

"Can I see the pictures?"

"No," I said, sitting back, away from him. "Why? What difference does it make?"

"You said yourself it's not a big deal."

"It's not." My throat tightened. *Don't you dare cry right now, Alexis.* "But I'm not going to be scolded like a kid who stole a candy bar from a drugstore."

He gave a quick, disapproving shake of his head. "Is that supposed to be a metaphor for my feelings? I guess I'm . . . the drugstore? A nameless corporate entity? Is that how you see me?"

Without a word, I got up off the couch and hurried to the bathroom, where I splashed cold water on my face. The girl staring back at me in the mirror was flushed, her eyes vivid blue against the angry red of her cheeks.

She looked wretched and flustered.

She looked scared.

She looked . . . weak.

I leaned against the wall for a minute, squeezing my eyes shut. Why did *every single tiny thing* in my life have to be difficult?

Finally, I opened my eyes and stared at my reflection. I was past the danger of crying, but I couldn't stop my heart from beating like a snare drum.

There was a knock at the door. "Alexis?"

"Just a second," I said.

"Open the door," Jared said. "Please. I didn't mean to upset you."

The longer I watched, the worse things would get. I flung the door open, like pulling a Band-Aid off all at once.

Jared stood across the hall, his hands in his pockets. "I trust you completely. If I gave you the impression that I don't, then I owe you an apology."

"I'm sorry. I should have told you," I said. "But it's only for school. I swear."

"Of course it is." His voice was as soft as velvet. He beckoned me toward him. "Come here."

Like there was a magnetic connection between us, I let myself be dragged across the hall into his embrace.

"We shouldn't do this," he whispered into my hair. "We shouldn't upset each other."

"I know," I replied, letting my cheek rest against his shoulder.

"Hey," he said.

By the time I'd raised my eyes to look at him, his lips were on mine.

I WOKE IN THE MIDDLE OF THE NIGHT, covered with my thick comforter and a coating of sweat, like someone had turned the heat up and left it blasting. As I went to push the covers off, I realized there was something in my left hand.

I turned the light on and sat up, pulling whatever it was out from under the covers. Something stung my thumb, and I flung the thing to the floor. Sticking my stung thumb in my mouth, I stared at the object on my carpet—

A single yellow rose.

Then I became aware that something else was wrong—something far worse than the rose.

It was a sleeve. A sleeve of pale purple chiffon, fluttering weightlessly around my arm.

And it was attached to a dress. *The* dress. The one Ashleen had worn.

The dress I was wearing now.

I climbed out of my bed and stood in the center of my room, grabbing at the gauzy layers and trying to figure out how someone could have changed my clothes entirely without waking me up.

I reached over my shoulder to see if there was a zipper in the back of the dress. There wasn't. A little more patting down revealed one under my right arm. I unzipped it, then went to slip the dress off—but I couldn't.

When I checked the zipper, it was zipped again.

I unzipped it once more, working hard to steady my breath, trying not to let the situation get to me. But again, when I went to raise it over my head, it wouldn't budge.

I decided to go with brute force. I lifted the skirt and yanked as hard as I could, determined to rip it to pieces if that was what it took. But as soon as the skirt was blocking my view of the room, I heard soft laughter.

And a voice.

"It doesn't come off."

The words were the quietest whisper, the merest hint of a voice in my ear. But through the layers of fabric I saw a shadow standing between me and the lamp.

A human-shaped shadow.

I was half naked, my arms in the air, but I didn't move. I didn't drop the dress.

I just stood like a lump, staring. My voice froze solid, like ice in my throat.

Finally, I whispered, *"Lydia?"*

Then the shadow moved, whipping around me faster than I could react, and in my struggle to catch up, to keep it where I could see it, I dropped the skirt of the dress and found myself face-to-face with my empty bedroom.

It—*she?*—was gone.

And something had changed.

There was another rose. It was closer to the door, which was now open a crack.

As I forced myself to calm down and not freak out—*yet*—I heard, coming faintly from somewhere in the room:

Vzzzzzzzzzzz

I backed slowly out to the hall.

There I found a third rose, and a fourth one a few feet farther, and a fifth, sixth, and seventh, leading to the foyer.

The urge to see where they led was irresistible.

I held my breath and followed the trail. When I came to the front door, I silently turned the dead bolt and pulled the door open.

There were more roses outside.

It was the middle of the night, and the temperature was in the low thirties. All I wore was the gauzy purple dress, not shoes or even socks. But I followed the line of roses laid out in front of me.

It was almost like I *had* to.

When I reached the intersection of our front walk and the sidewalk, I hesitated.

I could follow these roses forever, by the looks of things. And at the end, I would find . . .

What would I find?

As I started to step on the sidewalk, a freezing rush consumed my body.

The roses blinked out of existence just as someone grabbed my arm.

"Lexi?" Kasey stood beside me, bundled in her bathrobe and a pair of woolly slippers. "What are you doing out here? Why didn't you stop when I called your name?"

I started to open my mouth to ask what *she* was doing—the best defense is a good offense, after all—but she rolled her eyes and cut me off.

"Following you," she said. "Now, answer me."

"I was . . ." I glanced down at the bare sidewalk.

Then I looked down at my body. All I saw were my plaid Christmas pajama pants and a long-sleeved tee. No purple dress.

Could it really just have been a dream?

If Kasey had seen the dress, she would have said something.

"I was just . . . sleepwalking, I guess. Weird. Thanks for waking me up."

"Well, not like I'm going to let you run off in the middle of the night—" She stopped, suddenly realizing that girls running off in the middle of the night was nothing to joke about. "Lexi . . . was it—would you have kept going? Like Kendra or . . ."

She didn't want to say Ashleen's name. I didn't blame her. I didn't want to hear it.

"No," I said. "Of course not."

As my daze wore off, the cold took hold of me. It seeped through the skin of my feet and up through my legs.

Kasey watched me go all the way to my room before retreating toward her own bedroom. She looked like she'd rather plant herself down in the hall and guard my door than go back to bed.

"I'll be fine," I said. "Get some sleep."

After I closed the door, I looked around my room.

No roses, no purple dress. The covers of my bed were rumpled, and as I climbed back underneath them, I tried to convince myself that it had just been a nightmare. How could I *not* have nightmares, after what I'd been through over the past week? Of course it wasn't real.

That was what I told myself. And I repeated it in my head, an endless mantra, until I fell asleep.

But I didn't believe it. Not that night, and not in the morning, when I woke up to find a tiny spot of blood on the pillow and a scab on my left thumb, as though I'd been pricked by a thorn.

No, I wasn't fooling myself. I knew it hadn't been a nightmare—

Something had come for me.

18

I WAS SITTING IN ENGLISH CLASS the next day, trying to write an essay about *The Grapes of Wrath* without actually having read it. The room around me was silent.

"Sleepwalking? Ha. Not quite. I had to try three times to wake you up."

It took a couple of seconds for me to realize it was Lydia.

She sat on the teacher's desk. The teacher was leaning back, reading. Which is a good thing, because if he'd leaned forward he would have been staring directly through her butt.

"So what exactly was that little midnight stroll about?" she asked. "Or were you planning to blame it on me again, like everything else that goes wrong in your life?"

I pursed my lips to keep myself from accidentally answering. Kids at my school already thought I'd killed

Lydia. I didn't need them to know that I had regular conversations with her.

"I must admit, it was a pretty impressive little show."

I gave her a questioning look and beckoned her over. The kid next to me saw me moving my hand, so I pretended to be stretching my fingers.

Lydia came over to my desk. I flipped to a page farther back in my notebook and wrote: *What did you see?*

"You woke up, flipped out, spun around in a circle, and then walked straight out of your house, staring at the ground."

I raised my hand. "Hall pass?"

The teacher nodded.

"Don't bother," Lydia said. "I'm leaving."

And she vanished.

I spent the rest of the day doing something I never in a million years thought I'd do:

Wishing Lydia would show up to bug me again.

After school that day, Marley and I met in the yearbook office to scroll through the Student Council portraits. We narrowed it down to one or two of each person but couldn't agree on which pictures were the best, so we decided to leave it up to Elliot.

I carried the printouts over to her desk. She studied

each photo for a second and made her choices without hesitation.

"How do you do that?" I asked.

She tilted her head. "Do what?"

"Decide things so fast."

"Oh, that," she said. "Ninety percent of the time, I go with my gut."

"And your gut is usually right?"

She gave me an amused smile. "My gut is flawless. It's the other ten percent of the time I get myself in trouble."

I tried to remember the last time I'd trusted myself to make an important decision without agonizing over it. "I don't know about my gut."

"I think your gut is smart." Elliot set down her highlighter and poked a finger into her stomach under the YALE logo on her sweatshirt. "My gut tells me that."

I sighed.

She leaned forward, studying me intently. I nearly took a step back, but managed to stand my ground.

"You know what your problem is?" she asked. "You need to learn to trust—"

Here we go again.

"—yourself," she finished.

"Hmm," I said.

"What?"

"I just sort of thought my problem was trusting other people."

She waved her hand like the statement was a pesky fly. "Other people need to earn your trust. That's beside the point."

To earn my trust.

Huh.

"Tell me something, Alexis," Elliot said. "Why do you eat lunch alone?"

"I don't know," I said. "It's easier."

Elliot didn't ask, *Easier than what?* She just stared at me for a long moment, the same way she would stare at a layout that wasn't quite gelling. "We have room at our table, you know. You should eat with us."

"Wow," I said. Somewhere inside me was a happy little shudder—here was someone who knew me exclusively as a crazy, messed-up person, and she *still* liked me. But . . . even if Elliot felt that way, did the others? Or did they silently judge me? Would they judge Elliot for inviting me? "I don't think so. But thanks."

Elliot didn't even fidget like a normal person. She had to take a pen entirely apart and rebuild it. "You were there when she died, right? Lydia Small?"

I stopped short, my bones fusing together, locking me in place. I couldn't look at her. I stared at the surface of the desk until its faux wood grain swam in my head.

She slipped the spring back into the plastic barrel and screwed the pen back together. "What I'm getting at is, it's not like it was your fault. Even if you were there. You should stop punishing yourself. Or—should I say—punish yourself in a new and different way by eating at our table and watching Chad talk with his mouth full of food."

She gave me a look of such utterly honest understanding that a lump immediately formed in the back of my throat.

"A lot of stuff sucks. But that's life. Just eat with us." Elliot mistook my silence for resistance. "I'm asking you, Alexis. Consider it a personal favor."

I swallowed the lump and blinked before I could look up at her. "Why?"

"Why not?" She shrugged. "If you need a reason . . . it's bad for morale to have one of our staff sitting all alone by the trash cans. Take one for the team, all right?"

So the next day, when the bell rang for lunch, I walked past my usual table and took a spot between Marley and Demetrius. Not only was there enough lively debate to disguise the fact that I didn't have much to say, but there also seemed to be a healthy appreciation for people who were willing to be the audience. And even though I kept looking, I didn't catch a single suspicious glance thrown in my direction, the whole hour.

In other words, it was actually . . . kind of great.

19

THE DAY OF ASHLEEN'S FUNERAL, I faked a sore throat and didn't go. Not that my parents would have pressured me to. Even Kasey didn't say anything. The truth is, it was simple cowardice: I couldn't face Mrs. Evans and Ashleen's brothers.

For several days after, there was calm. No bright lights. No weird dreams. No new girls went missing. Kendra was still comatose, but the doctors said she could wake up any day. Of course, they'd been saying that for six weeks—but at least she wasn't getting worse.

As the early part of February passed, I started to have that weird feeling that I'd imagined everything. School went on as usual, things were stable with Jared, and I avoided making eye contact with Carter. I ate lunch with the yearbook kids every day, and Kasey dialed back her wide-eyed vigilance.

After school one Monday, I decided I deserved a break. A little fun in my life, for once.

So I set aside the whole afternoon to organize the kitchen junk drawer.

I divided the extra paper clips, thumbtacks, and rubber bands into little tin containers with clear lids, tested all of the pens and highlighters and threw away the ones that didn't write well, and then turned to the stack of takeout menus, random pieces of mail, and old maps that Mom stowed in there.

We'd lost almost everything when our house burned down—except what was in the cars. Such as, my pack-rat mother's collection of old maps. She had a glove box full, and after the fire, in her sentimental longing to hang on to anything from our old lives, she'd stashed them away before Dad and I could cull them.

Today is not your lucky day, old maps.

My cell phone rang, and I thought about answering it, but it was across the room and I was blissfully elbow-deep in promotional key chains, mechanical pencils, and magnets. So I let it go to voicemail. I knew there weren't any yearbook shoots that day, and Mom or Dad would just call the house phone if they needed me.

Then the house phone rang. I checked the caller ID. It was Jared.

I debated for a moment, then heard the siren song of the new drawer organizer Mom had brought home as a pick-me-up gift when I was sick (or should I say, "sick"), sitting on the counter waiting for someone to place it in a drawer and fill its compartments with tiny items. I could call Jared back later. So I left the receiver in the cradle and went back to organizing.

I stood facing the kitchen wall, with my back to the world, going through the stacks of papers.

One of the maps of Surrey was so old that it must have been printed when my mother was in high school. Silver Sage Acres and Megan's neighborhood weren't even on it.

"Well, *you* can go," I said, trying to fold it up. But its seams were so old and soft that I couldn't figure out which way it went. So I just folded it in quarters and took it to the recycle bin.

As I dropped it in, I noticed something: on the back of the map was an aerial photograph of Surrey, with the elevation changes marked in faint white outlines that radiated out from the hills.

And there was a small, gleaming white spot on it. Like the bright white light from TV and my photos—only in miniature.

Which made sense—it was a photograph, after all.

Leave it, Alexis. Forget it.

But I reached down into the bin to grab the map back out—

And that's when I heard it:

Vzzzzzzzzzz

I swung around, my hands gripping the edge of the counter.

Vzzzzzzzzzz. The sound continued on steadily. I started toward the foyer, hoping I could leave it behind by leaving the room. Or the house, if necessary.

"Hello?" I called. "Who's there?"

As I stepped around the corner—

"Me," Lydia said.

To say I jumped out of my skin would be an understatement. I screeched and slammed backward into the wall, bruising my back on the light switch.

"Jeez, Alexis," she said. "You scare easy."

For a good five seconds, I could only glare at her. Then I sidestepped around her and stalked to my bedroom, grabbing my camera, my jacket, my purse, and my car keys.

"Where are you going?" she asked. "Can I come?"

I turned to look at her.

"I'm bored," she said. "Besides, you'll probably end up demanding my presence eventually."

My most innate reaction was to say, *No thanks*— getting useful information from Lydia was one thing. Having her ride along like some sidekick was another. But something made me hold back. Was it . . . could it be . . . my gut?

"Fine, whatever," I said. "Come on."

I went straight out the front door and locked it behind me, without another word. Then I started down the sidewalk to my car. Lydia was already waiting in the passenger seat.

I cross-referenced the map with one that had actual streets on it, and followed that (no thanks to Lydia's horrific navigation skills) to a neighborhood built in the 1950s. The spot where the light was supposed to be was just a run-down brick house with white trim. The hair pricked up on the back of my neck as I pulled into the gas station across the street and looked around.

Kids were trickling down the sidewalk, alone or in pairs.

"Is there another high school around here?" I asked.

"Redmond," Lydia said. "I almost had to go there after we moved, but my mom gave the lady at the school district a bunch of free haircuts so I could stay at Surrey."

"What's so great about Surrey?" I asked.

"It's where my friends are." She shrugged. "Of course, I didn't know how many less friends I'd have once we moved to our crappy new house and Mom stopped stocking the fridge."

"That sucks," I said.

"Yeah, well . . . I found Aralt. So it didn't matter anyway."

"And look how well that worked out," I said.

She snorted. "Tell me about it."

I watched a girl stride along, looking totally relaxed and carefree, wearing oversized hipster headphones. A familiar stab of envy went through me. I'd been that girl once, but I'd never be her again. The closest I'd ever get to that kind of happiness was standing there, surrounded by gasoline fumes, watching somebody else enjoy it.

Then, as she passed the brick house, the girl stumbled and almost fell. She caught herself at the last second and kept walking, glancing around self-consciously.

"What exactly are you looking for?" Lydia asked.

I considered not telling her, but it wasn't like she could say anything to anybody else, right? So I explained about the bright light, and all the times I'd seen it—in my car, on TV, at night in the field, at Jared's house, in my photographs, and finally on the old map.

"Wow," Lydia said. "All that, and you thought it was me?"

I shrugged.

"Well, I can tell you it's not," she said. "In the first place, too much work."

"The light seems related to Kendra's and Ashleen's disappearances," I said. "So if it's here, I want to know why."

"So is it? Here?"

"I don't know yet," I said. "I just want to observe for a minute."

What I didn't want to tell her was that I was afraid of the light. Specifically, I was afraid of attracting its attention and ending up surrounded by the horrible laughter again.

Then came two boys, walking close together, looking down at a piece of paper.

Suddenly, one of them reared back, his voice loud and annoyed, though I couldn't make out his words. And then they were fighting, and all I heard as they continued down the street were their angry voices.

The next girl was tall, with dark skin and long braids, wearing a green-and-yellow cheerleading uniform. She walked with confidence—until she reached the sidewalk in front of the brick house.

Then she stopped and slapped at her arm, looking dismayed. She studied her hand, then took several steps back, like something had frightened her.

She made a sharp turn and crossed the street toward the gas station, walking right up to my car.

"I just got stung by a bee, and I'm allergic," she said. "I have an EpiPen, but if I pass out, will you call nine-one-one?"

I nodded—what else could I do?—and watched as she jabbed a small needle into her thigh. Then she sat down on the curb and dug through her bag for her phone.

"Do you need me to drive you someplace?" I asked. "To the hospital?"

"No, thanks. My brother'll come. He'll take me if I need to go. . . . I feel okay so far." She sighed.

"All right," I said. "I can wait here with you."

"If you don't mind." She studied the welt rising off of her forearm. "I swear, I got stung there last year, too. That house is totally cursed."

She went on talking, but I wasn't listening. I was looking at the house.

Cursed.

That was something I hadn't thought about. Could the bright light, the wandering girls, be part of a curse?

A few minutes later the girl's brother pulled up. She thanked me again and got into the car.

As soon as she was gone, I collected my courage, got the camera out of my bag, and walked to the edge of the road. I kept my distance—I was a good twenty feet from the sidewalk in front of the brick house.

I took a few pictures, expecting—hoping, even?—to see some kind of troublemaking ghost.

But all I saw in the frame was a spot of bright white light.

I stared at the image, trying to make sense of it.

"What are you looking at?" Lydia peered down at my camera. "I don't see anything."

"Really? Nothing?"

"What do *you* see?" She followed me. "What's in that house?"

"I don't know," I said, hoping no one noticed that the girl with the camera was apparently having a conversation with herself in the middle of the sidewalk. "You're the one who can walk through walls."

"I can, you know," she said. "I could go look. Want me to?"

I'd spent the past three months hiding everything from everyone. And now I was supposed to trust the one person who I thought hated me more than anyone else on the planet?

I sighed. "Sure, why not."

She disappeared. A minute passed.

I caught myself checking the time on my phone, thinking, *I hope she's all right.*

Lydia emerged a few seconds later and hurried across the street, not even flinching when a car drove right through her. She was too eager to share what she'd learned. "There's an old guy passed out on the sofa. He's drunk."

"Just a regular guy? You didn't see any other . . ."

She blinked. "Any other what?"

"Ghosts?"

"No." She gave me an accusatory glance—almost like her feelings were hurt. "Are you saying you can see *other* ghosts? I'm not the only one?"

"If it makes you feel better," I said, "you're definitely the most intrusive ghost in my life."

She shrugged. "A *little* better . . . I guess."

"Come on," I said. "Let's get out of here."

Her eyes went wide.

"What?" I asked.

"You really want me to ride with you?"

"*Want* might be too strong a word," I said. "But you might as well."

Truthfully, though, I guess I did kind of want her there. Amazing how having zero friends and absolutely nobody to turn to could make you look at a person (or a ghost) in a new light. Lydia could be snarky, but it was nice to have someone to talk to for a change.

As we drove back through town, I thought about Lydia's willingness to help. Maybe this helpful act was just that—an act, designed to lull me into a sense of false confidence she could spring some super-duper destructive attack on me when I least expected it.

I pulled off to the side of the road.

"Why are we stopping here?" She looked around. "Did you see another ghost?"

"So if it's not you," I said, "why are there always yellow roses?"

"What? What do flowers have to do with anything?"

"You had yellow roses at your funeral."

"You remember that?" She cocked her head to the side. "Wow. That's almost kind of—"

"Answer me!" I said. "Does that mean you aren't the one leaving yellow roses all over the place?"

"Of course I'm not." Lydia sighed airily. "I don't care about stupid yellow roses, okay? The funeral home picked them."

Really.

The funeral home.

"But *why*, Lydia?" I asked. "Why do you keep showing up? Just tell me the truth, all right?"

She crossed her arms and didn't answer for a long moment, like she was gathering every ounce of dignity she could muster. "Because . . . you keep calling for me. You call my name, and it's like . . . I figure I should check on you. Honestly, Alexis, you're like a helpless little baby. *Someone* has to save you. Are you happy now?"

With a magnificent *harrumph*, she faded out of view.

The thought hit me like a Frisbee to the head:

The bird charm wasn't Lydia's power center.

I was.

20

I STOPPED AT MY LOCKER and shuffled my books. My phone buzzed in my pocket.

The screen was cracked almost beyond recognition, but the alternative was some Iron Age castoff of Mom's—another sentimental holdover from our old lives. So I was toughing it out. The phone still worked all right—it was just a little harder to see, that's all.

It was a text from Jared: *Nature preserve?*

Can't today, I replied. *Have a shoot.*

:(x 1000000

"Oh, come on," I said out loud. *Call u later,* I texted, flipping the phone shut and turning back to my locker.

"Who are you talking to?" Marley asked, coming down the hall at warp speed and stopping just short of a hard collision with the empty locker next to mine—the one that used to be Megan's.

It was February 12, and we were scheduled to cover the final planning meeting for the student government–sponsored Valentine's Day dance, a.k.a. "The Sweetheart Shindig," which Elliot had immediately proclaimed the worst title on record for a Surrey High dance (and considering that in the 1990s, a club called the Pseudointellectual Society hosted "The Dead Fish Jamboree," that was saying a lot). I was, to put it mildly, less than totally psyched about this shoot.

I slung my camera bag over my shoulder and walked with Marley to the gym. Inside, a bunch of Student Council members were gathered in a ragged semicircle of folding chairs. Zoe was there, as was Carter, and about ten other kids.

Marley started by making them move their chairs closer to the windows, looking for natural light for my photographs. The pale late afternoon sunlight still wasn't enough to drown out the sickly green of the overhead fluorescents, so finally she made them carry their chairs outside and sit in a circle on the lawn.

I looked through my viewfinder.

"Excuse me, I can't sit in the sun!" Zoe complained. "I'll burn."

"How is it?" Marley asked, ignoring her completely.

"It's fine, except . . ." I said, "it reads more 'drum circle' than 'Student Council.'"

I felt a tap on my shoulder and turned around to see Carter.

"How about over there?" he asked, pointing to a spot on a nearby covered walkway where two stone benches faced each other. Soft, natural light reflected off the white walls, but there was enough shade to be interesting (and to protect Zoe's milky complexion, which was apparently going to be a priority for all of us).

"Um . . . yeah, thanks," I said, and then without being asked, he busied himself getting everyone arranged and keeping them quiet while I set up.

Carter was the last one to sit. He planted himself on a bench in full sun—even though Zoe was hiding in the shade. She looked tempted to join him, fragile skin and all, but there were no seats left. So she pouted and stayed where she was.

"Come to order," someone said. They started going through their agenda.

After a month of Elliot's lightning-fast meetings, where wasting time was the equivalent of robbing an old lady in an alley, their petty back-and-forth bickering made my brain itch. In a yearbook meeting, if we had four minutes' worth of stuff to cover, the whole thing lasted about four minutes and fifteen seconds. The Student Council kids seemed so entranced by the idea of holding a "meeting" that they could hardly focus on the business at hand.

On the plus side, it gave me plenty of time to take photos.

Afterward, the decorations subcommittee went inside—to wander aimlessly and argue, I imagined, based on their snippy discussions during the meeting—and the rest of the kids left, pairing up to gossip about ideas and people they disagreed with as soon as they were out of each other's earshot.

Marley and I made plans to meet in the morning, and she took off.

Then I turned to leave—and saw the circle of folding chairs still sitting out in the grass.

I might have left them, except that the night's forecast predicted rain, which would ruin the padded seats. One of Elliot's pet topics to rant about was the way our school spent tons of money on the athletic department but almost nothing on maintaining the *non*-athletic facilities and equipment. She'd practically picketed the front office when I told her I'd tried to take a picture of the Literary Society but couldn't find a sofa in the library that didn't look like it had been gnawed on by a pack of wild dogs.

So I enclosed my camera in its case, slung it snugly across my body, and grabbed a chair to carry it back inside.

Then I went back out and picked up another chair.

This was going to take all day.

"Here," said a voice. "Let me help."

Next to me, Carter lifted a chair and walked toward the gym. After setting it down inside, he turned around and went back for another. He could have lapped me, but he went slowly, so we were walking together.

I set down my final chair and rubbed my hands on my jeans to get the feeling back in my stiff fingers. I raised my head to see Carter standing there watching me.

"Thanks for the help."

He smiled. "No problem."

Then he just kept . . . standing there.

"Carter," I said. He gave a little jerk, like I'd sneaked up on him. "Can I help you?"

"Well, I don't know." He looked around the gym. "Could you build a time machine, go back to the day I volunteered to help plan this dance, and knock me unconscious?"

"Aw," I said. "Not psyched for the shindig?"

His expression was so dismal that it was funny.

Then we were both laughing, maybe a little harder than we should have been. But I think part of it was relief—this was the first time in months that we'd managed to break through the tension between us.

"Are you going?" he asked.

"To the dance? No, I don't think so." My nerves twanged like guitar strings. "Jared—I mean, my . . . boyfriend—he goes to a different school."

Carter raised his eyebrows. "I see. One of *those* boy-friends."

"What boyfriends?"

"You know, the kind nobody ever actually sees." Carter smiled so his dimple showed. "I'll bet he's an international spy or something."

For a moment, I didn't know what to say. Carter had seen him at various parties, and we both knew it.

It was almost like he was talking to me, joking around, because . . . he wanted to.

"Yeah, totally," I said. "And he lives in a mansion in Miami, and he's best friends with Chuck Norris, and he's a race car driver."

"And a millionaire?"

"Actually, no," I said. "A billionaire. But I *swear* he exists."

"And I *completely* believe you," Carter said.

"He's a movie star, too," I said. "And he's . . ." Behind Carter, one of the gym doors opened, creating a blinding rectangle of light. A figure stood silhouetted inside of it. "Um . . . right over there."

Carter looked surprised, then turned around and watched Jared come toward us.

Right before he came into hearing range, Carter turned to me. *"Awk-ward,"* he said in a singsong voice, and I laughed.

"Hey . . . what are you doing here?" I asked, when Jared got closer.

"Meeting you," he said. "What's the joke?"

"But you knew I had a shoot."

"Yes, but . . ." He looked at his watch, then looked up at me, perplexed.

I kept hoping that Carter would slip away into the background, but he didn't. He looked at Jared and asked, "We haven't actually been introduced, have we?"

I gritted my teeth. "Jared," I said, "Carter. Carter, Jared."

They looked at each other for a breath longer than they needed to before extending their hands for a curt, manly shake and doing that mutual chin-raise boy-greeting.

"I'm just finishing up," I said to Jared. "But—what do you mean, meeting me?"

"Nature preserve," he said. "Like we texted about?"

I started to reach for my phone. "I thought we texted about *not* doing that today."

"No," Jared said, his jaw twitching. "You said you'd call me later, so I just thought I'd meet you here."

"Yeah, but . . ." I glanced up at the narrow windows. The sun was on its way down. He *must* have known it would be too late to take pictures.

Not to mention that I'd planned to spend the

afternoon looking up news stories on Kendra and Ashleen.

"Sorry. I thought it was clear that we had plans." Jared shrugged, glancing in Carter's direction. "But I guess you have more important things to do."

He started to walk away.

I shot a flustered look at Carter and hurried to catch up with Jared.

"Wait," I said. "I'm done here anyway. Let me get my stuff, all right?"

He gave me a chilly look. "Do what you have to do."

I walked back to the bleachers, where I'd stashed my backpack.

Carter was already there, standing next to his own bag. He looked at me with narrowed eyes. "Does he always treat you that way?"

"No, Carter," I said. "Usually he beats me with a two-by-four. Does Zoe always treat you like a stuffed animal?"

"That's not funny," Carter said as I walked away.

"I'm not joking," I called over my shoulder.

Jared wrapped his arm around my waist when I reached him. "Don't be mad," I said.

"I'm not," he said. "I thought I was, but it turns out I'm not."

He pulled me close and kissed me—a long, serious kiss.

I pushed away, blushing and unsettled.

Because I knew he'd done it so Carter would see.

"Hungry?" Jared asked. "I can make dinner."

We were stretched out on the couch watching cooking shows. I lifted my head off his chest and looked at him. The lines of his face were loose and relaxed.

"I guess," I said. "I should call my mom, though. Are you sure you want to cook? You don't have to."

"I'm a very good chef," he said. "Self-taught. I'm looking for a chance to show off, in case you can't tell."

"All right," I said, getting up and walking around the room to stretch my legs. "Dazzle me."

His arms were around me before I knew what was happening. He dipped me low, like a dancer or Scarlett O'Hara or something, and kissed me until I saw stars.

He was slender, but his arms were solid, lean muscle. He was strong.

Stronger than Carter, I thought.

He lifted me to my feet. I felt a little wobbly.

"I meant dazzle me with your *cooking,*" I said.

His fingers traced through my hair. "I don't care what you meant," he whispered. "Is that bad?"

Breathless, I nodded my head and said, "No."

I called Mom to tell her I'd be home later, then sat on a barstool in the corner of the kitchen.

"Can I use your laptop?" I asked.

"You don't want to spend every minute admiring my mad skills?"

I tried to smile, but the thought of what I had to look up online was weighing on my mind. Jared went to his room and brought back his computer, handing it to me.

I kept one eye on Jared as he worked. He really did know what he was doing—he chopped vegetables like the TV chefs, so fast the knife was practically a blur. And he always seemed to be finishing one thing exactly when the next thing needed to happen.

But my real focus was the web browser. I searched furiously for any article that linked supernatural occurrences with bright lights. I followed a few links that led me to dead ends.

"What are you so focused on over here? Can you be done now?" Jared asked, lifting the back of my hair and kissing my neck. "Dinner's ready."

We sat down to eat at the dining room table, with two steaming bowls of pasta in front of us.

"Hang on," Jared said, disappearing into the kitchen and coming back with two glasses of red wine. He handed me one and held his up. "Cheers."

I clinked glasses, then set mine down. "I don't really drink."

"Not even a sip?" he asked.

I took the tiniest sip. The wine tasted like vinegar to me, but I forced my expression to stay neutral.

"So," Jared said. "I've been thinking."

"About what?"

He finished chewing and smiled. "Why you've been so tired lately. And I realized—you should quit yearbook."

"What?" I said the word with a mouthful of pasta and then had to swallow a too-big bite. "What do you mean?"

"I mean . . . what it probably sounds like I mean. You're overwhelmed, you have a lot going on, you're tired and busy, and you should quit. It's not like they're paying you."

"Of course they're not paying me." I pinched the bridge of my nose, where a tiny headache was blossoming into existence. "They don't pay anyone. That's not how it works."

"My school pays the yearbook staff," he said. "Minimum wage, applied to their tuition, but it's the principle of the thing."

I crossed my arms. "Well, I guess your school has a lot of money."

There was a chilled silence.

"That's not a *bad* thing," I said. "It's just . . . I like

yearbook. And I don't think I'm overwhelmed. I'm just busy."

He still hadn't spoken.

"I appreciate your concern, but that's not an option for me. I don't want to quit."

Jared took a big swig from his wineglass and shot me a baffled look. "Fine, then. I just thought . . . since it's cutting into other areas of your life . . ."

"What other areas?"

"Our relationship, for starters," he said. "Lately there have been days when I really wanted to see you, and I can't even get you on the phone anymore."

I glanced down at my food. Nothing had ever looked less appetizing. "I'm sorry."

"You know what? Forget it. I don't want to talk about it right now," he said. "I'd like to enjoy my dinner."

I sat back, silent.

Jared didn't eat, either. He just stared down at his bowl, holding his fork in a death grip. After a few seconds, he leaned back a little and sighed.

"I'm sorry," he said. "I think that's what they call an overreaction. Can you forgive me?"

"Sure," I said. My nerves were starting to feel like a frayed rope. I reached for my wineglass and gulped down a mouthful before I had time to dislike the taste.

Jared had softened. "Maybe you should tell me about yearbook. Since you seem to enjoy it so much."

So I did. I talked about Elliot, Marley, Chad, Mr. Janicke . . . all the shoots I'd done. Well, all the shoots except the ones with Carter. I thought that by putting names and anecdotes along with it, I could make Jared understand why it was so important to me.

By the time dinner was over, I'd finished the entire glass of wine, and my head was feeling fuzzy. I was still shy, underneath my alcohol-loosened tongue, and I suddenly wondered just how long I'd been going on about how cool Elliot was. It could have been five minutes or it could have been an hour.

"I should go home." I stood up, but the room swayed around me.

"Yeah, I don't think so, lightweight," Jared said. "You're going to have to hang out a while."

I called Mom and told her Jared and I were going to watch a movie, but I'd be home by ten. The words slipped around my mouth like a wet fish, but Mom didn't seem to pick up on it.

"You should probably drink some water," said Jared.

I shook my head, which was starting to ache. "I just want to sit down."

He helped me to the couch and turned on the TV.

I put my hand on his thigh. "Sorry," I slurred. "I guess I'm a featherweight."

He half laughed. "A fezzerweight?"

"Is that what I said?" The words were too thick to come out correctly.

"No." He softly swept the hair from in front of my eyes. "It's not. I shouldn't tease you."

I yawned in his face. "I'm so tired."

"But you *are* a featherweight." He leaned toward me. "A very cute one."

By the time the kiss was over, I was passed out.

"Alexis?"

My temples ached like I had a too-tight bandanna tied around my head. I opened my eyes to see Jared standing above me.

"Ow," I said.

"Hello to you, too." He took my hand and pulled me to a sitting position.

"I think my brain is full of ball bearings," I groaned.

"It's getting late," he said. "Are you okay to drive?"

"What time is it?"

"Nine forty-five."

That opened my eyes. I'd been asleep for two hours?

"I can take you home. I'll just drive your car and take a taxi back."

"I'm sure I'm fine," I said. "It was just one glass."

He looked sheepish. "Well, it was a generous pour."

"But *you're* fine?"

He smoothed my hair. His cool fingers felt heavenly on my skin, and I pressed my face against his hand. "I like wine," he said. "Dad's let me have a glass with dinner since I was thirteen."

"No, I'm okay," I said, standing. Then the room whooshed around me, and I sat back down, defeated. "But you have to let me pay for the cab."

"We'll figure that out later," Jared said. "I'll get my jacket. Where are your keys?"

By the time I got home I was ready to pass out again. I totally forgot about paying for the cab. It was all I could do to brush my teeth, change into my pajamas, and collapse into bed.

Sometimes you wake up because you're hot, or cold, or thirsty, or have to pee, or hear a noise. And sometimes you wake up because you just *do*.

I yawned and stretched and moved my arm out from under my pillow, shaking it lightly to get the blood flowing back into my fingers. My head still swam from the wine, so I snuggled back down on my pillow and closed my eyes again, trying to make the spinning dizziness go away.

Then I felt the slightest movement across my cheek.

My fingers touched something soft and wet, and I gasped, slapping at my skin furiously, as if there had been a spider crawling across my face in the darkness. I jumped out of bed and switched on the light.

On my pillowcase lay a single yellow rose petal.

I looked around. My head felt stuffy and I could hear the blood in my ears. It made the room seem silent—until I focused a little harder.

Vzzzzzzzzzz

"Hello?" I whispered.

But there was no answer.

My cheek burned, so I turned to the mirror to see if I'd scratched myself. My body felt weighted down, my mind thick. I was still out of it from being drunk—it was like I couldn't even force myself to stay alert.

The sound seemed to be coming from behind me. But I could clearly see in the mirror that the room was empty.

Without thinking, I reached down for my camera, aiming it at the mirror and shooting pictures of the reflection.

Looking down at the image, the first thing I noticed was that the exposure was way off. There wasn't nearly enough light in the bedroom, and I'd been too woozy to change the lens settings, which were adjusted for an outside shoot in the sun. Everything in the picture was darker than it should have been, which meant the image *should* have been a black, underexposed rectangle.

But it wasn't.

There was something there.

The air left my lungs completely, and my hands clenched the sides of the camera in a death grip.

What I had thought up to that moment was a bright splotch of light—in the woods with Ashleen, on the TV screen, and in front of the small house on the far side of town—was a ghost. The ghost of a girl.

But she wasn't like any ghost I'd ever seen before.

She was *moving*.

In a photograph.

Her whole body flickered slightly, like a neon sign about to burn out. The flickering gave the impression of a glow around her, and her form was slightly blurred, like she was making a million tiny movements. And even in my photo . . . she was *quaking*.

She floated directly over my bed, her body crooked and broken, arms askew and neck bent to a horrific angle.

The pose looked like she'd fallen—but she was hovering in midair. Her hair swung raggedly in front of her face, almost reaching my pillow. Her left arm hung down, and her left hand held a bouquet of yellow roses.

And she was wearing the purple dress.

The same one I saw myself in. The same one Ashleen's ghost wore.

Almost in a panic, I crashed into my dresser and then threw open my bedroom door, trying to get as far away from the ghost as possible. I ended up in the kitchen, with my back against the sliding door that led to our tiny patch of backyard.

"Lydia!" I whispered.

But Lydia didn't pop out of thin air. How long did it usually take her to come, I wondered?

Holding my breath, I looked back at the picture, at the trembling figure.

And then—she turned her head. The ghost in the picture *turned her head*. And looked at me.

Except she didn't have eyes. Where they should have been were just dark sunken patches of smooth skin, like two round shadows on her face.

But she saw me—I know she did.

Through a *photograph*.

I stood in shock, my breath coming in tiny puffs. I glanced at the hall, expecting to see a trembling cloud of white light float out of my bedroom.

Then I heard the sound again—*vzzzzzzzz*—coming from behind me.

Before I had the sense not to do it, I turned around

and took another picture, looking out the glass doors toward the yard. She was there. And she was closer—she filled almost the whole frame.

I stared at her waves of golden hair—which, up close, were covered in dirt. Where her hair and skin met, the skin was beginning to shrivel, raisinlike, and was laced with a thin layer of black. The layers of her purple dress were outlined in gray-green mildew, and her bony, desiccated left hand held a bouquet of rotting roses— only *held* was the wrong word. The stems seemed grafted to her palm, growing out of the skin like some grotesque, malignant tumor.

But the worst of it was the space where her eyes should have been.

It would have almost been better if there were disgusting empty eye sockets, because at least that would have been real—but this hollow smoothness was like something from a nightmare. It was impossible and horrible and yet it was right there in front of me—staring me down.

I thought, *I don't know if I can do this.*

"What—" I choked. "Who are you?"

I raised the camera and took another photograph. In this image she'd begun to lean forward through the sliding glass door, and her head and face and dress and flowers were actually coming right through it, as if the glass were nothing but a sheet of falling water.

I stepped back and snapped another picture.

Now she was in the kitchen with me.

"Wait—" I took one last photo and looked down at it.

She was smiling, revealing a mouth of blackened teeth, sharpened to points. Her gums were gray and decaying.

The *vzzzzz* seemed to waver and change, until it was a new sound:

Hissssssssssssss

And suddenly I understood something, down to the core of my being—

This was not a good ghost.

I swallowed hard, letting the camera fall to the end of its strap. My voice trembled like a flag in a windstorm. *"Go . . . away."*

Then she laughed—the horrible, musical, maniacal laugh.

That's when it clicked for me. Every time I'd heard that laugh—every time I'd seen the light—this *thing* had been there. This horrible, disgusting thing . . . this thing that had been in my bedroom—hanging over me— *watching* me.

In a burst of terror, I turned and ran, desperately trying to get away from the laughter and the teeth and the non-eyes. But the laughter came with me, like it was playing through headphones that were glued onto my ears.

I skidded around the corner and down the hall toward my room, gasping in shock as I saw another figure standing in my path.

At first I thought it was Lydia.

But this figure was solid, and I ran into it, and both of us went flying, and the next thing I knew, my sister was sputtering beneath me like an angry cat.

"What are you doing?!" she demanded, pushing me off her and getting to her feet.

I didn't answer because I was too busy looking behind me. The laughter was gone, but that didn't mean that she—it—whatever it was—wasn't still following me, hovering, grinning, hissing. . . .

"What's going on?" Kasey asked. "You look like you just saw a . . ."

I turned to her. I don't know what my face looked like, but her expression changed as though someone had flipped a switch. She went from irritated to dead serious.

"Lexi," she whispered, shaking her head. "What *exactly* are you doing?"

"Nothing," I said.

She looked in the direction of the living room.

"No," I said.

She whipped her head toward me.

"Kasey," I said. "Don't. Just go back to bed. *Please.*"

She glanced past me toward the end of the hallway. Her eyes came back to meet mine, and we stared at each other for a long, terrible minute.

Then, so fast her nightgown swished around her legs, she turned and stormed into her bedroom.

I got into my bed, but I didn't sleep. I just sat there with the light on.

I was so tired that I began to see swirls of color in my vision, but I didn't lie down, didn't rest my head.

Didn't even close my eyes longer than it took to blink.

For the whole night.

21

THE NEXT DAY, I got to school early and went to the yearbook office, where I found Chad hunched over a layout, as usual.

When I sat down at one of the open computers, I found that the internet was blocked.

"What's up?" Chad asked. "There's a lot of disgruntled sighing coming from your side of the room."

My sleepless night left me feeling like the world's grouchiest zombie. "I'm trying to look something up," I said. "But I can't."

He wheeled his chair over and looked over my shoulder before I thought to minimize the screen.

"'Supernatural yellow roses,'" he read. He sat back and looked at me.

"It's . . . a band," I said. "My cousin's punk band."

He thought about it, then nodded. "Catchy name. Do they have any songs out?"

"Probably nothing you've heard of."

He shrugged and reached for the mouse, going through a series of menus and typing in a bunch of long codes. Then he sat back. "Chad rules, firewall drools. Cyberstalk crappy bands to your heart's content."

"Thanks," I said. But none of my searches pulled up any relevant results. Nothing was written about a ghost that could move, or about ghosts wearing clothes other than the ones they died in.

I was fairly certain that the ghost who'd been in my room—though really she was more than just a ghost, kind of a *superghost*—was somehow the key to everything that was happening. If she was the source of the buzzing noise, the yellow roses, and the purple dress, then it was fair to speculate that she was the one who'd lured Kendra and Ashleen from their houses in the middle of the night to wander in the woods.

So if she was at the center of it all, the next logical step would be to find out her identity and her story.

It might help to take a closer look at my pictures. "Do you have the card reader?"

Chad wheeled back over to me, card reader in hand, and looked at my screen again. "'Dead girl in purple dress'?"

"It's . . . one of their songs."

"I never really figured you for the emo death rock type," he said. "But I guess it makes sense."

"Thanks," I said, grabbing the card reader and

pushing his chair back toward his own computer. Then I hooked the reader up and inserted the memory card from my camera. The pictures loaded, and I leaned closer to study them.

Nothing stood out to me in the daylight that I hadn't noticed at night.

But . . . the white spots . . .

"Hey, Chad?"

"Yes, Death Rock?" He wheeled over. "Should I just sit here with you for a few hours?"

"Help?" I'd opened Photoshop and loaded one of the pictures of Ashleen and the white spot.

Chad squinted. "This is your best work?" To him, it just looked like a poorly composed picture of a tree.

"No." I looked closer at the screen. "How do I make it darker?"

"You mean lighter."

"No, I mean darker."

"You *do* know this picture was taken at night, right?"

"Darker, please," I repeated.

"Image menu . . . adjust . . . exposure. Or levels. Play around until you have the extreme, black, ruined photograph of your dreams. Are we done here?"

"Like this?" I used the mouse to move the exposure slider down, keeping my eyes on the white spot.

It worked.

"Yeah, like that," Chad said. "Now you can't see anything. Mission accomplished. So, tell me why you're doing this?"

But I was too busy looking at the picture to answer. The white spot in the picture of Ashleen, faded down, was the exact same ghost I'd seen in my room.

"Live via satellite," Chad was saying. "It's Alexis Warren . . ."

She was still shaking. And she looked at me again.

Then—she moved closer.

I jerked away from the desk and pushed off of Chad's back, slamming him forward into the desk and shooting my own chair across the room.

"Turn it off!" I said. "Turn the computer off!"

"What—why would you—my *stomach*!"

I ran back and hit the power button on the underside of the monitor.

"I hope you didn't break my ribs," Chad said. "I mean, I'd kind of heard you were supposed to be mental, but I didn't know you were violent."

"I'm sorry," I said, breathing heavily and not taking my eyes off the darkened monitor. "I thought I saw a spider."

"Um, okay," he said, wheeling his chair away. Under his breath he whispered, *"Crazy."*

After a minute, I went back and disconnected the card reader. Then I reached down and held the computer's power button in until the machine shut off with a sudden sigh.

"Um, excuse me. You've used computers before, right?" Chad asked, looking up from his screen. "You know how to go to the menu to turn the power off? And how to eject a memory card? Are you *trying* to corrupt the hard drive?"

I couldn't answer. My fingers fumbled getting the card out of the reader and sticking it back in my camera. I went to the menu and selected ERASE ALL.

There was probably important information in those photos. Clues that could help me figure out what that thing was, and how it was connected to Ashleen and Kendra, and—most important—why it was sleeping in *my* house.

But I couldn't bear to let it live in my memory chip.

I looked at Chad, stuffing the camera back in my bag. "Did I hurt you?"

The way he looked at me, I knew he knew something was wrong.

"Nah," he said, his voice a shade gentler than usual. "You're just lucky my rock-solid six-pack broke the impact."

* * *

I completely ignored whatever my first period teacher was talking about, and spent the whole class sketching what I could remember of the purple dress. When the bell rang, I went over to the 200 wing, where my sister and her friends had lockers.

Keeping an eye out for Kasey, I went up behind Mimi Laird, whose bouncing red mane of curls made her visible from a hundred feet away. I tapped her on the shoulder, and she turned around, obviously surprised to see me.

"Can we talk for a minute?" I asked.

Mimi glanced around. If I had to put a word to it, I'd say she looked nervous. (Which further confirmed my suspicions that the whole ex–Sunshine Club thought I was a murderer.)

"Sure," she said. "What's up?"

"Not here. . . . In the bathroom, maybe?" I didn't want Kasey seeing us.

She put on a brave little smile and followed me. When I unfolded my drawing, she visibly relaxed.

"That's . . . nice," she said. "Are you into fashion now?" She cast a doubtful look at my non-fashionista outfit—jeans, T-shirt, and a hoodie.

"No," I said. "I saw this dress somewhere and I'm trying to figure out where it came from."

Mimi knew more about fashion than anyone I'd ever

met. She read every magazine and had an encyclopedic knowledge of all the designers and trends.

She made a skeptical face. "Where it came from?"

"Like, any particular store or whatever?"

Mimi quirked her mouth up. "Um . . . I don't know. Like, literally thousands of dresses come out every season. And a lot of designers did stuff that looked like that."

"*Did?* What do you mean?"

"Nobody's done tulip sleeves for two years," she said. "You . . . weren't going to try to wear this to prom, were you? Because I'm sure Kasey and Adrienne could help you find—"

"No," I said. "I just liked it."

Mimi nodded slowly, with the kind of caution you'd use around an unstable person. "Well, I'd say that style's two years old, at least."

"At least?" I said. "So it could be, like, ten years old?"

She bit her lip and looked down at the dress. "No. Two to three years, max. If that helps."

"It does, actually," I said. It gave me a window to look into. "Thanks. And . . . could you not mention this to Kasey?"

"Um . . . sure," she said. "Anytime."

I stopped at home after school to drop off my backpack and have a snack before Brighter Path. As I was sitting on the couch, with the TV droning on as background noise, the front door opened and slammed shut.

I sat up to see Kasey in the entryway. She left her backpack in the foyer and came over to the couch. Then she just stared at me.

"Um, hi," I said.

"What is it, Lexi?" she asked.

"Excuse me?"

"Why would you go to Mimi for help instead of asking me?"

I tried to hide my annoyance, but I guess it didn't work.

"Don't be mad at her," Kasey said. "She didn't tell me anything specific. She just said I should check on you."

"Great," I said. "Now Mimi's gossiping about me."

"It's not like that," Kasey said. "Mimi wouldn't gossip about you. She's just worried."

"Why would she worry about me?" I asked. "I didn't ask her to."

Kasey rolled her eyes. "You don't have to ask your friends to worry about you. That's just what they do. It's why they're your friends."

Did Mimi really consider herself my friend?

I'd certainly given up thinking of her that way. I'd lumped her in with the rest of the Sunshine Club girls— the ones who avoided me.

"If you need help with something, I'll help you," Kasey said. "I'm your sister."

She sat forward in her chair, her hair hanging in two loose braids over her shoulders, her jaw set, and a fierce look in her eyes.

"I'm fine, Kase," I said. "I'm sorry Mimi got you all worked up."

She sighed and sat back. Then her phone started ringing. She glanced down at it and stood up. "Just remember," she said as she walked away, "people want to help you."

Then I heard her say, "Keat? Hey," and shut the door to her bedroom.

I stared at the TV, not processing the images but letting them wash over me.

Maybe my sister was right.

Maybe it was time to ask for help.

I just couldn't bring myself to ask *her*.

When I pulled into the Sacred Heart parking lot, Megan was waiting for me.

Seeing her used to give me a glowy moment of happiness mixed with relief—the security you feel around your best friend. But as the weeks went by, the glow had gotten dimmer and faded out faster. I didn't know what we were to each other, but it didn't seem quite like BFFs anymore.

She hugged me, beaming her Brighter Path smile. She looked flawless, as usual, her hair in a perfect frizzless ponytail, her makeup understated but pretty. But lately she was . . . different.

Like a robot. In fact, she reminded me a lot of herself as a Sunshine Club girl.

"Welcome!" she said, in a chirpy voice that made me wince.

Megan had bought, mixed, and drunk the Brighter Path Kool-Aid—then gone back for seconds. She was basically the group's poster child; she was Brother Ben's second-in-command, and she loved nothing more than to sing the praises of him and his stupid club until I wanted to tear my hair out.

We started walking along the tree-lined cobblestone path that wound through the campus. I tried to think of a way to bring up the superghost—but Megan did it for me.

"It's so weird about that girl Ashleen," she said, shaking her head and smoothing her skirt. "Do they know anything about what happened?"

"No, nothing yet."

"It's sort of . . . off, you know? Sneaking out in the middle of the night. Dying mysteriously."

Could I really be hearing correctly? Megan was thinking about it. She was curious. Maybe she would be excited to hear what I had to say. And then we could work on this together—and fix it.

She clucked sadly. "I just can't help but assume they were in trouble somehow."

It wasn't what I'd been expecting to hear. "In trouble?"

She had the grace to seem a little uncomfortable. "I mean . . . they were messing with things they shouldn't have been messing with."

I could tell my stare made her nervous, but that didn't make me back down. "Are you trying to say that Ashleen *deserved* to die?"

"God, no! That's horrible." She swiftly spun away, but I knew Megan too well—her sharp denial was basically an admission. "Just that they probably weren't being careful. So it's not like it's a *surprise*, that's all."

"Like girls who dress a certain way and get attacked and—"

"No!" She snapped the word at me, and I could see I'd broken through her smooth, composed exterior. She blushed hotly and sped up, walking a few steps ahead of me.

I caught up. "Let's talk about something else, okay?"

She made an annoyed sound. "It's not like you to deliberately misunderstand me, Lex. I meant more like . . . like Lydia. You play with fire, you're going to get burned."

Shockingly, I felt the hair on the back of my neck stand up. "Lydia didn't know any better. She didn't deserve to die, either. Her death was a horrible tragedy."

Megan shot me a glance that I couldn't decipher. "Of *course* it was."

"I need to show you something." I knew it was a long shot. I even knew it was a terrible idea and even more terrible timing. But that didn't stop me from pulling out the drawing of the dress and handing it to her. "Have you ever heard of a ghost that, like . . . flickers?"

She'd been studying the picture, but when she heard the word "ghost," she shoved it back into my hands. "Why are you asking me this?"

"Just . . . no reason. Or . . . a ghost that can hold something? Like, in its hands?"

She turned to me, her body rigid. She swallowed hard and seemed to think before she spoke. "*No*, Alexis."

Did she mean "no" as in, no she hadn't? Or "no" as in, she was refusing to answer the question?

I pressed on. "What about ghosts who aren't wearing what they wore when they—"

"*Stop it*," she said, her teeth gritted. "Seriously. What are you doing?"

It was like a pit opened up in my stomach. Megan wasn't going to help me. Not in a million years. Even if she had information, she'd never share it.

"Nothing," I said. "Forget it."

I started walking again, and she followed. But something had changed between us.

When she spoke, her voice was low and lifeless. "How are you doing? You know, with Jared and all that?"

"We're fine," I said.

She stared up at the spindly, leafless treetops. "I guess it kind of makes sense that you guys are together."

My pulse quickened. "What does that mean?"

She gave me an uncomfortable glance. "You know, because you're both sort of—"

"Girls!" Ben called. He was standing on the path up ahead. "We're starting!"

"Sort of what?" I asked.

Megan gave her head a quick shake. "Nothing. Forget it."

Brother Ben was waiting for us at the door. "Howdy, Megs. And Lex. How are we today?"

Carter and Megan used to be the only people who called me "Lex." But considering Carter didn't call me anything at all anymore, and Megan only existed in the context of these weird, stupid meetings . . . Brother Ben could have it.

But "Megs"? Five months ago, I would have assumed Megan would pulverize anyone who said it to her face.

Now she just grinned at Brother Ben. "Happy Tuesday."

232

I started to take a seat in the fourth row, but Megan touched my sleeve. "Hey, let's sit up front."

I couldn't muster the energy to protest. I just picked up my bag and moved to the chair next to hers.

Ben stood at the front of the room and began the meeting, then passed the contraband box, then opened the floor for discussion. A couple of kids got up and spoke, but the testimonials ended faster than usual, which momentarily put me in a good mood. I thought I might get a few extra minutes to spend with Megan in the parking lot. Maybe once the meeting was out of her system, she'd calm down and actually act like my old best friend.

But after the last kid went back to his seat, Ben gave Megan a nod that seemed to suggest they shared a secret. She glanced at me (rather ominously, I thought) and stood up.

Uh-oh.

"So today we're going to try something new." Her eyes met mine, and she gave me a bright, encouraging, and one hundred percent artificial smile. "It's called the 'hot seat.' And it's basically sixty seconds where you stand up and people can ask you anything. And you have to answer honestly."

Oh, no. No, no, no.

A thousand times no.

"So, I was thinking . . . um . . . Lex? Do you want to go first?"

I shook my head. Nope. I did not.

She didn't lose her plastered-on smile. "Come on, it'll be fun!"

"Megan, no," I said, my voice low—almost a growl.

Ben stood up, his whole face one big *I told you so*. "Well, Megs, I guess your sales pitch needs some work."

People behind me tittered, more from a collective sense of discomfort than anything else, and Megan went red from her neck to her ears. As much as I couldn't bear this new weird Megan, I also couldn't bear to watch Ben make fun of her, knowing how she worshipped every word that came out of his stupid puffer-fish mouth.

"Fine," I said, standing up.

Megan's eyes were wide. "No, Alexis—you don't have to."

"I don't care," I said. "I'll do it."

Brother Ben rubbed his hands together like a villain who's finally got the helpless damsel tied to the train tracks. No doubt he'd been waiting a long time to probe my evil brain.

Megan was already looking regretful. "Sixty seconds starts . . ." She hit the start button and let a couple more seconds pass. "Right . . . now."

Hands went up around the room, but Ben ignored them all and looked right at me. "Why did you get involved with the occult?"

I glared at him. "Because I had to."

"Are you truly unaware of the danger you're dealing with?"

I let the question hang in the air before I turned to him. "Not by any stretch of the imagination."

"So why do you continue to do it?" he asked, a challenge.

"Who said I do?"

His nostrils flared. "Well, I think it's pretty obvious, judging by your attitude *alone*, that—"

"My attitude is fine," I said. "And I don't need to sit here and be attacked—"

"We're not trying to attack you." Megan clawed her way in, trying to defuse the tension before the situation exploded in her face. "We're trying to *help* you."

This was help? My insides felt like they were being twisted, and I felt a sudden shock of love for my sister—who, when she said she wanted to help me, meant it from the bottom of her heart.

Megan was giving me a chance to calm down, to take the easy way out. But I didn't want the easy way out. I was too angry. I'd been ambushed, and I was looking for a fight. Brother Ben had wanted this to happen, even if Megan was too blinded by her willful ignorance to see that. On purpose or not, she'd led me right into his trap.

And as much as I wanted to, I couldn't forgive that.

"The questions you were asking me before . . ." She let her voice trail off.

"What questions?" Ben asked. "What have you two been discussing?"

"Nothing!" Megan cried. "Nothing. It wasn't important!"

"Maybe not to *you*," I said, staring her down.

She looked at the floor.

"Now, hold on," Ben said. "Megs, if you've been backsliding, maybe it's *you* who needs to be on the hot seat."

Anything I wanted to say now would be like slapping my best friend in the face, so I stared at him, seething.

The mood in the room had become decidedly dark for a Brighter Path meeting, and Ben took notice and lowered his voice. "I don't know why you feel you need to be rude and hostile," he said, dragging his lips into what was supposed to be a smile. "We're all here to *support* one another."

"Support? That's what you call it?" I said, picking up my bag. "Telling us we're weak and helpless?"

"Alexis, I'm sorry!" Megan said. "I didn't know—"

236

"Maybe it's better that you go," Ben said. "Since you've proven yourself to be not only a liar, but a thief as well."

Megan was practically frantic. "No, wait. This is all wrong. Alexis—"

"Let her go, Megs," Ben said. "She's chosen her path. She knows what she wants."

What I *wanted* was to heave Megan over my shoulder and carry her out of there, straight to a cult deprogrammer.

No, that wasn't true. What I *really* wanted was for her to walk out on her own two feet.

I turned and looked at her. Her expression was sad, pleading—but she hadn't moved, not an inch, in my direction.

She was staying.

A sea of astounded eyes watched me from the rows of seats.

"Everyone has moments of weakness," I said. "But that doesn't make you *weak*."

I pushed the door open and felt a rush of winter air in my face.

I was walking away from more than just Brighter Path.

I was walking away from my best friend.

22

I STORMED ACROSS the parking lot and slammed the car door behind me, hurling my bag onto the passenger seat. "Lydia!" I called. "Where are you?"

She didn't appear. I turned the key in the ignition so forcefully I had a moment of fear that it might break in two.

"What? What is it?" Lydia faded into view in the backseat.

"I need your help."

"About time!" She smirked. "I've been waiting for you to give up on the albino Swede look."

"Not with my hair," I said, pulling out of the parking lot. "With something else."

"Like what?" she asked. When I didn't answer, she batted a hand through my arm. "Like what, Alexis?"

"You'll see when we get there," I said.

Lydia squirmed in her seat. "Can't you just call an exorcist? Or a tiny creepy little old lady, like in *Poltergeist*?"

"Lydia," I said, "if I got an exorcist, what do you think would happen to you?"

"Right," she said. "Never mind."

We were parked in front of the funeral home that had handled Lydia's services, and she was pretty jumpy. When I finally I told her that I wanted to get more information about the yellow roses, she freaked out and disappeared completely for a few minutes. Then she faded back in, looking embarrassed. I wonder if popping out of sight is the ghostly equivalent of peeing your pants.

"If there are any funerals going on, we're not going in, right?" Lydia said. "I can't. I won't. I hate funerals."

I wasn't wild about them myself. "I promise," I said, because the parking lot was empty. I pushed my shoulders back, held my head high, and went inside, with Lydia right at my heels like a nervous dog.

The lobby was carpeted in plush beige and wallpapered in soft olive-green paper with blue flowers. There was a small sofa, a side table with a lamp and a stack of magazines, and a desk with a small bell on it. I rang the bell.

"Hello?"

Lydia yelped in surprised, and I spun around to see a man standing between me and the door, silhouetted in the late afternoon sun.

"Can I help you?"

He moved into the light so I could see him. He had a long, wrinkled face and wore a jacket and tie.

"Hi," I said. "Um . . . I wanted to ask some questions."

He frowned.

I'd invented a few different explanations, figuring I'd use the one that seemed most appropriate in the moment. I discarded "my best friend is dying and wants me to find her a cool funeral home" and "I think I might want to be a mortician when I grow up" and went for the one that was closest to the truth.

"I'm a student at Surrey High, and I'm doing research on issues related to death and dying," I said. "I was hoping someone here would have a couple of minutes to talk to me."

He seemed to consider it, but was on the verge of saying no, I could tell. So I started talking again.

"What I've found is that our society seems to think of death as, like, this mysterious, horrible thing. When really, it happens to everyone. So I'm sort of researching the idea that death is more like a passage. And how funerals help people cope."

He checked his watch. "Well, I guess we could chat for a few minutes. Do you mind coming back to the office? We have an appointment coming in shortly, and I'd rather they not overhear us."

I followed him through a wood-paneled door. We passed a woman sitting at a desk, talking on the phone, and went into a glass-walled office.

"It's good that she's here," Lydia said, looking out at the woman. "So you don't have to worry about him murdering you and dissolving your body in a vat of acid."

I couldn't reply, so I gave her a withering glare.

"I'm Richard Henry Gordon," the man said. "And you are?"

Uh. "Alexis Ann Warren."

"What?" Lydia said. "Henry-Gordon is his *last* name. It's on the sign, doofus."

He gestured to a guest chair, then sat down at his desk. "Well, Alexis Ann, would you like some candy?"

"Would you like some *dead-people* candy?" Lydia asked. "Alexis Ann?"

"Um, no, thank you," I said.

"All right, then. Ask away."

"I was wondering about the ritual of having a funeral. What goes into that? Who makes all the decisions?"

He touched his fingertips together and leaned back, staring at an invisible spot on the ceiling. "Obviously, there are considerations such as religion, the wishes of the family, budget—that's a big one. Sometimes the deceased will have expressed certain preferences, and in that case, we make those a priority."

That was my in.

"Like—the kind of flowers?"

"Flowers, music, the casket, the format of the service, the location . . ."

"But are people specific about that stuff? If I said I want daisies, you would give me daisies?" *Or if I said yellow roses . . . ?*

"Provided your parents were supportive, there's no reason why we wouldn't."

"What if people don't have preferences about things?"

"That happens quite a lot. We're often left to make certain decisions if the family isn't feeling up to it. Usually, the more sudden and unexpected a death, the less the family is prepared to come up with specific answers. So we go with our tried-and-true standbys."

"Sudden, like . . . when kids die?"

He frowned and sat forward.

"Easy, Nancy Drew," Lydia said. "You're spooking him."

"Can you give me an example of your standbys?" I asked. "If a person came in and didn't have any preferences or whatever?"

"Well," he said, "in the mid-range, you'd have a solid pine casket, lined, with a split lid; some classical music, which we provide—"

"And the flowers?"

"Our standby flowers are yellow roses," he said.

Bingo.

"Do yellow roses mean, like, death?"

That actually got me a smile. "No. Yellow roses symbolize joy and friendship. But we've always used them. They were a favorite of my mother's. It's just preference. Bergen and Sons uses a lot of lilies. Victor Campos likes white roses."

I was guessing Bergen and Sons and Victor Campos were other funeral homes. "Kind of a signature," I said.

He shrugged. "You could call it that."

Yellow roses were their standby. Their default. That meant this ghost could be anyone.

"That sucks," Lydia said. "My mom was too sad to even pick flowers? I would have picked black roses."

I glanced at her to make sure she was okay. She just seemed bummed, so I turned back to Mr. Henry-Gordon.

"Do you do funerals for young people?" I asked. "People my age?"

"Of course." He gave me a sympathetic look, like he was about to deliver some pretty bad news. "Death can come for any of us, no matter how old or young we are."

"Ugh, he's creepy," Lydia said, perking up a little. "Do you think he saw me naked? I hope not."

I stared down at my notebook, trying to ignore her

and focus. "So you've done a lot of funerals for teenagers?"

"Yes."

"Can you tell me roughly how many . . . in the past three years, maybe?"

He leaned toward the computer and tapped a few buttons.

I tried to catch Lydia's eye, to get her to go around and look at the screen. But she was staring at the family portrait on the wall behind the desk. So I faked a coughing fit, stood up, and waved my hand through her body.

"God! Keep your hands to yourself!" she said, jerking away. "I'm already traumatized from being dragged here, and—"

I gave Mr. Henry-Gordon a meaningful look.

"Oh," she said. She walked around the desk and leaned over his shoulder.

"It looks like, in the past three years, we've done twelve services for teenagers."

"I can't read them," Lydia said. "He's scrolling too fast."

"Um, wow," I said. "Do you mind telling me how many were girls and how many were boys?"

He started clicking through again, more slowly.

"Okay." Lydia leaned over his shoulder. "Boy, boy, Claudine, Rachel, boy, Laina, boy, Quinn—is that a boy or a girl?—Jamila, boy, Grace . . . Lydia. Saved the best for last."

"Seven girls and five boys," Mr. Henry-Gordon said.

"Were they all sudden deaths?"

"I'm sorry, Alexis Ann, I don't know that I feel comfortable going into that level of detail." He narrowed his eyes. "I'm obligated to respect the confidentiality of our relationships with the bereaved."

"Yeah, whatever," Lydia said. "My screen says 'aneurysm.' If you can get him to scroll back, I'll tell you what they all say."

I only had one chance left. "Of course," I said. "I definitely understand. But could you tell me if any of them were—"

The woman who'd been on the phone knocked on the door and opened it. She cast a suspicious glance at my white hair, then looked at Mr. Henry-Gordon. "Your five o'clock is here."

He stood up. "I hope I've helped you some. I think it's a very interesting topic for a paper. If you'd like to take my card, you could e-mail me a copy when it's finished."

"You bet," I said, slipping the card into my pocket.

23

"So we don't know anything new," Lydia said. She was perched on the back of the toilet, watching me brush my teeth.

"Yes, we do," I said, dribbling toothpaste down my chin. I leaned over to spit. "We know the names of the other girls who have had their funerals there."

"What good does that do for us?"

"We look up those girls and find the one that looks like the ghost I keep seeing."

Lydia reached down and absently spun the toilet paper roll. "But why does the ghost seem to be obsessed with you? Do you think this town house is haunted?"

"I doubt it," I said. "According to Mimi, that dress was two years old. This neighborhood is newer than that."

Lydia glanced up. "Unless . . . maybe she died here before construction started. Or during it?"

"Hm," I said. "That's worth looking into."

"Alexis?" It was my mother's voice. "Who are you talking to?"

"I'm on the phone!" I called.

"In the bathroom?" Mom asked. There was a longish pause. "Well, okay."

Lydia cackled, so I grabbed my hairbrush and swung it lightly through her head. She recoiled, pressing her hands against her ears. "*Not* cool."

She followed me into my bedroom and sat on my dresser while I pulled the covers back and got ready for bed. I looked up at her, wondering why she was still around. Before, she'd never stayed longer than an hour or two, but today she'd been hanging out all afternoon. And from the looks of things, she planned to stay the night.

I tried to keep my voice light. "So what is this—a slumber party?"

"Ha," she said. "You *wish* you could have people as cool as me at your parties."

I almost pointed out that she didn't fall into the "people" category anymore, but I bit my tongue. No point in hurting her feelings. And then I realized—why should I care if she slept in my room? It was a billion times better than waking up to the superghost.

"All right, suit yourself." I climbed under the covers and turned off the light.

A few minutes later, I still hadn't fallen asleep. I was huddled under the blankets, covered all the way up to my eyes. I didn't want any more rose petals brushing against my face.

I lifted the blankets away from my mouth. "Lydia?" I whispered.

"Yeah?"

"Nothing." I flopped over and shut my eyes.

When I woke up in the morning, she was curled up asleep, hovering a foot above my dresser.

Lydia rode to school with me and split off once we got there, talking about some classes she wanted to sit in on. Apparently being dead can get a little dull, because Lydia hadn't exactly been academically minded when she was alive, and now she was all over the curriculum.

I actually thought it was a pretty decent idea. Maybe she'd learn something useful.

After that afternoon's yearbook meeting (twelve minutes long, for the record), I went to the parking lot and sat in my car, expecting her to show up. After waiting for ten minutes, I went home and gave the empty house a brief once-over, looking for her. She was nowhere to be found.

Well, no big deal. It's not like you're dying—no pun intended—to hang out with Lydia Small, I told myself.

As I pulled my phone out of my bag to charge it,

I saw that I'd missed a call from Jared. I went into the kitchen and called him back from the landline, turning on the speakerphone and setting it on the counter while I made myself a snack.

"Where are you?" he asked.

"Hello to you, too," I said, getting bread and peanut butter out of the pantry.

He sighed. "Hello. I called a few minutes ago. What were you doing?"

"Nothing," I said. "I just got home."

"I wanted you to come over tonight. Dad's working late."

"I can't," I said, pulling the jelly out of the fridge. "I have plans."

"What plans?"

"Nothing special. Just some research stuff I have to do."

I'd noticed that Jared made this impatient little sniffing noise when he was aggravated.

Sniff.

"Jared," I said, "I have to get this done."

"What is it? Look it up online. Or maybe I can help you. What's the topic?"

A list of dead girls and a ghost that hisses at me.

"I'm sorry," I said, spreading peanut butter on a slice of bread. "I can't."

"But you'll definitely come over tomorrow?"

"I don't know. Maybe."

"Come on."

"I don't know if—"

"Say yes."

Fine. Whatever. "Yes," I said.

"Promise?"

"Sure, I promise," I said. "Now I have to go."

"Okay," he said. "Work hard."

I hung up the phone and leaned down, burying my face in my hands for a moment.

"Lexi."

Kasey stood in the hallway, hand on her hip.

"Oh, hey—I didn't know you were here." I studied her face. How long had she been there? Long enough to hear me calling for Lydia?

"I just got home a minute ago. I was quiet because you were on speakerphone." Her voice was carefully even. "We need to talk."

I assembled my sandwich and started cutting it into quarters. "About?"

I expected her to say something about ghosts.

But she said, "About Jared." -

"Or we could talk about you minding your own—"

"Yeah, yeah, yeah," she said. "I should mind my own

business. But I'm not going to. So what's he mad about this time?"

"It's complicated. I don't expect you to understand." My head was starting to throb.

"Lexi," Kasey said, softer, coaxing, "do you think maybe there's a chance he's a tiny bit . . . controlling?"

"No," I said, rubbing my temples.

"But the way he talks to you—I mean, the way I hear you talk to him—"

"*No,*" I repeated. "You know, if you would spend more time cleaning up your dirty clothes and wet towels in the bathroom, and less time eavesdropping, you could save both of us a lot of trouble."

I meant it as a joke, but she gave me a wounded look. "It's just . . . when you talk to Jared, you sound like you're trying to pass a test or something. You never sounded like that with Carter."

"Yeah, and *that* landed me in 'happily ever after,' didn't it?" I said. "Besides, your boyfriend is three years older than you. If anyone has control issues, wouldn't it be Keaton?"

She looked hurt. "Keat's only sixteen. He skipped fourth grade. And he would *never* make me feel bad for not wanting to spend every waking moment with him."

"Kase, I appreciate that you care," I said. "I really do. But you're totally wrong."

I slipped my sandwich onto a plate and started for my bedroom without even putting the peanut butter and jelly away.

Before I could close the door, she said, "Wait!"

I stopped.

She took a deep breath, then said, "Why did you have those bruises?"

Instinctively, I turned my face away.

"Last month. There was one on your neck and one on your face. You tried to cover them up, but I saw them."

I blurred my eyes and stared at the dim rectangle of sky visible through my window.

"Tell me the honest-to-God truth, Lexi," she said, suddenly hoarse. "Is it Jared?"

"No." I cleared my throat. "I swear."

I wanted to make her feel better, but what else could I say? If I hinted at a ghost, she'd insist on knowing everything. She'd want to be part of it. And then she'd be in danger.

"Kasey, please," I said. "It was nothing—I just fell. You worry too much."

Then I reached out and ever so gently closed the door in her face.

Fifteen minutes later, Lydia and I were in the car, headed to the library to look up the names from the funeral home. She leaned away from me, her arms crossed in front of her chest. She'd been quiet for the whole drive, shooting me weighty glances.

"What?" I asked. "What is it?"

"I know you don't want to hear it, but your sister's right."

"Seriously, Lydia. I'm not going to talk about this with you," I said. "You know nothing about relationships. You're *dead*, remember? Anyway, I know what I'm doing."

"Oh, sure," she said. "You're totally in control, as always, right?"

I couldn't reply.

"I'm just saying, check yourself before you wreck your emotionally vulnerable little self, Alexis." Lydia shrugged and looked at herself in the passenger-side mirror. "It's obvious you'll take affection from whoever's willing to throw it at you right now."

"Can we not do this?" I asked. "Please?"

She threw her arms in the air like I was the one being stubborn and frustrating. "Have it your way."

"Thank you."

"Or, you know, just have it *Jared's* way. As usual."

I gritted my teeth and pulled into the library parking lot.

As great as the free office supplies were, having a

mom who worked at a place that sold computers and software was actually a major hindrance to my ability to get any research done at home. Mom had access to the best software consultants—and the best internet monitoring software. That is, when she left her laptop home instead of carting it around with her.

It seemed everybody's parents were clueless but mine. We had an old computer that we could use for typing papers, but internet access was highly restricted. Sometimes I wondered what on earth Mom thought we'd do if she didn't stop us—order ourselves some Russian mail-order brides? Send money to fake Nigerian princes?

It's not that I thought she was so wrong—and not like I was dying to create an online life for myself (just another place to not have any friends)—but it was inconvenient, to say the least.

If I ever had kids—which I wouldn't—I would make it a point to stay a little clueless about technology. Just to be nice.

Lydia hovered over me as I sat at one of the public computers. "I can't believe you didn't write them down."

She meant the names of the other girls whose funerals had been held at Henry-Gordon. To be honest, I couldn't believe it, either.

"I was a little stressed out," I whispered. "I had to

carry on a conversation with him. Why can't you remember them?"

"That is *not* my responsibility," she said. "You know, technically, I don't even have a brain."

"I am *definitely* going to quote you on that at some point."

The guy at the computer next to me glanced over in mild alarm.

"Not you," I said to him.

So far, between the two of us, we'd come up with four of the seven names.

"Claudine, Rachel, Quinn . . . Lydia, obviously . . ." Lydia's voice trailed off.

I stared at the monitor. Something with a *G.* Gabrielle?

No—Grace.

I typed "Grace + Henry-Gordon Funeral Home." The first result was an obituary. Lydia leaned in closer to read.

"Twelve," Lydia said. "Too young."

And she didn't look anything like the superghost, either. Dark straight hair, not blond.

Out of all the girls, the only one who came close was Rachel. She was seventeen and had medium-length blond hair. But I didn't see how Rachel could have become a ghost. According to the news articles, she was driving along when she was blindsided by a truck that ran a red light. Witnesses said she never saw it coming. Doctors said she died instantly.

No time to be afraid or angry or traumatized. Just here one second, gone the next.

Not a good recipe for a ghost.

Dinner was silent. Mom had apologized in advance; she had to make a presentation to the board later in the week and couldn't think about anything else. Dad was mellow and in a good mood, but he was never the driving force behind conversation. And Kasey and I didn't seem to have anything to say to each other.

I was finishing up, getting ready to take my plate into the kitchen, when Kasey tensed.

"Your phone's ringing," she said.

I sat still and listened, and made out the soft ringtone coming from my bedroom.

"Probably Jared," I said, about to push my chair back and stand up. Then I noticed, out of the corner of my eye, that Kasey was watching me.

So I stayed in my seat.

A second later, Lydia came wandering out of the hallway. "Who do you know with a 703 area code?"

I thought for a second.

Agent Hasan.

It took a huge effort not to rush away from the table.

Feeling like I was moving at quarter speed, I took my dishes to the kitchen, rinsed them and stuck them in the dishwasher, and was about to hurry down the hall to my bedroom—

When the doorbell rang.

"I'll get it," Kasey said, from her place at the table.

"No!" I called. "I'm right here."

I peered through the peephole, and my stomach knotted.

Lydia had stuck her head through the door. She pulled it back, eyes wide. "She looks mean."

Agent Hasan did look mean. She had dark hair in a severe cut that hung halfway between her chin and her shoulders. And every strand was perfectly in place—not even her own hair would test her authority.

Her eyes were brown and almost almond-shaped, and her eyebrows seemed to be perpetually raised in annoyance.

"Stay away from her," I whispered to Lydia. "I don't know what she could do to you."

Lydia took a step back from the door and disappeared.

I braced myself, then called out, "I'll be back in a few minutes!" to my family.

And I slipped out the door—out of the frying pan . . .

Straight into the bonfire.

* * *

Just like I'd sensed that she was there to see me, Agent Hasan seemed to sense that I didn't want my family to know she was there. So when I started walking down the sidewalk, away from the house, she followed me.

"Sorry to barge in." The hint of amusement in her voice told me it was a lie. She enjoyed knowing that she had freaked me out. "It's just that you didn't answer my call."

She must have already been in the neighborhood when she called. Which meant she'd gone to the trouble of coming all the way to Surrey—just to see me?

"What do you need?" I asked.

"I kept thinking about our conversation," she said.

I held my breath.

She turned to look at me, squinting her eyes a bit. "About how interesting it was that you would call me and suggest that there was something out of the ordinary going on—when you had no concrete reason to think so."

My lips were glued shut. If she thought she could trick me into incriminating myself, she was dead wrong.

"And I'm not a patient person," she said. "So when something like that gets in my head, I don't want to sit around and see if anything comes of it."

It was a breezy night, and Silver Sage Acres is a wind tunnel. I stuck my hands in my pockets and raised my shoulders up to my ears, hunching my chin down to warm my neck.

"I'm sorry to waste your time," I said. "You were right. I was just being paranoid."

"That would definitely be the more satisfactory outcome." She didn't say more satisfactory than what—or for whom. "But I do appreciate that you called me. It shows that you understand my role. And it gives me a chance to show *you* how important it is to *me* to help you stay out of trouble."

Right. Help me stay out of trouble. There was a threat in there, and you couldn't even say it was a veiled threat. It was loud and clear: *I'm watching you.*

"All right," I said. "Well, thanks."

She stopped and looked down at me, smiling like she'd just won the lottery but wasn't planning to tell anyone. "You're so welcome."

What had she seen? What did she know?

We started back toward my house.

You're almost there, I told myself. *Just stay cool for a few more minutes and you'll be fine.*

At last, we reached my front walk. I glanced up at the front window, anxious to get rid of Agent Hasan before my family noticed her presence.

"Don't worry," she said. "I'm going."

She made a half turn away from me, then spun back.

"By the way." She reached into her pocket. "I think you dropped something."

Her fingers uncurled, revealing my missing lens cap.

We both stared down at it for a moment, then she reached over and tucked it into the pocket of my jeans.

"You should really keep better track of your things, Alexis," she said. "You never know where they might end up if you don't."

I wouldn't let myself be scared speechless by her, so I forced out an abnormally loud "Thanks."

"That, for instance, was found fifty-four feet from Ashleen Evans's body."

I didn't answer. My throat tightened.

"But I'm sure you don't know anything about it."

I had to stay strong, or I'd crack into a million pieces. "No," I said. "Sorry."

"Well, good." Agent Hasan wiped her hands on her jacket. "Because I would really hate to think that you were part of the problem."

I started for the stairs.

"See you 'round, Alexis," she called.

I walked inside, afraid to look back over my shoulder.

24

THE NEXT DAY, I went to the *Wingspan* office before school started. Elliot was already there, wearing her PRINCETON sweatshirt.

"What's up?" she asked.

"How many different college sweatshirts do you own?" I asked.

"Not sure. Fifteen?" She shrugged. "I'm nurturing my aspirational self."

Um, okay.

She glanced up from the layout she was marking on. "You have the cheerleader shoot tomorrow morning, right?"

I nodded, looking at the intricate color-coded schedule on the whiteboard.

"Did you ever find the janitors to get the Dumpsters moved?"

"Oh, no." I slapped a hand to my forehead and sat down. "I totally forgot."

"Never mind," Elliot said. "I'll take care of it."

"No, I'm sorry—"

"Don't be sorry. I should have been more specific."

"I can do it," I said. "Their office is that little shed out by the field, right?"

She shrugged. "I don't mind getting some fresh air."

"Are you sure?"

"You know how most people say 'no offense,' but they secretly hope it does offend you? I swear I'm not doing that." She capped her red pen and set it down. "No offense, Alexis, but you look terrible lately. I'd rather you just relax a little than start passing out during photo shoots."

There was never any changing Elliot's mind, so I nodded.

"So . . . Chad said you had a little 'episode' the other day." From the way she went back to her layout and the carefully measured tone of her voice, it seemed like she was intent on not making a big deal out of it. "Of course, Chad's a busybody, so I wouldn't put it past him to exaggerate."

I shook my head and let my finger trace the edge of a desk. "He probably didn't exaggerate," I said. "If having me on staff makes people uncomfortable, then I'll quit."

Elliot practically threw her pen down. Her eyes were fiery and her voice was almost a growl. "Did he say that to you?"

"What? Chad? No, no—he was pretty nice, actually. Weirdly nice."

She sat back and relaxed.

"It's my own idea," I said. "I know a lot of people at school know things about me—or think they do—and I don't want it to be uncomfortable for you."

"Alexis, can I give you some unsolicited advice?"

"If I say yes, that would make it solicited, right?"

She grinned. "Smart. Yes. So listen. You're a fantastic photographer."

"Thanks."

She waved me off. "You're talented. You're smart. You're funny. You can put up with Chad. Therefore, you are a good person."

"Well, I—"

"Hush. I didn't start my advice yet. Here it is: Find the people who treat you the way you deserve to be treated. Tell everyone else to go to hell. And don't look back."

I sighed.

"Do you believe in God? I believe in God. And I think God makes people exactly who He wants them to be."

I blinked. "I—I don't know if I believe or not—"

Elliot shook her head. "You're missing the point."

No doubt. "Which is . . . ?"

"Which is, get over it. Forgive yourself. Stop assuming that you deserve the worst of everything."

I dragged my finger in a circle on the desk. "Easier said than done."

"Easy?" she repeated, raising her eyebrows. "Who wants easy? Easy's boring. Now, I have to get back to work. You go take a nap in the library or something."

I sighed again. "Thanks. I think maybe—"

"Don't think, grasshopper," she said. "Gut, remember?"

I'd promised Jared I would come over after school, but I made a detour first—to the small brick house near Redmond High.

I parked on the street, a few houses away, and got out of the car, my camera hanging around my neck. I tweaked the exposure way down and started taking pictures, expecting to see the girl in the purple dress.

The white light did hold a quivering, jittering figure—but not the girl.

It was a man. A boy, actually—a football player.

Held tightly in his left hand was a trophy. I couldn't—and wouldn't—get close enough to see what it said, but I zoomed in on the figurine on top of the gold pedestal: a football player cradling a ball under one arm.

The ghost was carrying something—just like the girl with her roses.

A *second* superghost?

He hovered about a foot over the sidewalk, looking

in the direction of the high school, with an expression of pure rage on his face—forehead furrowed, teeth gritted. He had short, slicked-back hair, and his uniform looked oddly old-fashioned. His shoes were simple no-name black cleats. If I had to guess, I'd say he died in the 1960s.

At least he had eyes.

And this guy, unlike the girl in the purple dress, didn't seem to notice me. His entire focus was directed toward the school. I cringed as another couple walked by. This time, the boy started hopping on one foot and saying, "Ow! Cramp! Ow, ow, ow, cramp!" as they passed the spot where the superghost stood.

I went closer and fired off a few more frames. Then I looked at my camera. Across the back of the boy's jersey, I could make out his last name: CORCORAN.

"Five minutes," I said. "Ten. Then we can hang out."

"Can't you do this at home?" Jared asked.

I was sitting on his couch with his laptop balanced on my legs. "Mom's laptop is the only computer in the house that gets internet. And she guards it like a junkyard dog. But I'll only be a minute. This is important."

He tried to remove my hand from the keyboard. I shook him off and went back to typing. In the web browser, I searched for *corcoran + redmond street*.

It pulled up an address listing: RANDALL CORCORAN.

When I went on to search for Randall Corcoran, what came up was his prison record. His most recent jail time had ended less than two years ago—it was fairly safe to assume that he was the drunk guy Lydia had seen passed out inside the house. So he wasn't dead.

Then who was the ghost? His football uniform had accents of green and yellow, like the girl's cheerleading uniform. So I tried *Corcoran dead Redmond high school*.

And found: "Redmond High Holds Memorial Assembly for State Champ Quarterback Phil Corcoran."

The article was dated 1965, and it was published in the *Los Angeles Times*, a much bigger newspaper than our local Surrey paper. Presumably this was a high-profile story because of Phil's triumphant performance at the state championship. He'd been a senior, the star quarterback of the football team, when he died of injuries sustained in a car accident.

But something didn't add up:

"We take tremendous comfort from the fact that Father Lopez was able to administer the Last Rites to Philip before he died," the boy's mother, Mrs. Joseph Corcoran, told the assembled students. "He died in a state of deep peace. He knew he was going to a better place."

Impossible.

Because people who die in a state of deep peace don't become angry ghosts.

They just don't.

"What are you looking at?" Jared asked, leaning over to look.

"Nothing," I said.

He hovered at my shoulder, scanning the article. "I wonder if that's the same Father Lopez from my school."

He lifted the computer off my lap and went to his school's website, clicking through a few screens to the headmaster's bio page.

"Yeah," he said. "Look. He was ordained in 1962 and served at Saint Viviana's on the east side of Surrey. That's right by Redmond High."

Gears started turning in my head.

"But why are you looking at this?" Jared asked. "It's pretty morbid."

"I . . ." I didn't have the faintest clue what to say. "One of my teachers was talking about this guy."

"And now you know who he is. So do the rest later," Jared said, head-butting my arm gently. "Spend time with me."

"Come on," I said. "Three more minutes."

"No more minutes." He wandered away. "Look, I'm going to go through your stuff. I'll totally rearranging your obsessively organized book bag. . . ."

That actually sounded fine, if it would distract him. One of the perks of being obsessively organized is that chances to reorganize things are like little treats.

"I'm looking at your science book. . . ." He took it out and set it on the floor. "I'm going to read your English journal. . . ."

That was just a reading journal where we summarized what we were reading for class.

"Go ahead," I said, turning back to the computer.

He was quiet for a minute—he really was looking through my stuff. I should have stopped him, but I needed the time for research.

"What is this?" Jared asked. He was staring at a piece of paper—the one with my drawing of the purple dress.

"Nothing," I said, reaching out to take it back.

He whipped it away, holding me back with his other arm.

"Seriously, Jared, it's just a stupid sketch."

He finally took his eyes off of it. "Why did you draw this?"

"No reason. Just give it back, please."

He smiled—but it was one of his fake smiles—and moved the paper a tiny bit closer to me. "I'll trade it for a kiss."

"Jared—"

He handed me the page, and when I'd folded it and slipped it back inside my bag, I felt hands on my ribs.

As soon as I turned back to him, our lips were pressed together.

Usually, kissing was a way to wipe the slate clean, to forget our petty arguments. But in that moment, a thought barged into my head like an uninvited guest: *If Lydia showed up now, what would she say?*

She would say he was distracting me. Trying to keep me from being mad about his jerkish, immature behavior.

I'm not going to lie. Kissing Jared could drive a girl to distraction in the best of circumstances. But when I was irritated, or thrown off guard, or made to feel dumb by his little I'm-going-through-your-stuff antics, I was extra susceptible.

And I couldn't shake the feeling that he knew it.

Jared stood up and pulled me with him. He walked me into the foyer and pressed up against me, his breath coming in hot puffs against my neck. I found myself backed against the wall. Then I felt the soft touch of his hands on the skin of my stomach, his fingers trailing around to my back, leaving thin lines of sparking energy . behind them.

"Want to go to my room?" he whispered.

To his room?

"No," I said, dipping my head to escape his kisses. "I really need to do some more work right now."

"Don't worry about that," he said, nibbling lightly on my neck.

Don't *worry* about it? I tried to picture myself and Carter together—me telling Carter I had work to do and him telling me not to worry about it. And not in a cutesy way, either—in a way that meant that he really expected me to stop worrying or thinking about anything but standing there, making out with him—because it was what *he* wanted.

But what about what *I* wanted? What about the things that were important to *me?*

Suddenly, what I wanted was not to even be in that house.

"Wait," I said, turning my head and setting my hands on his shoulders—firmly, but not quite pushing him away. "No."

He stopped and looked at me questioningly.

"I'm going to go," I said. "I really have a lot of work to do, and I'm not getting it done here."

"That's ridiculous," he said. "You're leaving? Because I don't feel like watching you sit and use *my* computer and ignore me?"

Okay, yeah, it *was* his computer. But if he couldn't find something else to do for a half hour while I worked on something that I'd made it really clear was important to me—

I mean, I could put up with it. I'd been putting up with it for nearly two months.

But why *should* I?

"Alexis," Jared said sharply. "You're acting like a child."

Everything in my body that had been warm and tingly turned cold when I heard the edge in his voice.

I gave him a sideways glance. He was looking at me as if I were crazy.

"You know what I mean," he said, softening. "Don't overreact."

I heard Elliot's words in my head: *Find the people who treat you the way you deserve to be treated. Tell everyone else to go to hell.*

Forget this. I reached for my camera. "I'm not overreacting, Jared. I'm leaving."

"Please don't."

"I have to." I knelt to put the scattered books in my bag. "I'll give you a call later . . . or tomorrow."

But when I turned for the door, I found him standing squarely in my way.

A moment passed between us.

"Excuse me," I said.

"Can't we behave like grown-ups?" His jaw trembled, like he was losing patience with me. "I don't understand. Things were completely fine two minutes ago."

Yeah, fine for him. Not for me.

"I *am* behaving like a grown-up," I said. "I'm going to go get some work done. Like a grown-up."

"You know what? Fine. Do it here. I don't care. I'll just find something else to do." But he didn't say it like he meant it. He said it like he wanted me to hear, in every word, how irrational I was being and how wrong I was.

"Don't worry about it," I said, reaching behind him and putting my hand on the doorknob. "I'll go to the library."

He looked down at me, his expression businesslike. "I would really prefer it if you would be mature for once, Alexis."

I stared at him. What would I do if he refused to move?

Don't be paranoid, I told myself. He wouldn't refuse to move.

Except . . . he didn't move.

And then my phone rang, making us both jump. I grabbed it from my pocket and answered without checking the caller ID. I'd have happily had a heart-to-heart with Agent Hasan at that moment if it meant getting out of that house.

I was vividly aware that Jared was watching me, so I forced myself to play it cool. "Hello?"

"Alexis?"

It took me a second to place the voice. "Carter?"

A wave of irritation flashed through Jared's eyes.

"Yeah, it's me. Are you busy?"

"Um . . ." I looked at Jared. "No."

"Okay. I have something for you. I mean, for you and the yearbook. I was thinking maybe I could run it over after dinner?"

"Where are you right now?" I asked.

"What? I'm home right now, but—"

"All right," I said. "I'll be right over."

"Really? Are you sure? Okay," Carter said. "If you want to. See you soon."

"Yeah. Bye." I slid the phone into my pocket.

Jared's face had fallen; his mouth turned down at the corners, and all of the tension had gone out of his body, from his jaw to his shoulders to his hands. "Please, Alexis—can't you stay? I'm really sorry. I know I can be a jerk. I've always liked being the center of attention." He gave a weak half laugh. "I mean, my mom used to tell me I should have a spotlight installed in a hat so I could wear it around."

I relaxed a little, taken aback by this first-ever mention of his mother. "Jared . . . what happened to your mom?"

"Happened to her?" He looked puzzled. "She's in Colorado with my stepfather."

273

Oh.

"So could you please just stay?"

Back up a second. If his mother was alive and well, then what was his pain, his baggage? I felt oddly like I'd been misled, although that wasn't true at all. I'd just assumed. And obviously I'd assumed wrong.

So that meant there was something *else* he was hiding from me?

"No," I said. "I can't. We can talk later."

I slipped around him and left, shutting the door behind me.

25

THE "SOMETHING" CARTER HAD FOR ME ended up being a vintage Surrey High sweatshirt that he'd seen at a garage sale.

"I mentioned it to Elliot," he said, laying it out on the couch so I could see it, "and she said she thought it would be cool to have a picture of it in the yearbook. I think it's from the forties."

I stared down at the sweatshirt, trying to focus. But I couldn't really get over the fact that I was standing in Carter's house—in his living room—for the first time since October.

"It's great," I said.

"Yeah, I thought it was pretty cool."

Since I'd just proclaimed it "great," I thought it might be wise to actually take a look. It had really baggy sleeves and tight cuffs, and the neckline was so high and tight it seemed like it would choke you. There was a threadbare red *S* on the front with a small embroidered eagle above it.

"All right," I said, scooping it up. "Thanks. I'll get it back to you soon. Or Marley will."

"No rush." Carter followed me into the foyer. "Thanks for coming on such short notice."

I shrugged. No need to tell him that the primary reason I'd agreed to come was that I wanted an excuse to get out of Jared's house. "No problem."

He brightened. "Thanks. So you're really into yearbook, huh? That's nice. I mean, I'm glad. They're good people."

I glanced around. "Where's Zoe?"

"Um . . ." Carter stood awkwardly, with his hands shoved into his pockets. "She's . . . home, I guess? I don't really know."

I reached for the doorknob. "Okay, see you later."

"I'll walk you out." He hurried to open the door for me. Then he followed me to the driveway, where my car was parked next to his. "Is this yours?"

"Yeah, I got it for Christmas."

He stood back and looked it over. "It's really . . . brown."

"Go ahead, say it," I said. "It's ugly."

"I'd never say that."

"Not out loud, at least."

And then he was giving me that impish Carter look, and my heart felt like two pieces of Velcro being ripped apart.

"It *drives*," I said. "That's what matters."

"Does it have a name?"

I opened the passenger door and set the sweatshirt on the front seat before I looked at him. "A name?"

"All cars have names."

"Does yours?"

"Of course."

It was a cool afternoon, and I was beginning to shiver. I hugged myself, thinking that it would be a great excuse for Carter to urge me to get into my car, if he was tired of talking to me.

But instead, he automatically took off his own sweatshirt. As he brought it near my shoulders, I flinched, and he stopped short.

The cold made me shake from my toes to the top of my head, but I said, "Don't. Please."

He nodded and backed off, looking abashed and a little disoriented. I felt the same way. Gestures like that had been second nature to us once, but now it was too personal, too much of a reminder of what we'd had.

What we'd lost.

"So," I said through my chattering teeth. "What's your car's name?"

"Ayn Rand."

I had to laugh. "Are you kidding?"

"No," he said. "What, is that dumb?"

277

"It's . . . unusual," I said. "I don't think you could call it dumb."

He was watching me closely. "It's good to see you smiling."

I shrugged. "Only on the outside."

He started to laugh, but then I think he realized it wasn't a joke.

"Alexis. We're . . ." He let the word fall. "I mean, Zoe and I—we're breaking up."

"Oh," I said. But inside, I was all: OH. "Um . . . I'm sorry."

His eyes sparkled. "I'm not sure I am. Anyway, I wanted to see you . . . I wanted to tell you."

"Why?" I asked. I didn't mean it the way it sounded. I just meant . . . *why?*

"I know you're with Jared," Carter said. "But I want you to know that if you ever need anything—or need to talk about anything—call me."

Was I with Jared?

I felt like a swirling vortex had opened up under my feet.

Carter's cell phone rang. He took it out of his pocket, and I saw the name on the screen: ZOE PERRY. He started to put it away, but I waved him off. "No, go ahead. I'm leaving."

After I'd sat down in the driver's seat, I looked up

to see that Carter was waiting for me to get settled so he could close the door for me. At the same time, he held the phone to his ear, listening patiently to whatever Zoe was squawking about.

I put my hands on the steering wheel, which had always been the signal for him to shut the car door. He did, and gave me a little wave before walking back to the house.

I turned the key, my heart aching like an open wound.

Two days later, and yet still somehow reeling from my conversation with Carter (it didn't help that everyone at school was talking about his and Zoe's breakup), I pulled into the Sacred Heart Academy lot and parked in a space marked WELCOMED GUEST. I assumed that meant me—even if I was uninvited.

I'd skipped sixth period, so their school day was still in session. As I walked to the main office, I could see random kids wandering around between classrooms. I felt the oddness of being a stranger in a strange school.

The front desk was staffed by a woman in a plain brown dress. She smiled at me. "Welcome. Can I help you?"

"Hi," I said. "I know this is super, um, not planned, but I was wondering if Father Lopez is here today."

She looked interested. "Yes, he's here. Did you have an appointment to speak with him?"

"No," I said, expecting to be turned away.

"All right." She stood up. "Let me just go check and see if he's available."

I told her my name, not that he would know who I was, and waited, my whole body on pins and needles. A minute later she came back and pulled open the swinging wooden door.

"Come on through," she said. "He's got a few minutes to spare."

I followed her to a small office with a high window and a giant desk. The man behind the desk—Father Lopez, I guessed—was old and bald, leaning over a book. A Bible. Yeah, I suppose that would make sense.

"Alexis? I'm Father Lopez. Nice to meet you." He stood up and shook my hand. "Won't you please have a seat?"

"Thanks for letting me come in," I said.

"All guests are cherished, expected or otherwise," he said. "What can I do for you?"

Um, yeah. Okay. I summoned all my nerve. "I have a really weird question. Do you remember a boy named Phil Corcoran?"

He narrowed his eyes.

"He was a football player," I prompted. "He died in 1965?"

Father Lopez's eyes lit up. "Goodness. Philip Corcoran. Yes, of course. Nice young man."

"And do you know who Randall Corcoran is?"

He sat back and looked at me. For a minute I was afraid he was going to ask me a question in response to my question. But then he nodded. "Yes. The younger brother."

Younger brother? Was Philip's ghost haunting his brother—possessing him, causing him to commit the crimes that had landed him in jail? That was what had happened with Kasey . . . a ghost took over her body and made her do bad things—almost murder.

"Randy was a nice boy, too. Always looked up to his brother. Just devastated by his death. If I recall correctly, when Phil died, Randy started a campaign to have the graduation ceremony canceled at their high school. He went to the school board meeting to make his case. It didn't work, and he got very angry. Dropped out of school. Went on to a life of some unhappiness, I think. I wonder if he's still alive. I should look him up," Father Lopez said, jotting a note down on a piece of paper. "See how he's doing."

"Okay," I said.

"It was the last thing Phil would have wanted—Randy's sad turn. But Randy wasn't thinking that way."

"What was the, ah, *first* thing Phil would have wanted?" I asked.

I'd meant my question literally—I was hoping for an answer like, *Phil would have wanted someone to take good care of his prized Babe Ruth–autographed baseball.*

But Father Lopez considered it with a philosophical look on his face. He turned to me and folded his hands. "What would *you* want? If you died, how would you want the people who care about you to feel?"

I squinted. "Um . . . sad?"

"Sad forever? To the point of not living their own lives? And always feeling guilt over what had happened?"

"No, of course not. Just for a little while. Not guilty, I mean—sad."

"Exactly. You'd want them to remember you but keep going. I'll never forget that school board meeting. Randy had brought his brother's trophy with him, as a sort of visual aid. And when the superintendent refused his request, he threw the trophy to the floor." Father Lopez leaned forward. "This was an object that was precious to him—Phil had given it to him before he died. And he was so filled with rage that he broke it."

So if *Randy* was the one who was filled with rage, why was *Phil's* ghost trapped on the sidewalk, hating on the Redmond High kids?

And why was Phil's ghost holding his broken trophy? Was he mad at his brother for ruining it?

My head was starting to hurt. I stood up.

"I hope I've helped you," Father Lopez said. "I'll admit I'm curious, but . . . I hope you'll come back if you have anything else you'd like to discuss."

I was about to give him my standard *Yeah, sure* line. But something stopped me. I didn't want to lie. So I just said, "Good-bye. Thanks again."

I walked back through the hall toward the exit, studying the framed photographs that lined the walls, trying to see if I could sense any sameness between these kids and me—anything that bridged the gaping distance I felt from them and their privileged experiences. I saw a couple of ghosts, but not many. A Catholic school was too close to being a church, and ghosts don't hang out in churches.

I glanced at one picture that had been taken at a dance.

And I froze, staring at the grinning brown-haired girl in the center of the photo—clearly alive, clearly not a ghost.

And clearly wearing the purple dress.

With my cell phone, I snapped a picture of the photo and booked it down the hall, practically hyperventilating. I ran to my car and sat in the driver's seat, staring at the girl and the dress on my cracked screen, trying to make myself believe it was true.

I zoomed all the way in on her face, looking for a connection between the girl and the superghost. It wasn't the ghost—this girl wasn't blond.

So who was she?

There was a knock on my window, and I almost jumped out of my skin.

Megan was standing outside of my car.

In my shock, I stared at her for a few seconds before she made a "roll down the window" gesture. I hit the button, and the glass sank.

"Um . . . hi," I said.

"Did you come here to complain?" she asked. "About Brother Ben?"

I set the phone in my lap. "No," I said. "I swear—"

"It's all right if you did," she said.

I stared up at her.

She swallowed hard and looked directly into my eyes.

"I quit Brighter Path," she said.

Something inside me leapt, like a unicorn jumping over a million rainbows. But I tried to stay calm. "Why?" I asked. "You liked it so much."

"I did, kind of," she said. "But only because it was safe. Or so I thought. But . . . it wasn't real. Do you know what I mean? It was fake. It wasn't really a brighter path. It was just a . . . box."

I wanted to get out of the car and hug her until she turned blue. I wanted to turn on the radio and have a dance party.

"Besides." She shook her head, looking disgusted. "The stuff he said to you—calling you a liar—and a thief? That really crossed a line. I mean, you can be rude, but you're no thief."

I froze, remembering the book of charms. "Um, actually . . ." I said, cringing, "there was one little thing."

Megan looked stricken. Then, to my shock, she burst out laughing. "Oh my God, Lex! Are you serious? You *stole* something from him?"

"It was well-justified," I said. "I swear."

She was still laughing, shaking her head in disbelief. "Well, that doesn't matter. He was still really wrong about a lot of things. You know, I just got tired of him talking about . . . my mom and . . . stuff."

I didn't want to say anything that might sound like "I told you so."

Megan looked down at me. "So why'd you come here?"

"To talk to Father Lopez about something." I didn't elaborate. If she wanted a normal ghost-free life, I had to respect that.

She nodded and dragged a finger across the car door. "You keep your car as clean as your house, don't you?"

"Naturally," I said.

Her gaze bored into me. "Are you really having ghost problems?"

It took me a second to overcome my staunch *deny all* mind-set.

But I nodded and held up my phone to show her the zoomed-in picture of the girl wearing the dress. "Do you know who this is?"

"Yeah," she said. "Marissa Hearst. She's a senior. What about her?"

I pulled the phone back into the car. "Do you really want to know?"

Megan began to fidget with her little necktie. "Maybe not the whole story. But is there something simple I could ask her for you?"

"Really?"

"Yeah," she said, shrugging. "That's not getting involved. It's just . . . talking to someone."

"If you could ask her where the dress came from," I said, "that would be amazing."

Megan reached for my phone and angled it to see through the cracks. "What dress? Okay, I see it. Jeez, what happened to your phone?"

I tucked it into the cup holder and gave her a small smile. "Do you really want to know?"

"Maybe I don't," she said, limping back a step from

the car. "But I'll find Marissa and let you know what she says, okay?"

"Yeah," I said. "Thank you. Seriously."

"It's nothing," she said, giving me a wave and heading for the school entrance.

But it wasn't "nothing" to me. It was practically everything.

I drove past Surrey High on my way home. The student parking lot was mostly empty, but I did see Elliot's giant wood-paneled station wagon. Which meant she would be in the *Wingspan* office. Which meant I could stop by and offload the pictures of the sweatshirt for Chad, and not have to worry about getting up early the next morning to do it before school.

Elliot had her laptop open and was busily typing.

"Prop the door open, would you?" she said. "It's the first warmish day in forever."

So I propped the door and went to the computer with the card reader.

"So sorry about that rando Carter thing the other day," Elliot said. "He could have just dropped the shirt off here. I think dating Zoe turned him insane."

I spun around and looked at her. "Did you just say *rando*?"

"Yeah, why?"

"It just doesn't sound like an Elliot word."

"I claim all words," she said. "I empower them by speaking them."

I believed it. Someday, Elliot would be president of the United States and saying, "These rando stock market downturns are not going to shake our national spirit."

"No worries about the shirt thing," I said. "It's pretty cool-looking. I got good pictures."

"Hope it didn't take you away from anything important."

"Ha. No. Not really. . . ."

"Hm?"

"Just . . . a boy."

She sniffed. "Sounds like you're crazy about him."

My laugh came out like a grunt. "*Crazy* is one word."

"Remember what I said, Warren. Follow your gut."

"Sometimes my gut's pretty rando," I said.

"Follow it anyway."

What was it about Elliot that made me believe everything she said?

"But what if following my gut will hurt someone?"

She moved her laptop out of the way. "You mean the boy?"

I nodded.

"At the end of the day, you have to do what's best for

you. You can't live for someone else. You can't let your guilt define your life."

"So . . ."

Her eyes sparkled. "So kick him to the curb."

I laughed.

"Um . . . hey." Elliot's eyes suddenly went wide. She was looking over my shoulder.

I turned around.

Jared stood in the open doorway.

"Hello," he said, his voice sounding oddly tight.

"Jared," I said, getting up. "This is Elliot. Elliot, Jared."

I watched them study each other and felt the full impact of Elliot's lack of self-consciousness. She didn't simper or fawn over Jared. She just nodded at him.

"Nice to meet you." Her eyes lingered on him for a moment longer than necessary, and then she turned back to her work.

He didn't reply. I walked to the door. "What are you doing here?"

"I came to talk," he said.

"I can't really talk right now," I said. "I'm working."

"Yes." His expression was blank, unreadable. "Right. I see."

"Um, Alexis? If you guys are done, we should really get started on planning that layout."

Elliot was standing a few feet away, her arms crossed in front of her chest.

I could feel Jared's gaze burning into me.

Follow your gut.

"We are," I said, standing as tall as I could. "We're done. Jared, I'll call you later."

He cocked his head to one side and looked at me.

"Good-bye," I said again.

He walked away without another word.

Elliot stared at the empty space in the doorway. "Sorry about that," she said, keeping her voice quiet. "You just seemed like you needed an out."

"I guess I did," I said. "Thanks."

She glanced at me, slightly preoccupied, then back at the door for a few drawn-out seconds. "I know him from somewhere."

Then she went back to her work.

That night, I sat in my room, able to concentrate on my schoolwork for the first time in forever. At the back of my mind, no matter how bad things got, there was a safety net now—Megan.

Not that I expected her to get very involved. But at least she hadn't shut me out. She'd listened. And she was willing to help. Even if it was just a little help, I felt a relief I hadn't known I needed, like someone had been winding a rope around me so slowly that I hadn't noticed its constriction until it was suddenly taken away.

I could breathe again.

My cell phone buzzed with a text message, and I glanced down. It was Megan.

Working on Marissa, she wrote. *Hopefully know something 2morrow.*

With a happy little tingle in my spine, I texted back: *Thanks.*

After a while, I put my books away, took a shower, and changed into my pajamas.

I'll be able to sleep tonight, I thought.

As I climbed into bed, I noticed that another text had come through on my phone. I picked it up, thinking the message would be from Megan—but it wasn't.

It was from Elliot.

Remembered where I met him. Used to be in Tree Society with his girlfriend. Hiked Maxwell with her once.

Tree Society was a volunteer group that planted trees and maintained the hiking trails around Surrey. Maxwell meant Maxwell Canyon. Elliot talked about it all the time, but she could never convince any of the other *Wingspan* staffers to hike it with her. That type of trail is best left to people who owned special hiking sandals and backpacks that are really just giant water bottles. In other words, people like Elliot.

But what was this about a girlfriend?

I texted her back: *He never talks about her.*

I laid down, switched off the light, and stared at my phone, hoping it wasn't too late for a reply. But apparently it was. Because I was asleep before a response came through.

And anyway, she never sent one.

I was deep in a dream about photography—walking through a strange city with buildings that stretched so high they disappeared into the clouds. And every time I took a picture of one, it shivered and changed into something else.

A sound came from a building behind me—a soft song. I started to walk toward its open doors, but they closed. I would have to climb in a window—

And then I woke up.

My phone was ringing, blaring out the sounds of this beyond-cheesy old song called "That's What Friends Are For"—Megan's ringtone. I hadn't heard it in forever.

I grabbed the phone and hit ANSWER, glancing at the clock. It was past midnight.

"Megan?" I said. "Hello?"

"Lex. Marissa just texted me back." Her voice shook with excitement. "That dress was *Laina's*."

Laina. The name sounded vaguely familiar, but I couldn't place it.

"Laina Buchanan?" Megan said. When I didn't react, she inhaled loudly. "Jared's ex-girlfriend."

I was still bleary-eyed and fuzzy-brained. Jared never talked about any ex-girlfriends. I just assumed he didn't have any who meant anything to him.

"Lex, this is huge." Megan finally got that I didn't understand the subtext behind what she was saying. "Laina's the girl who *died*."

That did the trick. "What? Died? Did you say died?"

"Yeah. In a hiking accident, two years ago."

I suddenly felt like I'd chugged an entire pot of coffee. "Are you at your computer?"

"Yeah."

"Can you look up *Laina Buchanan* plus *Henry-Gordon Funeral Home*?"

Typing, then a decisive click. "Yep," Megan said. "That's where her services were held. Well, there and at the school. She went to Sacred Heart since kindergarten."

"Okay," I said, although nothing was okay.

"What are you going to do?" Megan asked.

"I don't know. I have to talk to Jared, I guess."

"When? Tomorrow? You have to do it as soon as possible."

"Yeah," I said. "Tomorrow."

* * *

But I couldn't wait until tomorrow, which is why, exactly twenty-eight minutes later, I was standing outside Jared's bedroom window, tapping lightly on the glass. He hadn't answered my texts or calls, so I'd decided to pay him a visit.

I saw movement inside, a shadow emerging from the bed, and Jared appeared at the window in a plain white T-shirt and boxers. His eyes went wide. Before he could open the window, I pointed toward the front of the house and started running for the front door.

"What are you doing here at this hour?" he asked as he opened it.

"We need to talk," I said.

"At midnight? About what?"

We were both whispering. I led him into his bedroom and closed the door. He glanced at me, then went to his closet, opened the door just wide enough to stick his arm inside, and pulled out a robe. Then he closed it and . . .

Was I imagining things, or did he lock the closet?

"Talk about what?" he repeated, sitting down on the bed and switching his lamp on.

I took a huge bracing breath. "About Laina."

Jared jerked back as if I'd burned him. He looked up at me, practically twitching. "What about her?"

"Why don't you ever talk about her?" Not the most relevant question, in terms of conducting an investigation. But as his girlfriend, it was the first thing I wanted to know.

He shrugged. "What is there to say?"

"Well, for starters . . . how about, 'I had a girlfriend and she died'?"

"Why?" he said. "So you could start looking at me like everyone else looks at me? Like I'm damaged? Like I'm a display in a museum?"

"Of course I wouldn't look at you that way!" I said. "Jared—me, of all people—"

"No offense, Alexis, but I don't think you're as good at hiding your emotions as you think you are."

I sat back, wounded. I hadn't meant I would have those feelings and hide them. I meant that I, of all people, would understand why it sucks to be looked at like a sideshow freak.

Jared raised a hand to his mouth and started biting his thumbnail. "So that's why you came over in the middle of the night? Because you just learned about Laina?"

"Yes," I said. "But that's not a hundred percent of it."

He watched me, waiting.

And I realized—I'd backed myself into a corner. There was no way to take this further without explaining at least a little bit about ghosts.

"How did she die?" When I saw the look on his face, I said, "Please. Just tell me."

Jared stared at the floor. "She died . . . beautifully. Just like she lived."

I held my breath.

He looked up at me, seeing the alarm on my face. "I don't mean it in some sick way. I mean, Laina was never the type of person to ask *why me?* She believed that there was a plan, that everything had a purpose. So once she knew she wasn't going to make it, she was in a state of complete acceptance. She was . . . serene."

His voice had gotten so quiet I had to strain to hear the last word—especially over the tumult of my own thoughts, which were saying *No.*

No, it was wrong. Just like Phil Corcoran's death was wrong. The wrong kind of death to produce a vengeful ghost.

Jared continued, his eyes locked onto some invisible point on the floor. "She was staring up at the sky, and she couldn't speak anymore, but she was praying. Her lips were moving. She never went anywhere without her Saint Barbara medal—protection against sudden death— so she was holding that in her hand. And the sun came out of the clouds and the shadow moved off of her face, and then—"

He stopped himself.

"And then . . . nothing," he said. "She was gone."

"You were there," I said.

"Yes," he said. "I was there. I was the one who found her."

"Jared," I said. "I need to tell you something. And it's going to sound really strange, but you have to try to believe me."

He gave me a wary glance.

"I think Laina's a ghost. And I think she's the one who's been going after the girls who are missing." I swallowed hard, not wanting to look up at his face until I'd gotten it all out. "I think she's coming after me, too."

My eyes flickered up to see his reaction.

But there was none.

"Jared?"

"Yeah, I heard you," he said.

"I know how it sounds."

"You *know*?" He spun toward me, eyes flashing. "You know how it sounds to have the love of your life slandered—and called a murderer?"

"It's hard to explain," I said. "She's not herself. Ghosts are different. She's angry or scared and—"

"Alexis," he said, his teeth gritted, "you need to stop talking *right now*."

I did.

His hands were curled into almost fists, and he raked

them through his hair. His jaw clenched as if he were stifling a cry of physical pain.

"Please listen to me," I whispered. "She's hurting people."

He seemed to slow his breathing down through sheer effort, and I watched—the way you'd watch a lion if you were trapped in its cage.

Finally he looked up at me. "I knew you had issues, Alexis, but I didn't know it was this bad."

The air went out of my lungs.

His voice was perfectly calm. "I don't know if it's jealousy, or . . . some sort of bitterness, or just . . . I don't know, plain old-fashioned craziness. But I can't sit here and listen to you talk this way. So I'm going to ask you to leave. Please."

The weirdest part was, this was the Jared I knew. The Jared who could always coax or convince me to do things his way. This was the same tone he always used with me.

"I'll go," I said, standing up. He stood, too, and moved toward me like a sheepdog controlling a flock. I backed into the hall and walked to the foyer, my legs like jelly.

"I hope you stop and think," he said quietly, when I was standing on the front porch. "And realize that you're hurting people. And that you need help."

"Please just tell me one thing," I said. I took it as a good sign that he didn't slam the door in my face. "What was Laina's favorite thing in the world?"

His face contorted with pain. "Easy," he said. "Me."

I sneaked in the front door, shutting it an inch at a time and keeping my hand against it tensely until the lock clicked into place. Then I crept down the hall and into my room.

Lydia was sitting on my bed.

"Were you there?" I asked.

"No, I was watching Leno with your parents," she said.

I sighed.

"I'm kidding. Yeah, I was there. And I gotta say, Alexis, he clearly loved her." She nodded thoughtfully. "Way more than he likes you."

"Thanks a lot," I said.

"You know what I mean. He *luuuurrved* her. He likes you all right. Mostly because you do whatever he says, in my opinion, but whatevs."

"Do you have anything helpful to contribute?" I asked.

"I guess not," she said. "Just that it's weird that he locks his closet."

"I know, right?" I said. "What's up with that? Couldn't you look inside?"

She gave me an exasperated look. "I'm a ghost, Alexis, not a magical see-in-the-dark cat."

I rolled my eyes.

"But he's clearly in denial," she said. "It has to be her. The dress, the funeral home, the roses, targeting you out of jealousy that you're moving in on her man . . . It all adds up."

"But what did Kendra and Ashleen do?" I asked.

"You tell me." She shrugged. "I wasn't there."

I remembered Kendra fluffing her hair in front of Jared at the nature preserve. And Ashleen simpering over him at her house.

"They flirted with him?" I said. "That was enough to get them a death sentence? Then how bad is what I've been doing?"

"I'm not sure I want to know," Lydia said. "Anyway, it seems clear that we're dealing with the most psycho of psycho ex-girlfriends."

"Yeah," I said. "And the only way to get rid of her . . ."

"Is what?" Lydia asked.

So she hadn't been at the front door when Jared told me he was Laina's favorite thing.

Lydia didn't know . . .

That the only way to stop Laina was to destroy Jared.

26

I SLEPT SURPRISINGLY WELL once I managed to fall asleep, and awoke to see Lydia snoozing lightly above my dresser. I felt energized by the discoveries of the previous night, no matter how dark they were. At least now we had information. A place to begin.

"Look alive!" I said, patting Lydia on the head. My fingers turned to ice.

She woke with a start, looking around. I headed out to the kitchen, where my parents and Kasey were staring at a breaking news report on the TV.

I stopped at the end of the hall, goose bumps erupting all over my body. "What now?"

"Another local teen is missing," the female reporter said. "Her parents say they last saw her when she went to her bedroom to study after dinner."

I took a step forward.

"Wait, Lexi—" Kasey said.

A photograph came onscreen—a smiling girl with

a sharp jaw, black eyeglasses, and short curly hair.

Elliot.

"No," I said. "No."

Mom rushed to my side. "Alexis? Honey. It's okay." Her voice sounded like it was coming through water.

I began to feel faint, like my legs might give out. Kasey hurried over with a chair from the dinner table, and Mom eased me down into it. Dad brought me a glass of apple juice, which I couldn't hold because my hands were shaking so badly.

She doesn't fit the pattern, said the voice inside my head. I shook my head, banishing the voice. I didn't have the strength to deal with it right now.

"I'm sure she'll be all right," Mom said. "The police will find her."

Like they found Ashleen?

"Alexis, are you all right?" Mom backed away, leaving Kasey to pat my hand. "Let me call the office and tell them I'm not going to make it in."

"No." My voice echoed in the room, as though someone else were speaking. "I need to go to school."

"Lexi!" Kasey said. "You don't have to!"

"I want to," I said. "I need to be with my yearbook friends."

"I don't know," Mom said, but she was disarmed by the word *friends.* "Maybe you should stay here and—"

"Stare at my hands? Cry all day?" I asked. "No. I'm going to school. They'll have counselors there. Besides . . . you have your board meeting."

Mom looked hurt. "Oh, honey. That means nothing. Not if you need me."

A couple of years ago, I would never have believed I'd hear my mother speak that way about a board meeting, the holiest of holies.

Now, as much as I appreciated it, all I wanted was for her and Dad to go to work, and for Kasey to go to school and surround herself with popular kids.

Because I needed them all out of my way.

My parents were so used to seeing me take my camera to school that when I came out of my bedroom ten minutes later with my backpack over one shoulder and my camera bag over the other, they didn't even notice.

Kasey did, though. She looked up at me incredulously. "You're shooting *today*?"

"Just candids," I said, even though it felt like a steady electrical current was traveling through my body. It had been there since the moment I'd grasped that Elliot was actually missing—and that I was her only hope of survival.

"Of what?"

"People," I said. "Being candid."

"Alexis," Mom said, "are you sure you don't want us to drive you to school? Or you can stay home if you want. I know how worried you must be."

"I'm fine." I felt as stiff as the Tin Man before he got oiled. "I want to be there."

Kasey had been planning to ride with me (to keep me from having a breakdown and driving off the road, was my guess), but by the time she remembered to call Keaton and tell him she didn't need a ride, he was pulling into the driveway.

My sister shot a wary look at me and then grabbed her bag from the couch. "Are you sure you're okay? Why don't you just ride with us?"

I nodded. "I'm fine."

Keaton stood in the doorway, wide-eyed and earnest. "We have plenty of room."

"No," I said. "Thank you."

I watched them pull away from the house, then went back to my room and shut off the light.

Lydia appeared. "Why can't you find a non-drama boyfriend like your sister's?"

I felt like I was made of porcelain and might crack up at any moment—and not in a laughing way. "I can't do this today, Lyd."

"I'm just saying. Carter flipped out, Jared's Mr. Gloomypants—"

In spite of myself, my spine went rigid. "Carter did not flip out. That was Aralt's fault."

She made a face. "Whatever. Who dumps their girl-friend because she dyed her hair?"

"Stop. Please."

"All right, whatever." She gave a little jump and sort of floated to the bed, like a piece of paper in a breeze.

"Forget it." My nerves couldn't take any more argu-ing. "Just forget it."

"Let's go," she said. "We're doing the past perfect tense in French class and I don't want to be late."

"You'll have to get yourself there," I said, picking up my backpack and camera bag. "I'm not going to school today."

"Where are you going?" she asked.

"For a hike," I said. "Want to come?"

"Have you ever thought about writing all of your bad ideas down and selling a book of them? It could be called, like, *Alexis Warren's Surefire Ways to Die Young.* Hey, I could be your spokesperson."

I didn't answer, but not out of stubbornness as much as the fact that I was trying to conserve my energy for the rest of the trail. We'd only gone about a quarter of a mile, and I was already completely out of breath. I took another swig of water and then went back to taking pictures.

"And why do you think she would be here?" Lydia asked.

"Because she hikes here. It's her favorite trail. She always talks about it." I stopped, pretending to be looking off into the distance but really just trying to catch my breath so I could talk. "And the other girls ended up in places they knew. Outside of town."

Lydia floated effortlessly beside me. "Why?"

"I don't know." I hauled myself up a set of steep stone stairs.

"She's probably dead already," Lydia said. "If she tried to hike this trail without water . . . and it's actually kind of hot today."

I silenced her with a pointed glare.

"Fine, fine," she said. "I see how you are when it's somebody you like. Talking about death is only funny when it's me."

"It's not funny," I said. "I wish you weren't dead."

She stopped. "Really?"

"Lydia, seriously?" I said. "Of *course* I do. Now keep moving."

Mercifully, she retreated into thoughtful silence for a while, so I could save the air in my lungs for more important things than talking—like breathing. We made slow progress, stopping every twenty or thirty feet so I could take pictures.

I hadn't hiked Maxwell Canyon since seventh grade, and experiencing the trail's difficulty firsthand just added one more level of awe to Elliot's already mystical aura of superiority. My thigh muscles screeched with pain, and my lungs would have been screeching, too—if they'd had any air to spare.

Lydia drifted away, and I kept going. I got into such a rhythm that it took me a moment to realize there was actually a person in my photographs.

Elliot.

My heart just about imploded.

"Lydia!" I called.

"What?" She came toward me so fast that for a moment she was just a gray blur.

"She's dead." My voice came out sounding sandpapered. "I saw her . . . She's dead."

I leaned down to look more closely.

"That? No, that's not a ghost," Lydia said. "I can see her, too!"

I dropped the camera. It swung from the end of the strap.

We looked at each other.

Elliot was alive.

I snapped into action. "You go ahead!" I said. "Go up the trail and find her. Stay with her. Don't leave her. I'll follow you!"

Lydia obeyed without a word, hurrying up the trail.

I opened my cell phone.

NO SERVICE.

"No, come on," I said, shaking it.

But no bars appeared.

A minute later, I heard Lydia cry out in a panicky shriek. "Alexis! Alexis, come quick!"

I was already exhausted, but I forced myself to run, hurtling up the steep incline toward the sound of her voice.

Lydia intercepted me. "I tried to stop her, but I couldn't—and it was so weird, it was, like, hot, and—something's wrong. Something's really wrong. *Look.*" She held up her arms.

Her hands were much fainter than the rest of her body.

Lydia looked like she was about to throw up. "It's where I tried to grab her," she said. "Everything went hot, and then . . ."

"Don't worry," I said. "We'll figure it out. But first we have to stop Elliot. Which way did she go?"

"That way," Lydia said, pointing with her barely there left hand.

I took off down the trail. Within a minute I saw Elliot—she was maybe seventy-five feet in front of me.

"Elliot!" I called. "Wait!"

She wasn't running away; she wasn't even walking fast. In fact, she was stumbling every few steps. Her bare feet were covered with blood and bruises.

I caught up to her easily, grabbing her arm.

"Elliot, stop! It's okay. You're safe now."

But she wouldn't stop. It was almost like she *couldn't*. Even when I got in front of her, she ran right into me. I lost my balance and fell, nearly landing on a cactus.

"See?" Lydia said. "She just keeps walking!"

I tried again to pull Elliot out of her stride, but it was useless. She never so much as raised a finger to fight back, but she was so much stronger than I was that she basically shrugged off everything I did to her.

"Come on," I cried. "Please."

We were on a long straight stretch of the trail, so I got in front of her and walked backward, thinking I'd be able to reason with her.

But as soon as I got a good look at her face, I knew there was no use.

Her eyes were glazed over. She didn't even seem to see me. Her face was streaked with dried-out tearstains. She breathed through her mouth in a shaky, shallow rhythm, and her lips were dry and cracked, the corners coated in a crust of dried saliva, blood, and dust.

Her jaw trembled in silent, arid sobs.

She really couldn't stop.

And she was terrified.

"Elliot, please, wait," I said, grabbing her arm. It didn't work; she just dragged me along with her.

If I couldn't make her stop, I could at least keep her from dying of dehydration. I lifted my water bottle and poured some into her mouth.

But she didn't make any effort to swallow it. It just leaked out all over her filthy sweatshirt.

"You have to stop her," Lydia said. "It's too hot. This trail's too difficult. She'll die of exhaustion."

"I know," I said. "But I don't know *how*."

"Can't you block the path?"

"She'll just go around me."

"There's a narrow pass a little way ahead. If you can block the far side and trap her in there, she won't be able to keep going. She'll *have* to stop."

It was worth a try. I ran ahead.

The narrow pass was about twelve feet long and three feet wide, bordered on its sides by the cliff and a ten-foot boulder. I wedged a bunch of big branches between the rocks on the far side, blocking off the passage just where it started to widen again. Then I hung back and watched the trail for Elliot.

Finally, she came. She was slower now, growing weaker and weaker. In addition to the painful gasp of her breath, her lungs made a hollow wheezing sound, like a little sigh.

She went into the pass.

I stepped out behind her, setting another thick piece of brush across the near opening. I watched her get to the other end, bump up against the branches, and slowly turn around, dragging her left leg.

Her face was flushed red, but there were deep gray circles under her dull eyes.

"Elliot, stop," I pleaded, as she got closer to me, foot by agonizing foot. "Please."

Lydia appeared, her face pale with dread. "It's not going to work."

"Wait." I turned to Lydia. "*You* can stop her. You stopped me that night I was walking outside. What did you do? Try it on Elliot!"

Lydia's mouth dropped open. She glanced down at her hands. "It's . . . different than with you. It's . . . it's . . . *meaner* now."

Right. It was different because I was Lydia's power center. She *had* to protect me in order to save herself.

"How can you be so selfish?" I said.

Her eyes flashed with pain.

"You'll do it if it means saving yourself," I said. "But to help an actual living person, you refuse?"

Lydia looked at me like I'd slapped her. "What do

you mean?" she cried. "I was never trying to save myself!"

"Lydia, I'm begging you! *Don't let her die.*"

I don't know if ghosts can cry, but Lydia was about to. She gave me a hurt look, then grimaced, closed her eyes, and charged forward, plowing into Elliot.

But she didn't go through her and come out the other side.

She disappeared completely.

Elliot stopped walking and swayed on her feet for a moment. Then she looked at me, and there was a glimmer of recognition in her eyes.

"Alexis," she whispered. Her voice had a slight vibration to it, like when you talk into a fan. "Don't come too close. It's not safe."

"Where have you been?" I asked. "What happened to you?"

"I don't know." Then suddenly she looked up at me, her dazed eyes full of hope. "This is a dream, isn't it? It's just a nightmare."

I didn't know what to say.

"It has to be." She almost smiled. "That explains everything. I *knew* it wasn't real. It's too horrible to be real."

"Come with me," I said.

"No. I don't have much time. I need to keep going."

"Why, Elliot?"

She raised her finger to her lips, lost in thought. "I'm trying to get somewhere . . . trying to find something."

"I'll help you. Just come with me. Drink some water."

I reached out to touch her arm, and she jerked away. "No, I'm not—I'm trying to get *away* from something."

Then she looked at me. Her eyes went wide with horror.

"I'm supposed to get away from . . . you, Alexis." She looked down at herself. "Are you—are *you* doing this to me?"

Suddenly she went into a frenzy, like a trapped animal. She scrambled over the branch that was blocking her exit and gave me a hard shove.

"Stay away from me!" she cried. "Stay back! Leave me alone!"

"Elliot, listen to me," I said. "This isn't real! It's not me you need to get away from!"

But it was too late. Elliot's eyes clouded over. The air around her seemed to shiver, and all of a sudden, Lydia's nearly-invisible form fell out of her body and landed in a heap, too weak to stand or float.

"Lyd?" I said. "Are you okay?"

Elliot started to trudge away, down the trail.

Lydia waved at me, her arm just a faint blur in the air. "Follow her," she rasped.

I tried to plant myself in Elliot's way, but she shoved me backward, toward a short incline behind me. I tried to steady myself, but my foot slipped on a patch of loose gravel, and I lost my balance and I fell back, landing hard on my side.

Elliot stood still, staring down at me.

Suddenly, her neck went slack and her head hung low, her chin touching her chest. My throat constricted as she raised her head and looked at me.

Her eyes were empty black holes.

She took a step closer. I went to back away, but my path was blocked by two big rocks.

Elliot kept coming toward me. Only it wasn't Elliot.

"Laina?" I whispered. "What do you want?"

She didn't answer. She stood a foot away from me, looking down. I could have reached out and grabbed her legs.

"Please don't hurt my friend," I said. "Take me instead. *Please.*"

From the darkness of the eye sockets, blinking eyelids emerged—Elliot's terrified eyes. "Alexis?" she cried in a strangled whisper. "Oh my God—please—I can't—"

It worked, I thought. *Laina's letting Elliot go.*

"Hurry!" I said. "Run! Run away!"

"I'll be back," she said. "We need to get help."

She made a move to go past me, down the trail.

Then, with a grunt of surprise, she jerked and started moving backward.

But not walking—she was being *pulled.*

"No!" she yelped. "No! Let me go!"

My body was frozen, and my voice was frozen, and my mind was frozen, watching Elliot struggle like an antelope being dragged away by a pack of lions. Her bare feet stumbled helplessly against the trail.

"Why?" she cried. *"Why is this happening?"*

I forced myself to my hands and knees, crawling up the hill.

"She's getting away." Lydia was too weak to move, but she urged me on. "Alexis, hurry! She's getting away!"

I got to my feet, ignoring the shock of pain emanating from my ankle with every step I took.

I came around a bend in the trail and stopped short.

Elliot was standing at the very edge of a cliff, fighting against Laina's hold on her.

"No," I said. "Don't."

When Elliot saw me, she stopped resisting.

She looked at me with an expression of calm—almost acceptance. "This isn't your fault, Alexis."

Then she doubled over, like someone had punched her in the stomach.

And she plunged backward off the edge.

I heard screams, and I thought they were Elliot's . . .

Then I realized they were my own.

I started for the cliff, but Lydia moved in front of me.

"Wait," she said. "It's no use. She's gone."

"No," I said. "Don't say that. I can save her. I have to go find her."

"Alexis." Lydia reached out, and I felt the weight of her hand on mine. "It's like me, remember? It was too late to save me. And it's too late for Elliot. She's dead. You have to get out of here."

"No," I said.

I tried to move, but she held on to me.

"I'm sorry about before," she whispered. "I wasn't trying to save myself. I swear." She faded almost all the way out, then back in again, like the heavy blinking of a person who's trying to stay awake. "I . . . I have to go."

And she disappeared.

I sat hunched over in shock, wondering where Lydia had gone, and if she was okay. Or had I bullied her into trying something she wasn't strong enough to do and . . .

Had I really done it? Had I killed her again?

My hair, matted and tangled, hung in front of my face. My hands were scratched and cut, but I was too numb to feel anything.

The world seemed empty and useless. Even the landscape around me was alien and hostile—jagged rocks jutting out of the ground; rough, rocky cliffs and hill-sides covered in cacti and weeds that would cut your skin like a paring knife.

There was no use imagining the worst at this point, or being afraid of it.

I was living it.

After a couple of minutes I forced myself to start moving again. I had to find Elliot. I believed what Lydia said, that I couldn't save her. But I had to see for myself. So I limped down the trail until I reached a gentler slope that led me down into the narrow ravine. My ankle tweaked with every step.

I spotted her body from fifty feet away, lifelessly sprawled on the rocky ground. Her jaw was slack, her arms splayed out at her sides. She was very dead.

I knelt next to her anyway and reached up to brush a lock of hair away from her eyes.

She looked so peaceful—and that was horribly wrong.

Because Elliot was never meant to be peaceful. She was supposed to shine and blaze like a Fourth of July sparkler.

"I'm so sorry." My voice was low, as if she and I were having a difficult conversation.

But of course there would be no more conversations.

Suddenly her hand shot up and grabbed my wrist.

Her eye sockets melted to darkness. She bared her teeth and pulled me down close to her face.

A rotten stench—the scent of death—puffed into my face.

"I'm doing this for you," she hissed.

Then she fell backward onto the gravel.

I'm doing this for you.

Not *to* me. Not *because* of me. *For* me.

The sun was bright overhead and the inside of the car was growing warm.

I'd hauled myself up to the main trail and trudged back to the parking lot, but that was as far as I could make myself go.

I need water, I thought. I'm dehydrated.

But I really didn't care.

The hills off in the distance began to blur together into a mass of rusty browns and dull grays.

Girls would just keep dying. There was nothing I could do to keep them from dying. And it was somehow my fault. Not that I would ever figure out why or how it was my fault, since Lydia was gone—which was also my fault.

There would be no answers.

There would just be more dead girls.

27

MORE CARS, CARRYING HIKERS, came and parked alongside me. That meant it wouldn't be long before someone happened across Elliot's body. I hoped they would. The sooner they found her, the less her family would suffer.

Finally, I started my car and drove home. I was so distracted that I nearly ran a red light and had to swerve to keep from hitting a guy on his bike.

I parked and wondered vaguely what my next step should be. Call the police? Call Agent Hasan? Turn myself in?

There was no getting around Jared's being Laina's power center. Aralt had been tied to the girls in the Sunshine Club as his power center, but he was governed by his *libris exanimus*, the book that contained him between stints with clubs.

Laina was just a ghost. I mean, she was a superghost (what that meant, exactly, I wasn't sure), but as far as I could tell, she wasn't controlled by any sort of book.

Or . . . was she?

My mind flashed back to Jared's locked closet door. Did the closet contain something he didn't want me to see? Something to do with Laina?

No. Impossible. He'd been truly shocked when I'd tried to tell him that she was a ghost. That was the kind of reaction you couldn't fake.

I walked into our town house without bothering to wonder if there would be anyone there. Mom had her board meeting. Dad had gone to work—there was no point in his staying home if Kasey and I were at school.

Only we weren't.

I'd skipped school—

And Kasey was home, too.

She stepped into the hallway, staring me down. "What's going on?"

"Nothing," I said. "I just decided to go for a walk instead of going to school."

"A walk?" Her gaze traveled up and down my filthy beat-up body and my torn, stained clothes.

"Yeah."

"Where did you go last night?" she asked.

There was no point in denying it. I blinked. "Out."

"Lexi . . ." Her hair was pulled into a low loose bun. Her hands were on her hips. She looked like a character from a TV show about lawyers. "You always leave . . . right before the bodies are found."

"What are you saying?"

"If she's making you hurt them, tell me," Kasey said.

I had to take a step back and lean against the wall to keep my legs from giving out. How on earth could my little sister know about Laina? And how on earth could she suspect me of being a murderer?

I shook my head. "I just learned about her last night, Kase."

"Don't lie to me," she said. "I heard you talking to her a week ago."

"Really? To Laina?" I asked, my investigative side forcing my hurt-slash-shocked side to take a backseat. "A week ago? Was I asleep?"

"What?" She quirked her head to the side, puzzled. "Who's Laina?"

We stared at each other.

"I heard you talking to *Lydia*," she said.

"Oh, that. No, Kase," I said. "It's not what you think."

She swallowed hard. "I know what it's like, Lexi—to be lonely, and to think a ghost is your friend. Does she tell you what to do? Does she promise you things? Is she . . . is she making you hurt those girls?"

"No," I said. "Kasey, you don't understand. Lydia is—"

I cut myself off and took a shaky breath. As much as I'd wanted to protect my little sister and keep her out of this world, it was too late now.

"Lydia's my friend," I said. "But not in a bad way. She's not hurting anybody. She's helping me." *Or she was—until I killed her.*

Kasey's eyes narrowed. She didn't believe me—and after what she'd been through, I didn't blame her. Everything I was saying was something she could have said about Sarah.

"I don't know what to tell you," I said. "I mean, you either believe me or you don't. But I wouldn't lie about it. You never lied about Sarah."

She thought about that. "Not to you."

"Lydia's not behind this. She's not hurting those girls—and neither am I."

"Then why did you find Kendra?" she asked. "I mean, it was so obvious, once I thought about it. And Ashleen—that was your lens cap they found, I know. I checked your camera."

I wanted to shout at her, shake her. She wasn't supposed to be doing this. She was supposed to have a normal, happy life, and be a normal, happy girl. She was supposed to be pretty and popular and sail through high school, letting me absorb all of the pain, all of the suffering.

But what if—the thought hit me hard—what if that wasn't what she wanted?

What if she wanted to help?

She was fifteen years old. I'd been fifteen when I fought Sarah.

Just like I had the right to fight . . . so did she.

"In October," I said, "right before Lydia died, she threw chemicals in my face. They got in my eyes, and I was afraid I was going to go blind. So I retook the oath, and Aralt started fixing my eyes. I never got the chance to read the abandoning spell because Lydia burned the book."

Kasey's mouth dropped open. "*Aralt* is doing this?"

"No," I said. "He's gone. But my eyes . . . they're different now."

She stared right into them, and I fought the urge to turn away.

"They're haunted," I said. "I can see ghosts in photos and on TV."

"My God, Lexi," she breathed. "Why didn't you say something?"

I choked. "Wait—before you freak out. There's more."

And I told her about Lydia.

She had to put a hand on the wall as I spoke. Then

she backed into my room and plopped down on the bed. "I can't believe you didn't tell me. I would have helped you. With all of it."

"I didn't want you to help me," I said. "I wanted you to be safe."

She raised her eyebrows and gave me an angry look. "You think I want to just live a clueless, stupid life while you're out there suffering? Are you out of your mind?"

"Possibly," I said. "Believe me, I've considered it."

She pulled me down and wrapped her arm around me, resting her head on my shoulder. "I can't be happy if you aren't happy. I'm not going to let you sacrifice yourself for me."

"But you have a chance to be normal," I said. "And I don't think I do."

"Well, I don't want it," she said, with a decisive shake of her head. "I don't want to be normal."

I was overcome by emotions, but for once I didn't burst into tears. I just sat there feeling somehow like I was the little sister and she was the big sister. She was the protector and I was the one who needed protecting.

"Now," she said, "tell me absolutely everything."

So I did. I started with the bright light and the girl—Laina—taking control of Mom's car, and I told her everything that had happened since then.

She stopped me sometimes and asked questions,

which I answered as well as I could. She was trying to work out a way for us to get into Jared's closet.

"Stop," I said. "Did you hear that?"

"Hear what?"

The rumble of the garage door.

"Mom's home," I said.

Kasey ran to my window. "Lexi . . ."

"What?" I said.

"It's not just Mom. It's Dad, too." She turned to look at me. Her face was white. "And Agent Hasan."

We stared at each other.

"She's going to take you to Harmony Valley," Kasey said. "Like she took me."

Harmony Valley was a mental institution located in the middle of nowhere, about fifty miles outside of Surrey. It was where Kasey had spent almost her whole eighth grade year.

"I know," I said, because I did. The moment Kasey said her name, I knew why she had come. "I—I could run."

"You can't run," she said. "She'll find you."

I guess I knew that, too. "But *you* can run. Don't ever let them know we've talked about this."

"Tell her *nothing*," my sister said. "Not a thing. She'll act like she's your friend, but she's not."

"Go! Hide!" I snapped, steering my sister toward her bedroom.

"No, I'll leave," she said. "I'll go out through the backyard."

I followed her to the kitchen and opened the door for her, wanting to shove her out to safety. But she stopped on the threshold and hugged me.

"Keep quiet, behave, and she'll have to let you go," she said. "Eventually."

"Don't come see me. I don't want her to think you know about any of this." Suddenly, a cold line of fear went up my back. "And Kasey, don't try to deal with Laina alone. Promise me."

"I promise." She kissed my cheek and ran off through the backyard. She could hide in the side yard until everyone was inside, and then she could get out of the neighborhood.

But me?

I was stuck.

Mom's face was gray. She rubbed her cheeks with the backs of her hands and stared down at the floor. Dad sat next to her, looking at me.

I was across from them, and Agent Hasan stood over us all.

She was oddly non-smug.

"You can't just *take* her," Mom said.

I saw the way Agent Hasan's mouth opened to

answer, and then she stopped herself.

There was really no need to say it: she could. Just like when she'd hauled Kasey away.

Two hours earlier, she'd come in the door bearing a file of official-looking legal papers that had silenced my parents. While I waited on the couch, she sat at the kitchen island with them, and occasional phrases rose above the murmur of their low voices: *Danger to herself and others. Evaluation and treatment. Signed by the judge.* But even if Agent Hasan hadn't had her stack of papers, I would have believed that she could "just take" me. As far as I could see, that was her whole mode of operating: "just" doing things. And never facing the consequences.

Dad leaned forward to straighten a stack of perfectly straight coasters on the coffee table. "How long are you thinking she might be . . . away?"

Agent Hasan shook her head. "There's no way of knowing. That information tends to reveal itself after the initial evaluation period."

Mom and Dad didn't ask what kind of evaluations were included in that period. And I didn't either. After all, Kasey had gone through them and survived. . . . Then again, for all her ill-advised ghost involvement, Kasey was just a regular girl; she didn't have haunted eyes like mine.

Maybe I'd end up as a taxidermied specimen in some top-secret government science lab.

"Alexis, if there's anything you want to tell us . . ." my mother said. "Maybe there's another way to deal with—with whatever you're going through."

But I wouldn't tell them a thing. The less they knew, the better. I was positive about that. Ignorance is bliss, and the opposite of ignorance is the opposite of bliss.

Agent Hasan's presence implied that there was something supernatural going on. But my parents didn't ask for details. Maybe, in the backs of their minds, they somehow connected me to the missing girls.

Maybe they were afraid to ask.

Because I hadn't once claimed to be innocent of anything.

Agent Hasan checked her watch. "We should probably get going. Alexis, if you want to pack some clothes, maybe some books . . . nothing electronic, please."

I nodded and walked to my bedroom, grateful to have orders to follow so I didn't have to think. I pulled a bag out of my closet and started putting clothes in it— jeans, T-shirts, pajamas—the comfortable loungey stuff Kasey had worn during her ten months away.

Would I be gone for ten months?

Or longer?

Like . . . forever?

28

I SAT ALONE IN THE BACKSEAT of Agent Hasan's car while she drove. About forty-five minutes later, we headed down a long twisting road that went through a small tree-lined canyon and past a couple of horse farms.

A black iron gate opened to let us pass beyond the tall fence that bordered Harmony Valley. We parked at the back of the building.

Would people at school—would Jared and Megan— even know what had happened to me, or would I just disappear like a political prisoner in some second-world country? Kasey might tell Megan, but I doubted she would call Jared.

A man in gray pants and a lab coat came out the double doors, flanked by two massive orderlies. The man spoke to Agent Hasan, and then she came and opened my car door.

"Let's go," she said.

I kept my arms folded in front of me and followed her inside.

* * *

Harmony Valley was a private facility. The main lobby and visitors' lounge were nice, if a little generic—kind of like a hotel for business travelers. Visiting Kasey, we'd never crossed into the area where the patients spent their time living, eating, studying, watching TV, and attending therapy. So I'd always assumed the rest of the building was as nice as the parts we saw.

Wrong.

I followed Agent Hasan down a hallway painted in an ultraglossy shade of two-day-old oatmeal. The ceilings were striped with fluorescent lights, and the floor was an endless line of mismatched linoleum tiles. Every twenty feet or so we passed a solid-looking door with a small wire-reinforced window. Each one had a small numeric keypad instead of a lock. I slowed minutely to try to see inside some of the rooms.

"Keep up," Agent Hasan said over her shoulder.

At the end of the hall was a windowless door with a sign on it that read PRIVATE. Agent Hasan shielded the keypad with her body and typed a series of numbers. The door opened with a mechanical *click*, and we walked in.

The room was sparsely furnished, with a line of counters against one wall, a hospital-type bed in the center, and a table with two chairs on either side pushed back in the corner.

Agent Hasan glanced at me. "On the bed."

"No, thank you."

"Alexis." Her tone was heavy with warning and impatience.

"I'm not getting in the bed," I said, trying to keep my voice steady. "I'll sit in a chair like a normal person."

"Normal person?" She laughed humorlessly and gave me an exasperated look. "Go ahead, then. Sit."

So I did, edging myself into the chair in the corner—the one that faced the door.

A second later, Agent Hasan came over and sat opposite me. "So. Want to tell me what's going on?"

I didn't look up. Based on Kasey's advice, I had a brilliant plan, which was to ignore her questions for all eternity, if necessary.

"Did you know that the only signs of struggle on Elliot Quilimaco's body are your handprints?"

I flinched at the mention of Elliot's name. "I believe it."

"Do you admit to manhandling her?"

I raised my eyes. "I had no choice."

She leaned closer, coming in for the kill. "How'd you find her, Alexis? How did you know where she was?"

"She liked Maxwell Canyon," I said. "She hiked there all the time."

"What about Ashleen?" she said. "And Kendra?"

"Same as Elliot," I said. "They knew those trails."

Her lips turned down. "Kendra was found a mile and a half *off* the trail."

I channeled all my energy into counting the scratches on the table in front of me. If I let my attention waver for even a moment, I lost count and had to start again.

"Look, I don't care," Agent Hasan said. "I'm trying to make this easier on you. But if you don't want to accept my assistance, it's no skin off my back."

I remembered what Kasey had said—*She'll act like she's your friend, but she's not*—and looked up at her, on the verge of saying something snide.

But when I saw the way her sharp eyes were pinned on me, I swallowed my words and went back to studying the tabletop.

Agent Hasan stood up, the feet of her chair shrieking as she pushed it away from the table. "I think you need a little time to cool off. See you in a while."

"I hope you don't mind sharing a room," Nurse Jean said, pointing to an open door in the hallway.

Inside were two twin beds, each with its own nightstand, and two sets of shelves. The bed farther from the door looked slept-in, and there were a few items on the shelves—some clothes, a couple of magazines, a few books. Everything large enough to hurt somebody was bolted down.

I put my bag on one of the shelves and sat on the unoccupied bed, trying to bounce lightly. But the mattress was about as bouncy as a pile of warm sandwich meat.

"Now, you just get settled. Free time ends in thirty minutes, so you might as well just get ready for bed. We'll get your medication set up in the morning."

"Medication?" I repeated. "I don't think I need any medication."

She peered at me over the top of her clipboard. "You can talk to your doctor about that tomorrow."

But I didn't have a doctor. I wasn't even sick.

Or was this what Agent Hasan meant when she said she "takes care" of problems?

Face it. If I tried to tell the truth—that I was only there because a top-secret government agent knew I was somehow involved with a ghost and a string of killings—people would just assume I'd come to the right place.

Was this what Agent Hasan did so she didn't have to justify putting people in jail? She dumped the offenders in a mental hospital and kept them too doped up to talk?

"I see you've brought some of your own things, but I'll have to take them and look through your bag before we can leave it with you. So you can just go ahead and sleep in these." She handed me a hideous pair of loose, salmon-colored cotton pants and a matching V-neck shirt. Then she wished me good night and left, closing the door behind her.

I flopped backward on the bed and stared at the ceiling until my roommate came in.

She had brown hair cut bluntly to her chin and a thin, long face. She looked less than thrilled to be sharing a room. "I'm Haley," she said, sounding like the basic act of talking to me required a huge sacrifice on her part.

"Alexis," I said.

"So . . . do me a favor," she said. "Just don't try to stab me in the middle of the night, or anything, okay?"

I didn't know how to react to that. Was it a joke? Had her previous roommate tried to stab her?

"You know . . ." she prompted, "if the voices say, 'Stab your roomie,' at least give me a head start. Maybe we should switch beds so I can be closer to the door."

"Voices?" I said. "What voices?"

Now she looked alarmed.

Then I remembered what our cover story had been when Kasey was locked up: that she had schizophrenia and heard voices in her head telling her what to do. That was probably what the kids here were being told about me.

Don't worry, I thought about saying. *I'm not schizophrenic. I'm just being stalked by the ghost of my boyfriend's dead girlfriend.* Yeah—*that* would make me sound sane.

"I mean . . . I don't hear any right now," I said. "I'm on a good run."

A few minutes later, as Haley and I were getting ready for bed, Nurse Jean came back with a tiny paper cup. "This just got called in for you," she said, handing it to me.

I caught Haley trying to get a glimpse at the contents of the cup.

I gazed down at four pills—a blue one, a pink one, a black-and-white one, and a tiny white one. Quite a mix. "What are they?"

"I don't have that information," Nurse Jean said, shaking her head. "But I'm sure your doctor discussed it, didn't he? And you can always ask him about it tomorrow."

"I don't have a doctor," I said. I had a government agent who was trying to lock me away like a problematic mouse in a trap.

Jean gave me a quick smile, and I realized she thought I was just being crazy. Of course everyone here had a doctor. That's how you got here—if you were a regular person, that is.

"But what if I don't want to take any pills?" I asked.

She sighed. "First, we have a little talk about what our shared goal is here at Harmony Valley. Which is healing, naturally."

Or shutting people up. "And then?"

"Then I inform you that, as an involuntary patient, you are technically *required* to take any medication prescribed to you by your doctor."

It made my skin crawl to think that Agent Hasan had decided that I had to take these pills—and I didn't even get to know what they were.

"And then?"

"And then we strap you down and deliver the medication by injection." She said this last bit with the same unbending cheerfulness as the rest.

I swallowed the pills.

Haley seemed relieved.

I went to the bathroom and brushed my teeth. By the time I got back to the room, my thoughts were turning fuzzy, and I was practically swaying on my feet. Nurse Jean saw me and came to help me into bed.

"What was in those pills?" I asked. "What are they for?"

"I imagine your doctor will discuss those details with you," Jean said, checking the chart on the door. "Most likely just a little help getting to sleep."

I nodded. They were working, all right. My mind was loose and slow. "Feels like being drunk."

"I don't know about that." Jean smirked as she helped me lie down. "I guess it depends on what you've been drinking."

"Wine?"

"Maybe if you take your wine with a shot of tranquilizers." She pulled the covers over me and tucked them under my chin.

The next few days were uneventful—or maybe they only seemed that way because the drug-induced lethargy never seemed to leave my system. I spent a lot of time feeling unmotivated and loopy. Apparently, whatever it took to be accepted by Haley and her friends, I wasn't doing. So I ate, lounged, and watched TV alone. But it didn't bother me.

It also didn't bother me that I could never quite get my mind to focus on Laina. Every time I tried to think about it, I got distracted. Usually by a TV show, which turned into a string of TV shows, which led to mealtime and bedtime and the usual succession of distrustful looks from Haley and then my cup of pills.

Still no sign of Agent Hasan.

My parents came for a visit, but it didn't stand out in my memory. Pretty much a lot of sad-dog faces and apologies, even though they hadn't done anything wrong. They brought me presents—a couple of books, raspberry-scented lotion, comfortable T-shirts, and yoga pants. Kasey sent her love, they said—looking disappointed in my sister's apparent callousness at not showing up in person. But I was glad she'd stayed away.

No therapy for me, group or otherwise. And while I was too drugged to be acutely worried, it did occur to me that if this went on much longer, I might really go crazy.

But at least Laina seemed to be appeased. A week into my stay, there had been no new missing girls, and I hadn't had any purple dress dreams. Maybe my being locked away was just as good as my being dead.

On the seventh or eighth day, I was sitting on the couch, dividing my attention (poorly) between a talk show and a game of checkers that was progressing a couple of feet away from me, when the nurse called my name. "Alexis?"

I looked around, my eyes finally settling on her.

"Visitor," she said.

My parents again? Maybe Kasey? I shot to my feet, glad to have a distraction from the endless lack of distractions.

But it wasn't my family. It was Jared.

In spite of my loneliness and boredom, I stopped at the threshold of the visitors' lounge and considered turning back. All I could think when I looked at him was that wherever he was, Laina would be too. And she would be waiting and watching for a chance to get rid of me—or somebody else.

But his smile was so warm, his eyes so sweetly anxious—and I was so close to falling into a pit of loneliness—that I found myself disarmed. I walked toward the love seat where he was waiting. He stood up and moved to hug me.

"I'm sorry," the nurse said. "No physical contact."

"Of course," Jared said, like he was an old pro at this. "Sorry."

I was already sitting. I didn't really like to be on my feet too long. My meds made me dizzy.

Jared turned to me, his face etched with concern. "Are you all right?"

"Yeah," I said. "Who told you I was here?"

"Your sister."

Right. Except . . . there was something wrong with that, wasn't there?

"I just wanted to make sure you were okay," he said.

"I'm fine," I said. "It's fine here. Totally . . . fine."

I was a little light-headed and a lot confused. I had a pretty distinct memory of Jared booting me from his house when he thought I was defaming Laina's memory, and yet here he was, acting as if we were right back to normal. And what exactly was "normal" for us, anyway?

Did he know about Elliot? Yes, of course he did. Why didn't he ask about her? Or tell me how sorry he was?

Why didn't he ask why I came to Harmony Valley?

Ask me why I'm here, said the back-of-my-head voice.

Or maybe . . . was I remembering wrong? Had there been a text, a phone call?

No—there hadn't been anything like that. He'd been furious that night.

So why wasn't he mad anymore? And— Wait, what was the other question?

My cupful of pills was doing more than just putting me to sleep at night. It was stirring my thoughts like cake mix.

Jared reached out and took my hand. I stiffened, waiting for the nurse to say something, but she didn't notice.

"When you get out," he said, "things are going to be different. I know I'm over the top sometimes, but it's really important to me to try to work things out."

I stared at him, thinking, Why? I knew how crazy it must have sounded when I'd gone to him to talk about Laina. And I could only imagine how much it had hurt him to hear me accuse her—her ghost—of being a murderer. If the shoes had been turned—I mean, if the tables had been turned—*stupid pills*—I would have been just as angry.

So why wasn't he angry anymore?

All of that trickled through my head, but none of it

made it out of my mouth. Instead, I said, "Um . . . okay."

He smiled. "I wish I could kiss you."

I was actually really glad he couldn't.

"Alexis! Who's this?"

I looked up and saw Haley, who hadn't so much as said good morning or good night to me since the first night. She was on her way back to the rec room, but she paused in front of us and gave Jared a vivid smile.

"Um, Jared. My . . ."

"Boyfriend," Jared said.

Haley's eyes went as round as basketballs. "Wow, you're so nice to visit Alexis. I mean, a lot of guys wouldn't stick around once their girlfriends went . . . you know."

"Yes, well, nice to meet you." Jared turned toward me, angling himself so Haley was talking to the back of his shoulder.

"You too!" Then she toodle-oo'd off through the double doors.

Jared didn't even seem to notice her leave. "I really mean it. When you get out, everything will be better."

"I don't know," I said. I wasn't counting my when-I-get-out chickens until they hatched. As far as I was concerned, there weren't even any when-I-get-out eggs lying around.

His hands squeezed mine. "What we have is special.

And I'm not going to let that go. Yes, I was mad at you that night, Alexis, but that's because I didn't understand. And you didn't understand, either."

"But why didn't you ever tell me about her?" I asked.

"You didn't ask. Besides, the whole thing was, you know, horribly painful. Why would I talk about it?"

Because she was a huge part of your life and she died, maybe? But I didn't say it. I could hear the tension behind what he was saying. "What didn't I understand?"

He lowered his voice. "What she's doing."

I grabbed my hands away. "What who's doing? What do you mean?"

He smiled warmly.

"Jared, do you mean you believe me about Laina? You think she's doing something? Her . . ." I glanced around. "Her ghost?"

He leaned in close to me, and I couldn't escape the laser beams of his dark brown eyes. "I think she is, Alexis. I think I figured it out. See—we were supposed to be together forever, her and me."

I stared at him.

"But that's never going to happen, right? So here's what I think: she didn't want me to be alone." He reached up and caressed the side of my face. "So she found me *you* instead."

29

I HADN'T FELT THIS AWAKE IN DAYS.

"Wait," I said. "Laina *found* me for you?"

"She and I were a couple for two years." There was a dangerous lightness to his words; Jared's tone was never light unless he was forcing it to be, which meant that inside, his emotions were churning like a brewing storm. "We didn't say boyfriend and girlfriend. We said *soul mate*. We knew we were always going to be together."

I started to stand up.

"Stay." He tugged on my hand—hard enough to throw off my less-than-perfect balance. "You would have liked her a lot. She was the best person I ever knew. But then . . . she died." The lightness evened out into a horrible calm. "So I guess I needed to find a new soul mate."

I drew in a shaky breath.

Jared needed someone else to love—and Laina chose me for him.

Did that mean she would do whatever it took for us to be together?

Including murder?

He gave my hand a little shake. "Don't you see? *That's* what she's doing. She wants us to be together because she loved me so much that she doesn't want me to be lonely anymore."

The room began a slow rotation around me. I put my hand out to stop the spinning, but Jared thought I was reaching for him. I felt his fingers close around mine.

"It's like . . . our destiny," he whispered. "And she's trying to help us."

My words came out like a declaration of surrender. "What does that mean—how is she helping?"

"I think I'd better start at the beginning," he said.

This is important. I tried to keep eye contact. But it was hard because Jared's gaze was so glitteringly intense. I had to force myself to stare at the spot right between his eyes.

"We'd been friends since preschool, and then we were in the same classes—except fourth grade—all the way to junior high. Which is when we fell in love. A lot of kids say that and don't mean anything, but for Laina and me it was real." He blinked. "Do you believe me?"

I nodded.

Now he was clasping my hand so tightly I couldn't

feel my fingers. "The only tiny thing about Laina was . . . she was kind of a flirt. So one day when we went out hiking, she was sort of talking to another guy, and I said something about it. Well, she got really mad. Told me she wouldn't walk another step with me."

I felt my blood turn cold.

"I didn't *want* to leave her. You have to believe me." Jared's fingers were wrapped around mine like a vise grip. "But she ordered me to. So I said I'd wait for her in the parking lot."

I tried to pull away, but Jared wouldn't let go.

"Two hours later, she's not there. Three hours, still not there. I got mad. I figured she'd taken a side trail and called her mom to come get her or something. So I went home." His hand was starting to shake. "*I went home.* I left her there. And she . . . she got lost. She ended up off the trail. And she wandered for hours. . . . It was winter, so it was really cold, and . . ."

"Please stop." I didn't want to hear any more.

"We all went out looking the next day. We combed the park. And I'm the one who found her."

I knew this part:

She was staring at the sky and holding her Saint Barbara medal.

And as the shadow of a cloud moved off her face . . . she died.

Jared's lips were pulled into a painful smile. "I promised I would never forsake her memory. I would never leave her behind."

As the story ended, his grip finally loosened, and I pulled away.

"I'm sorry," I said.

"Yeah, well. Me too." A smile blossomed on his face. "But it's going to be great now. You'll see. She even looked like you, Alexis. She was your height and your build, and she had platinum blond hair, like yours."

Wonderful. I closed my eyes for a moment, to collect my thoughts. "Here's the thing, Jared . . . I think you're wrong."

"About what?" he asked.

"About us. Being meant to be together. I don't think it's going to work. I think . . ." Thoughts were crystallizing in my mind. "I don't think that's what she's doing. Because she's attacking me, too."

He looked almost amused. "You don't think it's going to work?"

I shook my head helplessly.

"But Laina clearly thinks it is." He shrugged as if that settled it.

"But I don't *want*—"

"Alexis." His eyes turned hard. "Could you *please* try to think of someone besides yourself for a minute?"

I fell silent.

"I mean, all of the things she's done—" He lowered his voice. "All of those girls—she did it to keep them away from me. She did it for you. Anyone who ever tries to interfere with us—she'll take care of them. That's how much she cares."

Jared's face turned into something twisted and ugly. *"Kick him to the curb,"* he said in a mimicking tone.

Elliot's words.

So Laina had been there—she'd heard Elliot. It wasn't just about flirting. It was about anyone who tried to come between us.

"She *knew* me, down to the tiniest part of my innermost soul," Jared said. "And if she wants us to be together, that means it's the right thing."

I decided to change tactics. "I just don't think it's a good idea," I said, keeping my voice light. "I was just thinking about you. I mean, Kasey was here for ten months. What if they make me stay that long?"

"Alexis, it's so important to me that you get well." He smiled. "Of course I'll wait for you. I mean, think about it. If I didn't care about you, I wouldn't have called your therapist and told her there was something wrong."

"My therapist," I repeated.

"Yeah," he said. "Dr. Hasan."

I closed my eyes.

"She called Dad a few weeks ago. She said your parents had asked her to call. She left her number and said she'd like to know if you ever behaved strangely."

Another piece of the puzzle clicked into place: the reason Jared didn't ask why I was at Harmony Valley was that he *knew* why. He *was* why.

"What did you tell her?" I whispered.

"Don't worry," he said. "Nothing about Laina. I just said you were talking about ghosts and acting a little off. She was very nice. She seems really committed to your care. And I think that's great."

"No. It's not great." I stood up, looking down at him in horror. "You need to leave."

"Now you're getting mad?" he said. "That's not fair. I'm just trying to help you."

"But—" I was so angry, there were stars in my vision. "If you believe that Laina's ghost is involved in the killings—then you *know* I'm not crazy. If you think Laina exists—"

"Maybe if that were your only issue, Alexis," he said. "But let's be honest. You've had a little trouble letting go of your past. Besides, I like the thought of you being here. Being . . . protected."

Being trapped.

I was speechless.

"I think it would be best if I came back another

348

day." He abruptly got up and walked to the nurse's station. A few seconds later, Nurse Jean came over and stood above me.

"You're getting a little worked up, I hear," she said to me. "How about a nap before dinner?"

"Walk me to the door?" Jared said.

I did, but only because I had something to say. Before he could ring the bell to be buzzed out, I took a deep breath and said, with as much conviction as I could muster, "Jared. I'm *not* your soul mate. We're not meant to be together."

Jared was watching me with a faint smile on his face, as if I were a precocious child reciting lines from a play I didn't understand. "That's exactly what your sister said when she came to talk to me," he said, touching me on the nose. "But you're both wrong."

Then he walked out.

Haley actually spoke to me that night. "Your boyfriend's cute."

"Um, yeah, you probably need to leave that subject alone," I said.

She gave me an indignant sniff. "And he puts up with you, so he must be a saint."

"Haley," I said. "Trust me. You don't want to have anything to do with him."

349

"That's what I'd say, too," she said. "Never mind. I can get my own boyfriends."

Ten thirty was lights-out. I lay in my buzzing twilight daze and listened to the slow, even sound of Haley's breath in the dark. Maybe that was why I was such a zombie during the day—the sleeping pills didn't actually seem to make me sleep. They just turned me to jelly.

Details slid out of my grasp, but the blunter points of the matter were lined up like building blocks in my head.

The last time I checked the clock before I finally managed to doze off, it said 12:38 a.m.

I dreamed about leaving Harmony Valley and going home to find my entire house—floors, walls, ceilings, every possible surface—covered in a thick layer of grit and grime, like wet coffee grounds. My parents didn't seem to notice, but Kasey wouldn't stop sobbing about it. I tried to console her by showing her that she could wipe it off, but when I touched it, my skin began to bubble and ooze.

Then Kasey walked away from me, bumping into things as she went—*clank, thump, thud*—and I looked down and saw that the skin on my legs was bubbling, too. It felt different, though—there was pressure—scraping—

I bolted upright.

Haley's bed was empty.

Then an arm reached up over the side of my bed, the hand bent like a claw, and dragged across my pajamas like it was trying to grab hold.

For a moment I just stared, trying to figure out what exactly was happening. Then I jumped out of bed and turned on my reading light.

Haley was on the floor between the beds, flailing like a beached mermaid, her arms reaching hungrily for me. Her eyes were open and staring, her mouth slack. Her feet were completely tangled in her sheets, leaving her unable to walk or even stand up.

The floor around her was littered with things that had been on the nightstand between us, swept off by her groping arms.

My first instinct was to open the door (triggering an alert at the nurses' station) and run away down the hall. Then I realized that this might be my only chance to gather actual information about what was going on.

I pressed my hands together, so tightly I could hardly feel my fingers, and made myself speak.

"Laina . . . ?" I asked. "Is that you?"

Haley opened her mouth.

Hissssssssss

I slammed back against the wall, watching

her claw hungrily at the air like a horror-movie monster.

"Why are you doing this?"

She twitched in frustration. *"Come closer,"* she whispered.

"No," I said.

She bared her teeth and snarled at me.

"What do you want?" I asked. "Is this about Jared? You can have him. I don't want him. You need to leave me alone and stop hurting people."

She turned her attention to her legs, but she was too clumsy to unwrap the sheet.

I looked around for something that could be used to defend myself if she did manage to get up off the floor. Of course, I didn't find anything—the whole point of this place was that they didn't keep weapons lying around.

Haley's arms gave one last convulsive effort, and she fell back limply to the linoleum, her eyes closed.

I watched for at least a full minute, then took a step closer. "Haley?"

Nothing. Only the slow, even breathing of a sleeping girl.

One step closer.

I knelt down to touch her shoulder.

Her eyes popped open and her mouth widened like the maw of a shark going after a seal. She grabbed my hand with one of her own and yanked on me so hard I lost my balance and fell on top of her.

Her other hand grabbed for my neck, but I put out both of my arms and pushed off of her body as hard as I could, slipping out of her reach.

It took me a second to catch my breath.

She let out a hopeless sigh. *"You must love him,"* she hissed.

"No!" I said, my back to the wall. "No! I don't! I never will! *Go away!*"

It was the wrong thing to say.

Her eyes narrowed with resentment. Then, before I knew what was happening, Haley's hands squeezed around her *own* neck, the fingers and knuckles turning white. I ran over and tried to pry them away from her throat before she suffocated herself.

She was choking, gasping for air, but her hands never let up their iron grip.

And the whole time, her lips were curled into Laina's bitter, vicious smile.

I fought to get my fingers underneath hers. I'd much rather have her try to strangle *me*, because then at least I could get leverage. But this was like trying to pull apart two boards that have been bolted together.

The gasping and choking grew more desperate, until Haley was deathly silent.

Time for drastic measures. I flipped her over so she was facedown. Then I hooked my elbows through hers and pushed my arms apart, dragging hers with them. Finally I managed to pull her hands off of her throat.

I waited until I heard her take a ragged breath before I relaxed.

Then I heard, in Haley's normal voice, "What the . . . ? What are you—"

She craned her neck to look at me, and gasped.

Oh, crap.

"Haley, wait!" I said. "It's not what it looks like!"

I was going to tell her I could explain. But she didn't give me a chance.

She let out a scream that could have peeled the paint from the walls.

30

AGENT HASAN SAT PERFECTLY STRAIGHT, her hands folded on the table in front of her. She had her usual air of detachment, but it was different, somehow—every few seconds I caught a flash of something behind her eyes. . . . Was it caution? Fear?

"I am *very* much hoping you'll enlighten me," she said slowly, "as to why you found it necessary to attack your roommate in the middle of the night."

I could tell her exactly what I'd told everyone else— that I didn't know why I'd done it. Which was beginning to look like a golden ticket to a lifetime at Harmony Valley.

Or I could tell her the truth.

I decided to try the middle ground. "I have a reason," I said. "But you wouldn't understand."

Her eyes widened, and she leaned forward. *"Try me."*

"I can't." My voice was stretched thin. "But it's a good reason."

She tapped her fingers against the table. "When I brought you here, that wasn't supposed to be an invitation to earn yourself a permanent stay."

"Well, maybe you brought me here for the wrong reason," I said.

She gave a half laugh and looked at me. "I'm starting to think the same thing, believe it or not. That is, I'm glad you're here—because you're clearly dangerous. But I have a theory, Alexis."

A theory?

"You called me to say there might have been some kind of supernatural activity involved in Kendra's and Ashleen's disappearances. At the time I thought you were being a little paranoid. Then I get a call from your boyfriend saying you're going on about ghosts. So at that point, I think—maybe so. Maybe it *is* supernatural."

My heart soared with hope.

"But it's not, Alexis," she said. "And I think you know it."

My soaring heart did a tailspin. "What—what do you mean?"

"I mean that as far as my team and my equipment can tell, there is not and has never been a ghost involved in those girls' deaths." Her blank face transformed. Her half smile disappeared, and she was suddenly as serious as death. "So maybe there is no ghost, Alexis. . . . Maybe there's just you."

It took a second for me to comprehend what she was saying—

That she blamed me—not an evil spirit, but *me*—for what had happened to Kendra, Ashleen, and Elliot.

"That's ridiculous," I said. "I'm not a killer."

"It's ridiculous that since you've been here, the only new attack has been on your own roommate?"

I didn't answer.

"It's ridiculous that every one of the girls who's been targeted has been linked to you in some way—after she's gone missing? We know about the anonymous tip, Alexis. You left fingerprints all over the pay phone."

"I'm telling you," I said. "I'm trying to save them!"

"And *I'm* telling you—there is no ghost." She sat back and gave me a coolly appraising glance. "So maybe what you've been trying to save them from is yourself."

I got transferred to the blue ward, which meant the pajamas were blue instead of sickly pink. But there were other differences: one patient per room. Two nurses' stations instead of one. Twice as many orderlies. And we didn't get trays when we ate—we got paper plates.

I was falling down the rabbit hole of risk assessment. What came after blue, I wondered. Green? Yellow? And what was the final level? What color pajamas did you get when your room consisted of four padded walls and a mattress? When your days were spent in total isolation?

Gray, I thought. *Then Lydia and I can both be in the gray void.*

I could end up staying at Harmony Valley forever, locked away in some inner level, never coming into contact with the outside world. Some people really did live like that—the dangerous ones. The killers.

And as I sat and stared at the soap opera playing on TV (in the blue ward, the remote was kept at the nurses' desk), I realized—why shouldn't I? Why shouldn't I be locked away, kept isolated from the world and the outdoors and other people?

Just say Jared was right, and Laina wanted us to be together forever. Say she was attacking girls who tried to keep us apart. If I were stashed in some basement bunker, no more girls *could* try to keep us apart. So Laina would be happy. And Jared would be happy.

And I would be . . . safe. Safe from being the reason other people got hurt.

Suddenly it didn't sound so awful. I mean, it sounded *awful*, but it sounded like the kind of awful I could learn to live with. Not nearly as bad as standing back and watching innocent girls die.

Now all I had to do was convince Agent Hasan to

sink me deeper into the belly of Harmony Valley. And somehow I didn't think that would be too hard to do.

"Alexis?" One of the nurses beckoned me over to the desk. She handed me a letter in an open envelope. "This was dropped off for you. We didn't read it—we just had to check to make sure there weren't any unauthorized items inside."

I nodded and sat down, opening the letter.

It was from Jared.

Dear Alexis,

I know you'll understand someday.

Until then, I'll keep loving you, and only you.

And Laina will make sure no one comes between us.

Yours always,

J.

The nurses were used to my cooperation by now. So my night nurse didn't notice when I tucked my four pills under my tongue and kept them there instead of swallowing. As soon as she was gone, I spat them out and tucked them under the side of my mattress.

No more twilight haze for me. I needed to be alert—so I could say the exact right things to Agent Hasan.

I tossed and turned all night, my body yearning for

the forced relaxation of the medication. At one point I almost reached under the mattress for one of the pills.

But I resisted.

The next morning I was wide awake—wired, even. I jittered through breakfast and hurried to the nurses' station to request a meeting with Agent Hasan.

I'd made up my mind—I was going to tell her that she needed to find a way for me to stay at Harmony Valley forever.

The nurse was on the phone, a deep frown on her face. She lifted her finger in a "just a sec" gesture. "Yes. Well, she's actually right here—"

Who, me? I stared at her. I was the only patient near the desk.

Suddenly, the game show playing on the TV behind me was interrupted by a volley of trumpet music.

Feeling like I was moving in slow motion, I turned around and watched the BREAKING NEWS banner come on-screen.

"Yet another Surrey teen is missing in what police are now calling the most bizarre series of deaths on record in Dennison County. According to the chief of police, the Federal Bureau of Investigation is prepared to get involved."

How could I be so stupid?

Even if *I* was locked up . . . *Laina* wasn't.

There were plenty of ways for girls to try to come between Jared and me—whether I was there or not.

And then two pieces of information stood out like framed photographs in my mind:

One, that Kasey had gone to talk to Jared.

Two, that she'd told him we weren't meant to be together.

So I didn't even have to wait for the picture to come up on the screen.

I knew Laina had taken my sister.

I SAT ON MY BED. LOCKED IN MY ROOM.

Which is what they do to you, I guess, if you start yelling about needing to talk to a woman whose name isn't even on record with the hospital. Especially if the name is "Agent Hasan." That really plays into the paranoid-delusional-conspiracy-theory reputation you've got going.

I'd only stopped yelling when they'd threatened to sedate me.

If I let that happen, Kasey's odds of surviving went from slim to less than none. So I would behave. Even if it meant I was exploding inside.

My sister was in mortal danger. And I was beyond stuck.

I would fight Laina. I would fight her with every last hint of life in my body if I could save my sister. But that was impossible. I couldn't even *get* to her.

Despite trying to hold myself together, I collapsed into jags of gasping sobs every few minutes.

There was no way out of Harmony Valley.

I fell sideways onto the bed and grabbed the corner of the pillow in my fist, twisting it tightly in my hand, my body shaking from the effort of not completely losing control of myself.

If only I had an ally. If only I hadn't forced Lydia to try to stop Laina when she knew she couldn't. Now she was in the gray void and I was completely alone.

"Lydia," I whispered. "I'm sorry . . . I didn't mean to kill you again."

"What? Of course you didn't, stupid."

I sat up.

Lydia was sitting on my dresser. "Sorry I haven't been around. I had something to take care of. I see your life's going awesomesauce in the meantime."

"Lydia—"

She raised her eyebrows. "Careful, Alexis, or I might think you're glad to see me."

I jumped off the bed and ran over to her, throwing my arms around her in a hug. I could actually feel her cold body in my arms, feel her hand awkwardly patting my head as I sputtered out apologies. The closer we got, the more solid she became to me. And maybe that went both ways.

"Shh," she said. "Calm down. I'm fine. I just needed a little R and R."

I took a step back, drinking in the sight of her—a familiar face.

A friend.

"She got Kasey," I said.

Lydia frowned. "I know."

"I have to save her," I said. "But I don't know how to get out of here."

"And that's why today is your lucky day," Lydia said. "Because I do."

Lydia—using memorization techniques from her years in the drama club—had learned the electronic access codes to all of the doors that led from the blue ward to the service exit on the side of the building. She could rattle off long strings of numbers to the tunes of songs from *The Wizard of Oz*.

So all I had to do was get myself to the doors and through them when no one was looking. Which was actually easier on the blue ward than it would have been on the pink ward. There was so much more security here, the nurses were almost complacent.

Plus, Lydia also knew the code to the supply closet, so I could change out of my blue pajamas into a pair of dark gray orderly scrubs. I snagged a pair during the confusion of a fistfight in the rec room and hid them under my mattress. There was the question of my white hair—but a lot of the orderlies wore scarves on their heads that matched the color of the ward they worked on. So I ripped a square from one of my blue pajama shirts and fashioned it into a little headkerchief.

But getting out was just the first part of my problem. I needed a ride back to Surrey. And even if there had been a steady stream of taxis or buses passing the mental hospital, I seriously doubted that any of them would pick up a random girl hanging out on the side of the road.

After lunch, I sat on the bed, twiddling my thumbs to expel my nervous energy. Lydia showed up, looking highly pleased with herself.

"The girl in 8A has a phone," she said. "It's in her bottom drawer, behind the clothes."

So I waited until the call for afternoon therapy (which I didn't have, since Agent Hasan's long-term plans apparently included letting me die of boredom), and I sneaked into room 8A and dug through the girl's drawer until I found the forbidden cell phone.

The first person I called was Megan. But there was no answer. I didn't leave a message—I didn't want her to have to deny anything if the police came to ask her whether we'd talked.

I sat staring down at the keypad, knowing there was one more number I could try.

But what if he didn't want anything to do with me?

What if he was just disgusted that I'd gotten myself into trouble again?

And then I remembered how he'd said *If you need anything—*

If I'd ever needed anything, it was now.

So I held my breath and dialed. And he picked up with an unsure, "Hello?"

"Carter?" I whispered.

There was a pause. I was afraid he was going to hang up on me. *"Lex?"*

"Yeah, it's me."

"Your sister—"

"I know, I saw it on the news."

"Where *are* you? I've been so worried—"

I took a deep breath. "I'm at Harmony Valley. And I need your help."

My skin prickled continuously through dinner. I couldn't stop thinking, *Is he on his way? Is he really coming?* Maybe he'd called my parents the second we got off the phone. Maybe he'd just lied to keep me from freaking out.

No. I couldn't believe that about Carter. I had to believe that he would keep his promise.

So after dinner I wandered back into my room and grabbed the orderly uniform, stuffing it into my waistband and then strolling back through the hallway, hoping nobody would notice my bulging midsection. At exactly 7:25 p.m., I slipped into the seldom-used bathroom on the far side of the rec room and changed, dumping my blue pajamas into the trash and tying the kerchief around my head. I waited until 7:30, when every single person on the ward sat down to shout at *Jeopardy!*, then I slipped out of the room and walked along the back wall toward the door.

Lydia recited the code. I typed it in.

And it worked. I was through.

Getting to the second door was easy because the hall was empty. Lydia called out that code, and I put it in.

Through.

"One left," she said. "Easy-peasy."

But this one wasn't so easy-peasy. I would have to pass the security desk, where a wizened old guard kept his eyes on everyone who passed. I hung back and watched him talk to people, questioning them. He knew everyone by sight.

"It's not going to work," I said through my teeth, as Lydia stood by and watched him.

"It will. Just be ready to move on my cue."

She walked down the hall and through the counter that he sat behind. A second later, I heard a deafening *CRASH!*

"Now, Alexis!" Lydia called. "Go!"

Careful not to look like I was rushing, I strolled down the hall, past the desk. I glanced up from the corner of my eye to see that one of the shelves on the wall behind the man had totally collapsed, spilling office supplies, files, a coffeemaker, and other accumulated clutter all over the room. The guard's back was toward me. He didn't even look up as I passed.

As I reached the exit, Lydia caught up with me and recited the final code. When the little light on the keypad flashed green, I turned the handle and pushed the door open, feeling the rush of cool winter air on my face.

"Hey, wait!"

I froze.

"Stay cool," Lydia whispered.

"Hold the door!"

I turned to see a guy in a pair of jeans and a blue polo shirt that read KATZ FOOD SERVICE hurrying toward me, carrying a box under each arm.

I held the door, and he gave me a smile as he walked through. "Thanks."

"No problem," I said.

The door closed behind us.

I was out.

I sat on a bench and leaned back, trying to look like any other employee just getting off work. It was dark outside, so the security cameras wouldn't show my face.

"It worked," Lydia said. "I can't believe it actually worked."

"I can't believe you're back," I said. "I seriously missed you, Lyd."

She turned away, but I could see the hint of a goofy, pleased smile on her face. "Stop it, Alexis. You're such a drama queen."

I kept my eyes peeled for Carter's Prius, not letting myself wonder if there was a chance he wouldn't show.

He did show. He pulled into the lot, drove right up to the bench, and paused long enough for me to jump into the car.

We sat there, both a little stunned.

I swallowed hard and looked at him. "Thank you."

This wasn't "Hey, since you're up, can you grab me a Coke?" This wasn't "Spot me twenty dollars?" This wasn't even "Can you feed my cat for three weeks while I'm backpacking through Switzerland?"

This was busting someone out of a mental health facility.

This was *major*.

Carter shrugged. "Anytime."

We pulled out onto the road without any trouble. Lydia sat in the backseat, her face pressed up against the glass.

"So," Carter said. "Any chance you want to tell me anything?"

"About what?" The words came out automatically. My standard fear response. Deny, deny, deny.

"About anything," he said. "Or not."

"Um," I said.

"It's okay. You called me. That's enough. All I wanted, Lex . . ." He cleared his throat. "All I ever wanted was for you to call me when you needed help."

Elliot's words played in my head like an audio recording. *People have to earn your trust.*

I stared at Carter's profile as he watched the road.

And I thought:

You came when I called you.

You came without knowing why you had to come.

You said you'd always be there when I need you, and you meant it.

"It's a ghost," I said. "It's another ghost."

I told him everything, start to finish. I was getting used to saying the words now, and I found that things I'd stumbled on when I was talking to Megan and Kasey came out easily. No matter what Agent Hasan said, I couldn't blame myself for this. I couldn't present the situation as if it were my fault. I could have moments of weakness, I could even invite trouble for myself, but that wasn't what I'd done this time.

I didn't do anything wrong.

I was only trying to help.

Carter listened, not as shocked as I would have expected him to be. But then I realized—he, like me, and Megan, and my sister, had been through this twice already. He believed in ghosts and he knew how dangerous they could be.

"So, it's chasing other girls away from you," he said.

"Away from me and Jared."

"And it's punishing them if they try to come between you."

"Yeah."

"But why is it attacking you?"

"I don't know," I said. "I mean, it's not *just* attacking me. It's kind of obsessed with me. It comes to my house and sleeps in my bedroom."

"Jared thinks she's trying to get you guys to be soul mates?" He couldn't hide the distaste in his voice.

"Yeah."

"Then maybe . . . what if she's not really attacking you?" he asked. "What if she's trying to get you closer to him?"

I sat back.

The day at the nature preserve, when my car had spun out of control—

It hadn't spun randomly. It started by trying to turn left instead of right.

Because Jared had turned left?

And on New Year's Eve, when Laina came after me in the field . . . it had driven me right into Jared's arms.

I tried to remember all the other times she'd shown up.

There was the night we quarreled in the car after Ashleen's party. And the night Jared found out I was taking yearbook pictures—with Carter. It was like she was showing up to bully me, or punish me. . . .

And those long stretches of time when there was no sign of Laina . . .

They were stretches when things were going well between Jared and me.

"I think you're right," I said. "She's not trying to kill me. She's just trying to get me to go to him."

Now that Jared was on board with that plan, what hope did I have?

Halfway into town, Carter glanced at his gas gauge. "Sorry, I need to stop and get gas. You can stay in the car. Want anything from inside?"

"No," I said. "But I have to pee."

He parked and started the gas pumping while I went around to the back of the building. The light was on and the door was shut, so I couldn't tell if the bathroom was in use or not. I took a step back and looked around. The property butted up against a densely wooded area.

And then, through the trees—

I saw a flash of bright light.

Laina?

Did that mean my sister was out there?

"Kasey?" I called.

The light was deep within the woods, but I could see it moving through the trees.

I glanced back at the car. Carter had gone inside. If I stopped to tell him where I was going, I might lose sight of the light.

"What are you doing?" Lydia asked, appearing next to me.

"I see her," I said. "I see Laina."

Lydia stared into the woods. "You really think your sister is here, of all places? What are the odds of that?"

It didn't matter what the odds were. "What am I going to do, Lyd, not go?"

I tore across the grass and into the trees, trying to follow the light. After I'd gone a hundred feet or so, it faded from my view—or got so far ahead that I couldn't see it.

I paused, panting, and looked around.

"Call Carter," Lydia said. "He'll come help you look."

Right. I still had 8A's cell phone in my pocket. I reached down to grab it.

But I didn't get the chance.

The ball of white light came at me like a tiger lunging at its prey, and everything went white.

And then it went black.

32

KEEP GOING.

The words faded into my consciousness like the first glow of a sunrise.

I heard crunching, and it took a moment for me to identify the sound: footsteps. Feet walking on leaves.

My feet?

I tried to open my eyes, but they were weighed down by an all-consuming heaviness. My lungs, too, seemed leaden and reluctant. I heard ragged breathing—my breathing?—and felt a tearing pain in my chest.

If I concentrated, I could seek out the awareness of my feet, feel the texture of the forest floor beneath them. But my concentration was slippery—as quickly as I found it, the awareness slid out of my grasp as if it had been nothing more than a shadow.

Run! It was an order, and my body was obeying.

The footsteps came faster and faster, and then suddenly I seemed to be floating. There was a stunning impact, a moment of uncertainty.

I opened my eyes.

I was lying on the ground, surrounded by trees.

When I tried to put weight on my wrists to push myself up, a blazing pain shot through both of them. But it faded after a moment, and I pressed up off the ground and sat on my heels.

Keep moving.

My thoughts came like a thick, dark liquid slowly pouring out of a bottle. As soon as enough of them had lined up back to back to back in my head, I realized that something was very wrong.

My hands, feeling detached from my body, plucked at the silky layers of purple fabric on my body.

The dress. I was wearing it.

I must be dreaming.

I got to my feet, and suddenly my left hand was filled with a bouquet of yellow roses.

And I was walking. The trunks of trees passed by me, each one leaving a series of vertical echoes imprinted on my vision.

Where am I going?

I hated it—this helpless wandering, this sense of dread, of looking for someone, endlessly searching.

Was I running from someone?

From Laina?

No, no, it was the other way around—I was looking for someone. . . .

For Jared.

I have to find him.

It was wrong, but I couldn't make myself stop. I had to keep searching for him. And the only way to search was by walking.

So I walked.

The night sky sank into a deep indigo. The air cooled around me.

And I kept walking.

Gradually I grew thirsty. Surely I could stop somewhere, rest, soothe my parched throat.

No. Don't stop.

I didn't stop.

More time passed—how long? An hour? Two hours? My legs burned. I couldn't even feel my toes anymore. My feet were numb from the cold and from the constant pricking of pine needles.

"Please," I said. "I'm so tired. I need water."

I couldn't stop, though.

It wasn't that I tried and failed—it was that I didn't even know how to try. Some force was pushing me onward, farther into the deep, cold night.

Worst. Dream. Ever.

After maybe an hour of unanswered pleading and babbling, I decided to save my voice and my cracking throat. My thoughts drifted away while my body drifted ever forward.

My feet caught on something and I stumbled, reaching out to catch myself. My right hand grazed a tree before I got my balance again, and I lifted a stinging knuckle to my mouth and tasted blood.

"Five minutes," I croaked into the night. "Please. Just let me stop for five minutes."

Don't stop.

And that was when it became clear to me—as clear as anything could be in my foggy mind:

This was no dream.

I was walking. I was searching for someone who was twenty miles away. I wasn't going to find him, and I wasn't going to stop—Laina wasn't going to let me stop—

Until I fell down and died.

I don't know how much later it was—long enough that I got a cramp in my side and an intense radiating pain in my hip. I ignored them, though, because I had to. I had no choice.

"Alexis!"

I ignored the sound of my name the way I ignored the pain in my abdomen.

"Can you hear me?"

Yes.

"Stop! Stop walking! Listen to me!"

Something came between me and the haze. I walked toward it, unable to stop, and ended up walking right through it. My cold body got even colder.

"*Ow!* Stop! Stop moving right now!"

I didn't hear the rest. I was already gone.

Another hour passed—or two? Maybe even three.

The moon was arcing gently across the sky. My hands were puffy; the skin felt so dry I thought it might peel off. My fingers were fat little sausages, and when they touched each other or the skirt of my dress, they burned, like the flesh was being chafed right off of them.

I would have cried, but my body was so dried out there were no tears left to cry.

Please let me wake up.

Please let me wake up.

Please let me wake up.

But I knew I wasn't asleep.

33

SOMETHING STUNG MY ARM. Not that a whole nest of wasps could have stopped me.

I slowed for a moment to dry heave into the roots of a tree, but as soon as I was done, I stood up and started walking again.

Another sting on my arm. Then on my neck. And my face.

Then I realized what the stinging was—

Rain.

Water.

I tried to open my mouth and catch some on my tongue, but my head lolled on my neck, and my tongue felt almost too swollen to get through my lips.

"Stop!" yelled a voice. The same voice as before.

Lydia.

"Stop it right now, Alexis! I mean it—stop walking! Are you trying to *die* out here?"

But I didn't stop—I couldn't.

I was looking for Jared, like Laina had. Except she hadn't found him in time.

And neither would I.

But Lydia seemed determined not to let that happen.

"Look at me!" she shrieked, right in my face. "Look at me!"

My eyes were open, I was sure of it. But I didn't see her. Everything was a dull gray haze.

"All right," she said. "Fine, Alexis. You leave me no choice!"

No choice. I knew all about that.

Something swept through me, like a stiff wind blowing by. I felt a whole-body chill.

It didn't stop me.

"All right," she said. "Here I come again."

Another whoosh went into and out of my body, like air was being propelled through my skin. I got even colder.

"Fourth time's the charm, right?" She was panting with effort.

If I could control my mouth, I would have told her, *This is pointless. You might as well go away. It's never going to work.*

But then the oddest thing happened.

Instead of walking, I was lying on my back. And my eyelids felt as light as helium balloons.

I stared up into the clearest night I'd ever seen.

Lydia stood over me, looking down. She was much fainter than usual—though not as pale as she had been after the encounter with Elliot. Her ghostly gray skin was extra gray, and she looked exhausted. "Are you . . . are you dead?"

"I don't know." I could feel the dry skin in my throat cracking as I spoke. "Am I?"

She sank to the ground next to me. "No, I guess not."

"Are you?" I asked.

"Well, yeah—but not how you mean."

"I'm so tired," I said, starting to let my eyes slide shut again.

"No!" she said. "You can't go to sleep. Don't even think about it."

So I looked up at her instead.

Her black eyes burned down at me. "You have a cell phone in your pocket. It's off. Can you reach down and turn it on?"

"Not a chance." The words floated out of my mouth, piggybacking on a shallow exhalation.

"Try."

I moved my almost lifeless arm, a millimeter at a time, toward my pocket.

I found the phone, and my fingers crawled over the

keys, looking for the power button. A second later, the little chime sounded. It filled the air around us like a symphony.

"Now call someone," Lydia said. "Call nine-one-one."

No. If I called them, I'd be in the hospital for days, and I couldn't let that happen. I had something I needed to do.

My finger reached for the keypad, and I found the little groove on the number five, then dialed with my fingers, by touch.

I listened through the night for the ringing. It didn't come.

Lydia leaned over to look at the phone. "Frack. No signal. You have to walk."

A dry laugh, almost a snort, burbled out of me.

"I'm serious," she said. "You have to get up and walk."

"Yeah, no," I said.

"Are you forgetting about Kasey?" she asked. "About your sister?"

I blinked.

Kasey was in danger.

Minutes later, I was somehow on my feet, stumbling through the woods behind Lydia, who ducked and scampered around like a wood sprite, checking the path ahead to be sure it was clear.

I don't know how long I walked before she said,

"Here! Over here! There's a road! Mile marker eighty-seven!"

I got to a point where I could see the break in the trees and sank down, my back against a thick trunk.

I closed my eyes.

"No, Alexis," Lydia said, waving her hand in my face. "Are you kidding me? No, no, no. Uh-uh. You're not going to die *now*. Dial. Call Carter. Right now."

I turned my head to escape her fingers. "I can't. I'm too tired."

"You will," she said. "You're going to do it for your sister."

I lifted the phone and typed in a number.

Then I sent a text message:

vaughn hwy mile 87

The effort drained the last of my energy. The phone plunged out of my hand.

"Nope," Lydia said. "No sleeping. Wake up."

I sighed and closed my eyes.

"You *have* to wake up. I mean, think about it . . . if you die, I totally win."

I lifted one eyelid to look at her.

She nodded smugly. "Yeah. Think about what a jerk I am. Think about how I almost sacrificed all of you guys for Aralt. Think about—"

"No," I whispered. "That wasn't your fault."

"Of course it was."

"No," I said, fighting to keep my eyes open. My lashes kept slipping down like a broken curtain in a theater. "And . . . I'm sorry I let you die."

"*Let* me die?" Lydia sat back and looked at me in disbelief. "Um, if I recall correctly, I was completely kicking your ass. You tried to stop me." She looked out into the distance. "Alexis, I don't blame you. I never really did. I was just mad. Mostly . . . at myself, I think."

She ripped a handful of grass out of the ground and threw it in frustration. "I am. I'm mad at myself. What a waste of a life. What a waste of a death."

"No," I said.

"Yes," she said, turning to me. "And *that's* why you're not dying tonight. You're going to rest and drink some electrolytes or something, and not die. Because I'm not watching someone else die for no reason. It's stupid. It's the stupidest thing in the world."

Already, my head was starting to clear. My body was still exhausted, but I wanted to live. She was right. I had to stop Laina and save my sister.

But there was something I needed to say.

"Lydia," I said, "the reason you feel like you need to protect me is because . . . every ghost has a power center. And I'm yours. I thought you should know."

"What?" She sat back, eyes wide. "I beg your pardon?"

"I want you to have a choice," I said. "Or at least know why you're doing this. It wasn't fair—what I made you do . . . with Elliot."

"Oh my God," she said. "I cannot *believe* you, Alexis."

I thought she was horrified by my confession, horrified by the fact that I'd kept this information secret. I expected her to get up and leave.

"Do you think the whole universe revolves around *you?*" She pursed her lips and stuck her nose in the air. "You are not my power whatever. And that is *not* why I'm doing this. Where do you think I've been for the past week? I was trying to keep my parents from throwing away the mix CD my dad made for me when I was five. Do you know how many phone books I had to flip open, how many internet searches I had to type, letter by letter, before they took the hint and made this . . . sort of lame . . . little display? So get off your ginormous high horse. You are not my power thingy."

All this time. All of the effort. The way she'd swallowed her pride and started working with me . . .

"Is it really so hard to believe that I'm helping you because I *want* to?"

I stared at her, and she sighed.

"Okay, yeah, you're right. It sounds hard to believe. But . . . I don't know what to say. I wanted to help you. I'm sorry."

"Lydia," I said, an impossible thought dawning in my mind, "you're just a good ghost."

She reared back in disbelief. "Ha!"

"No, I mean it. Most ghosts are bad, but some are good . . . like angels."

Her eyes went wide for a moment, then her expression relaxed. "If I'm an angel . . ." She looked up at the trees. "Does that mean that when I've filled my purpose—like, something I'm destined to do—I'll go somewhere? Somewhere that's *not* the transitional plane?"

"I don't know," I said. "Is that what you want?"

"I'm not sure," she said, hugging her knees to her chest.

"Well, then, maybe . . ." I thought of Megan's mother, Shara. Her ghost had disappeared after helping us. I felt a sudden twinge of dread and realized, to my utter shock, that I didn't want Lydia to go anywhere.

She started speaking, like she was confessing. "Did you know my mom has a cat now? He's like a zillion years old. I used to see him in the neighborhood—he was all skinny and weird-looking. He's still weird-looking, but she let him in the house and he follows her around and he's, like, pleasingly plump now. He totally worships her. And she . . ." Lydia's voice broke. "She calls him Lydia. She talks to him like he was me. And he just sits there and listens, and . . . there are so many things she

387

never said to me, Alexis. But she says them to the cat, and she tells him to tell me when he sees me. And I swear, he listens to every word she says."

"I'm so sorry, Lydia," I said.

"No, you don't understand." She turned to me, blinking back ghostly tears. Her face practically shimmered in the moonlight. "That's a happy story. My mom's going to be okay. And that means my purpose isn't helping her. Maybe it's helping *you*."

Headlights. An engine cutting off. Footsteps.

"*Alexis!?*" The footsteps broke into a run. "Alexis, where are you?"

"Over here! We're over here!" Lydia yelled, before remembering that people couldn't actually hear her. She gave me a nudge.

"Here!" I called. "I'm here!"

In the distance, the footsteps hesitated and then started again, heading toward us.

Carter's face appeared between the trees.

"Alexis!" he cried. "Are you all right?"

"I need water." My throat burned.

"What happened? I waited for you for twenty minutes and then I realized—" He took off his jacket and wrapped it around me. Then he lifted me off the ground and started walking.

* * *

As we approached the road, I heard another voice. For a moment I thought someone from Harmony Valley was after us.

A person came crashing through the woods toward us. "You found her?"

"Is that Megan?" I asked.

Carter paused for her to catch up with us. Megan gently tucked a strand of hair behind my ear and stared into my eyes. "What happened? Is she—"

"She's okay. Let's get her in the car," Carter said.

"I'm riding with you guys," Megan said. "I'll just leave my car."

He drove, and Megan sat in the backseat with me. We stopped at a convenience store and Carter went inside. I could feel Megan's eyes on me like a mother lion watching her cub.

"Kasey," I whispered.

"I know," she said. "We were all out looking for her when Carter called me."

"It's too late," I said. Tears sprang to my eyes. "There's no way . . ."

"There is a way," she said. "There's a chance. The ghost was with you for a long time tonight, right? Like, hours?"

"Yeah."

"Well, I don't know exactly what's going on," she said, "but I have some ideas. And one of them is that this ghost can't be in two places at once. Which means that when it was with you, Kasey may have had a chance to stop and rest . . . or find water. Or even get help."

"How do you know that?" I asked. "I mean, what makes you think that?"

"It's based on what Kasey told me. She came to see me. She wanted to prove that you were innocent."

Carter came back with a bottle of Gatorade and two bottles of water. I chugged the Gatorade, then promptly leaned out the window and threw it all up. So I sipped the water instead.

He turned to look at me. "Are you sure you don't want to go to the hospital?"

"I'm sure," I said. "I just need to drink more. Maybe eat. And then I need to find my sister."

I glanced at the clock and gasped.

It was 4:45 in the morning. We'd lost a whole night.

No way was I stopping until Kasey was found.

"Did you tell my parents I was missing?" I asked, hoping he hadn't. I didn't want them distracted from their search.

"No," Carter said. "But they knew you left Harmony Valley. They called to ask if I'd heard from you—"

"Me too," Megan said.

"And I said I hadn't. Maybe I should have told them, but—I know you don't want to go back there."

I nodded, then took another sip and closed my eyes—but this wasn't going-to-sleep-forever eye closing. I was just resting.

"What happened to you—it's what happened to those other girls, isn't it?" Megan asked. "Only they never woke up. How did you wake up, by the way?"

"Lydia," I said. "Lydia's a ghost. She helped me."

There was silence.

"Lydia's a *good* ghost?" Megan asked dubiously.

"One of the best," I said. "Believe it or not."

"Not *quite*," Megan mused.

"Hey!" Lydia said, popping into view in the front seat.

"So what now?" Megan asked.

"We find my sister," I said. And I didn't care if I had to knock Kasey unconscious or break her kneecaps or tie her to a tree.

Laina wasn't going to take her away from me.

34

As WE DROVE, Megan's phone rang. She glanced down at it and looked at me. "It's Savannah."

"Savannah?" I asked. Levitating-tarot-card-charm-book Savannah?

Megan shrugged. "I needed help. So I told her everything. She's really smart. Kinda nuts, but . . . hello, Van? . . . Hmm . . . I don't know. She's right here; I'll put her on."

She handed me the phone.

"Hello?"

Savannah was as chipper as a chipmunk. "Hi, Alexis! Long time no talk! How are you?"

"Worried," I said.

"Okay, down to business." I heard her flipping the pages of a book. "The girl ghost isn't wearing the clothes she died in?"

"No," I said. "She couldn't be. Nobody hikes in a fancy dress."

"Was it, by any chance"—more page flipping—"the dress she was *buried* in?"

I blinked. "That seems really likely. Is that common for ghosts?"

"Nope, not at all." She was quiet for a second. "So, when she moves in your pictures, that's not common for the ghosts you see?"

"No," I said.

"Right," she said, more to herself than me. "Very kinetic."

"Kinetic? Is that bad?"

"Just weird," she said. "Undead energy is usually passive. That's why most ghosts wait until you find them before they start messing with you."

The way Sarah had left my sister alone until she'd found the haunted doll.

"But this thing is lashing out, right?" Savannah said.

"Yeah," I said. "It's really aggressive."

"And it's fixated on you?"

"Yeah."

"And the first time you ever noticed it, was that tied to any really charged emotional event?"

I thought back to the nature preserve. Jared and I ran into Kendra. . . . But before that, I had the episode with the little boy ghost. And then—

"We kissed," I said, avoiding Carter's glance in the rearview mirror. "Jared and I accidentally kissed."

"Huh," Savannah said. "That could do it."

"And the flowers," I said. "It's weird that she's holding flowers. Ghosts don't usually do that. Although there's this other one across town with the same thing— aggressive, bright light, moves in pictures . . . and he's holding a trophy that his brother broke."

"So the flowers could be important."

"No, I'm pretty sure I know what her power center is," I said.

"You know about power centers? So you've read Sawamura?"

"Yes," I said. "I think . . . it's Jared."

"Ha," Savannah said. "Typical. I mean, sorry, but I doubt it. Do you know how rare that is? Like, point zero-zero-three percent of power centers are living beings. Yet somehow, every amateur ghost hunter wants to think they're the exception to the rule. Further evidence of our human-centricness."

Finally, I thought. Some good news. If Laina's power center were just some object, then I would have no problem destroying it. Heck, I'd burn down her whole house if that would do the trick.

"Keep thinking," Savannah said. "I'll call you back."

And she hung up.

Megan was watching me. "Smart, huh?"

"Scary smart," I said. "I'll have to apologize for stealing her book."

"Don't worry." Megan shook her head. "She's got tons."

We were closing in on Surrey.

"So where would Kasey go?" Megan asked. "If the other girls went to places they were familiar with . . . where does Kasey hike?"

"She's not much of a hiker," I said. "I guess . . . she likes . . ."

My stomach seemed to free-fall.

"What?" Carter asked.

"She likes the waterfall," I said. "The little one at the middle of Stewart Canyon."

"Stewart Canyon," Megan repeated, frowning. "That's where Laina died."

Carter made the turn on the highway that led east of town.

The problem was, how could I hike? I hardly had enough strength to stand.

"I'll go," Carter said, as if he'd read my mind. "I know you can't. I'll go up the trail and find her."

"I'll go with him," Lydia said. "I can float."

"Thank you, Carter," I said. "But I can't *not* go with you."

"You need to find the power center for this ghost, right?" he said. "You and Megan take my car and go find it. Go to that girl's house, wherever. Find it and get rid of it."

And leave him out there in the wilderness with Laina, to fight her alone?

But what choice did I have? Besides—if Laina got the idea that her power center was in danger, she might leave Kasey and Carter alone and come after us.

"Lydia's going to go with you," I said. "If you need her help, just ask her, and she'll do what she can, okay?"

"Sure," Carter said. He sped into the parking lot and stopped the car.

"I mean it," I said. "She's really great."

"Aw, shut up," Lydia said.

I got out to go around to the driver's seat.

Carter and I practically ran into each other at the front of the car. He pulled me into a hug.

"You're shaking," he whispered.

"Carter," I said. "Please be careful."

"I'm not scared, Lex. We're going to save your sister."

He turned and started for the path.

"Wait—" I said.

He turned back.

I rushed forward and grabbed him by his arms. "Thank you."

It wasn't what I'd wanted to say—but the words I wanted to say seemed impossible. There had never been a worse time.

"Lex," he said.

I stared up at him. His blue eyes locked onto mine. And we kissed.

It was a fast kiss, an efficient one. But it felt like rain on the desert.

He pulled back first. "I love you, Lex. Whatever happens, don't forget that."

I had to catch my breath. "I love you too."

"I'm going now."

"Okay—be safe!"

"I will!" he called, jogging away toward the path.

Lydia passed me as I walked toward the open car door.

"Don't try to kiss *me*," she said. "See you later."

Megan didn't say a word about the kiss. She was looking for Laina's address.

"There's a Tim Buchanan on Albright Street . . ." she said. "And . . . yeah, Tim's the name of the dad in the obituary."

"How do we get to Albright?" I asked, swinging out of the parking lot.

"Go left. The turn's in four miles."

Megan's phone rang again.

"It's Savannah. Hello? You're on speaker."

I knew immediately that something was up.

"You guys, this is crazy," Savannah said. She was about to burst. "It's crazy."

Megan and I exchanged a wary glance. *Crazy* didn't sound ideal. I would much rather she be exclaiming about manageability.

"Your ghost?" Savannah said. "Is not a ghost."

35

"EXCUSE ME, WHAT?" MEGAN SAID.

I had the presence of mind to slow the car down and pull to the side of the road.

Your ghost is not a ghost.

Did that mean that I *was* responsible?

"It was the kiss," Savannah said. "And the football guy's trophy. So that got me thinking. If the dude's brother broke the trophy, it's not the *ghost* who's upset. Ghosts don't care as long as you don't mess with their power center. But that Corcoran guy didn't die your typical ghost death, right?"

"Right," I said. At least I could say that much with confidence.

"So who's traumatized? Who's the one who can't deal with the death?"

The one who can't deal with the death?

"Randy," I said. "His brother."

"Exactly," she said. "And who can't deal with Laina's death?"

399

I got dizzy and had to grab the steering wheel to keep from tipping over.

"Jared," Megan said.

"Exactly," Savannah said. "This thing that's out there attacking people? It's not Laina's ghost. It's a poltergeist. It was probably formed during what must have been one heck of a kiss, when Jared was suddenly overwhelmed by this tornado of emotions."

I sat back and rested my head against the seat.

It *had* been a heck of a kiss.

"So he's controlling it?" Megan asked.

"No. Probably not. He probably formed it and released it. Like when water boils over in a pot, you know? He had all this trauma and he couldn't deal with it. So it boiled over and became this chaotic, manic energy. I mean, it's still tied to him on some level—but not on a conscious level."

"So it's a free agent?" I said. "It's just acting randomly?"

"Not necessarily. I mean, think about the football guy. He hates high school kids, right? Because the brother who lived hated his high school classmates. So when this energy came into being, it probably played off of what Jared wanted in that moment, which was . . ."

I looked up at Megan. I could hardly breathe.

"A soul mate," I said.

Savannah sighed. "And that would be *you*, my friend."

Poltergeists, it turns out, don't have power centers.

Poltergeists have *sources*.

As Savannah put it: "Say you have a faucet in your kitchen. Water's coming out of it. You don't want any more water, so you turn off the faucet."

"So we have to get Jared to turn off the poltergeist?" Megan said.

"That's one method," Savannah said. "Unfortunately, this guy sounds cuckoo for Cocoa Puffs and I think you're going to have trouble convincing him that this thing is just his loneliness and guilt manifested."

"True," I said. "He believes it's Laina. He's *glad* it's Laina. He's not going to be turning off any faucets."

"So is there an alternative?" Megan asked.

"Sure," Savannah said. "If you can't turn the faucet off, just . . . blow up the kitchen."

Megan glanced at me. "As in . . ."

Savannah took a deep breath. "What I'm getting at is that Jared would have to die."

I'd gotten rid of ghosts. I'd seen death firsthand. But under no circumstances could I bring myself to kill a human. So I would just have to find a way to reason with

401

Jared and get him to change his mind about Laina. There was no answer on his cell phone, so I drove by his house. Megan and I rang the doorbell and waited.

It was five thirty in the morning—someone had to be home.

After a minute, the door opened and Mr. Elkins stood there in a bathrobe, scratching his head.

"Alexis?" he asked. "Jared told me you were . . . uh . . . out of town."

"Is he home?" I asked.

"No. He was working late on a project at a friend's house, so he just spent the night."

"Well, I think I left my mom's computer power cord here. Can I come look for it?"

He glanced at his watchless wrist.

"She has a seven thirty flight to Los Angeles," I said. "I told her it was too early to disturb you guys, but she insisted."

"Her mother's priorities are totally out of whack," Megan added.

Mr. Elkins waved us inside.

We went into Jared's bedroom and looked around.

"What are we looking for?" Megan said. "Don't you think we should focus on finding Jared?"

But I was staring at Jared's closet door. It was unlocked. I grabbed the handle and pulled it open.

And then I could only stare.

It was plastered with pictures of Laina, newspaper articles about her, photocopied pages from yearbooks . . . and beneath all that was a small table covered in framed photos and small votive candles.

Hanging above it, suspended from the clothes rod by a long lavender ribbon . . . was a bouquet of dried yellow roses.

"Oh my God," Megan whispered. "It's a shrine."

I leaned in to look at the framed pictures, feeling like the Jared I thought I knew had just died in front of my eyes.

They were photographs of Laina in her coffin. Her eyes were closed. She wore the purple dress. And in her hands was a small bouquet of yellow roses—the same one that hung inches away.

"The poltergeist wears the purple dress because that's how he remembers her," I said, "the last time he ever saw her."

Jared never cared about me. I was just a substitute, a warm body . . . a stand-in.

I set the first photo down and glanced over the rest of them. My gaze stopped on one in a shining crystal frame.

It looked like a copy of the one of Laina in her casket. I almost didn't look closer.

But then I did.

I got a nice long look at it.

The frame slipped out of my hands, hitting the wood floor and shattering.

"What?" Megan swooped over. "What is it?"

I knelt and carefully plucked the photo out from the pile of glass shards.

"That's . . ." Megan covered her mouth with her hands. "Alexis . . . that's . . ."

It was me.

Or rather, it was a picture of Laina's body—with my face. Jared had Photoshopped *my* face on to *her* body.

My eyes were closed, like I was asleep—or dead.

When had he taken pictures of me sleeping?

Then it hit me in a flash—the night I'd drunk the wine and passed out.

The wine . . .

Maybe if you take your wine with a shot of tranquilizers, the nurse at Harmony Valley had said.

And I knew—that was exactly what happened.

We thanked Mr. Elkins and left. He said he was going to go back to sleep. But as we pulled out of the driveway, I saw him on the phone, peering out the front window at us.

"Who's he calling?" Megan asked.

"Probably Agent Hasan," I said. "He thinks she's my therapist."

But I'd been locked up when Kasey went missing. So by now Agent Hasan would have to know I wasn't the one behind the attacks.

Still, she'd be looking for me.

"I don't have much time," I said. "They'll realize Carter came to get me, and they'll be looking for his car."

"Where would Jared be?" Megan asked. She'd taken over the driving, since I was getting a little woozy. "What friend's house?"

"I don't know," I said, and I realized that, even though Jared often talked about his friends, he'd never introduced me to a single one. Did they even exist?

"Call him again," she said. "Maybe his phone just didn't wake him up before."

Just as I raised the phone to dial, it rang.

"It's him," I said.

"Answer!" Megan said.

Suddenly, my mind went blank. What was I supposed to say? How did I explain what was going on?

Jared didn't just accept the idea that Laina was a ghost—he thought it was the best-case scenario. So how would he react when I told him she wasn't even real? And that it was *his* fault that girls were dying?

"Hello?" I said.

"So you stopped by my house and woke up my father. . . ."

"I need to talk to you."

"I'm not sure that's a good idea. I think you really belong back at Harmony Valley, Alexis. It's safer for you there."

His voice had an odd, paternal quality. Caring, but on the verge of outright ordering me around.

But I had to make him happy. He had to agree to see me.

"Maybe you're right," I said. "Can't we just talk about it?"

He sighed. "I don't understand what there is to talk about."

"Jared," I said, my voice breaking, "my sister is missing. And Laina came after me last night. She almost killed me."

There was a long pause.

"I'm sorry about your sister," he said. "But she really should have minded her own business."

I stared at the phone as if it were emitting poisonous gas.

Don't scream at him. If you scream at him, he'll hang up, and Kasey will die.

"Where are you?" I asked. "Please. Let's talk. Please."

"Fine. We can talk."

"Thank you," I said.

"Meet me in twenty minutes. At the overlook at the top of Stewart Canyon."

He hung up.

The overlook?

"Call Carter," Megan said.

I looked at her.

"Lex, I can't get to the overlook." Her face was white. "My knee—I can't climb up there. Call Carter and have him meet you."

I tried Carter's cell and got his voicemail immediately. "No signal," I said. "He's in the canyon."

"Then call the police," Megan said. "You can't go up there alone."

"What are the police going to do?" I asked. "He hasn't done anything wrong. I'm the runaway mental patient, remember?"

"But—they can at least keep him from hurting you."

"It doesn't matter," I said. "They can't stop Laina."

Megan had turned the car back in the direction of the canyon, but her hands tensed on the wheel.

"I have to talk to him," I said. "I have to get him to understand about Laina. And he'd never do that if anyone else was there. He's too stubborn. My only chance is to talk to him alone."

"I hate it," Megan said. "I hate this idea."

It wasn't my favorite idea, either.

But there were no other options.

"Will you wait here?" I asked.

Megan had parked on the side of the road. We had a few minutes to spare.

The lookout at Stewart Canyon wasn't an official part of the park. In fact, going there was highly discouraged because the trail was rough and steep and there were sections where a careless hiker could slide over the edge and fall a couple hundred feet.

But everyone still went there. It was especially big on summer nights, when groups of kids would meet there for parties. The police knew about it, but they hadn't done anything yet—because no one had gotten hurt there.

Yet.

"Yes, of course I'll wait," Megan said.

"All right. If I'm not back in . . ." I checked the time on my stolen phone. "Forty-five minutes, then you can go for help."

She winced. "Forty-five minutes is a really long time, Lex."

"It takes almost twenty minutes just to get up there and back," I said.

She leaned across the seat and hugged me. "I'm so sorry. If I'd just listened when you needed me—"

"Forget it," I said. "You were doing what you thought you had to do."

"No. That's an excuse," she said. "Not a reason. I was just afraid. I wanted to be safe . . . and keep everyone else safe."

"Keep everyone else safe from ghosts?" I wanted to tell her that no club in the world could manage that. There were too many ghosts. And too many unlucky people.

She looked confused. "No—safe from me."

"What?" I sat back and looked at her. "You were never a danger."

She shook her head. Her mouth was open like she was going to speak, but it took a while for the words to come out. "I lied to you—when you needed me. When you trusted me. And I tortured your little sister. I would have killed you, Lex. I can never trust myself again."

"Megan," I said. "Seriously? No one thinks you're responsible for that. You were *possessed*."

"But I remember doing it." She sniffled, holding back her tears. "I wanted to kill you."

"I tried to murder my whole *family*. In their *sleep*. With a *butcher knife*."

409

She made a confused noise. "It's different. That wasn't your fault."

"And what you did wasn't yours, so stop feeling bad about it," I said. "I've spent a lot of time with you, and I never once worried about my personal safety."

So that was why she was so desperate to be part of Brighter Path. She wasn't being self-righteous. . . . She was just scared that somebody else would get hurt and it would be her fault.

Now *that* I could relate to.

"I mean it," I said. "Stop feeling bad."

She gave a minute nod of her head, then glanced at the clock. "You should get going."

"Yeah," I said, opening the door.

"Lex," she said, as I was about to shut it.

I leaned down to look at her.

"If you don't come back safe . . ." She gave me a wry smile. "I'll kill you."

36

"WHAT I'M ABOUT TO SAY is probably going to be hard to believe," I said. "But if you'll listen to me, I think it makes sense."

I'd said it aloud five times, but I knew I could have repeated it to myself a thousand times and that wouldn't make it any easier to say to Jared's face.

I'd made it halfway up the trail, stopping every hundred feet or so to rest. The adrenaline that was keeping me going had begun to run out, and my legs felt like hunks of stone. Climbing was especially hard—some of the steps were three feet from the previous rock. Much better navigated by summer-energized kids than me.

Still, I knew I'd make it. There was no question in my mind that I would be able to climb to the top.

Finally, after dropping to my hands and knees and crawling up the sloping hill like a baby, I reached the wide plateau that looked over the crevasse of the canyon below. City officials had at least put a guardrail at the top, knowing that kids would come here and drink.

Jared was sitting on the guardrail, facing me.

The jagged folds of the rocky walls that bordered the trail were behind him, and beyond that, the small sprawl of Surrey. I could see the high school, where in less than an hour, hundreds of kids would gather for another normal day in their normal lives. I could see the building where Dad worked—the tallest one in town, soaring all of seven stories. The sun had hit its top floor and was reflecting bright orange light off the windows.

It had been a while since I'd been up here. The view was gorgeous. The almost-spring sky was fighting for color after the washed-out whiteness of winter. Interconnected wisps of pink-and-yellow clouds froze in long streaks overhead; the sky behind them was pale purple.

As I got closer, I could see that Jared looked rough. He hadn't shaved. His hair wasn't combed. And his light brown shirt had yellow stains under the armpits and was streaked with dirt.

"How long have you been up here?" I asked.

He gave me a long, distant look before he answered. "Since yesterday afternoon."

In spite of myself, I felt a twinge of protectiveness toward him. "Have you had food and water?"

"Do you think I'm an idiot, Alexis? I wouldn't come

412

up here without supplies." His eyes flickered with annoyance. "So you want to talk? Talk."

"It's about Laina," I said.

He was staring at the ground, and the left side of his lips almost turned up in a hint of a smile. "Do you know how much I wish that she was here with me . . . instead of you?"

"I'm sure you do," I said, trying to ignore the fact that he was basically saying he wished I were dead. "Jared, I've been thinking. And what you told me about her—how she was so peaceful when she . . . at the end . . . People who die that way don't become ghosts."

He looked up at me, confused.

"That's good news. Laina had everything she wanted when she died. She was at peace. She moved on. She went to a better place."

"Yeah. That's what I believed, too." He bent down and scooped up a handful of gravel and sand and chucked it off the side of the cliff. "Until you started talking to me about her."

"But I was wrong."

"Wrong? But you know what she looked like. You know about the dress."

"I saw something, Jared, yes—but what I saw wasn't Laina." I shifted uncomfortably on the curved metal railing. "This is probably going to be hard to believe . . . but if you hear me out, it makes sense."

He was listening, at least. I had his full attention.

So I ran through the basics of what Savannah had told me. How this spirit wasn't Laina at all, but a separate creature entirely. And it wasn't doing what Laina would have wanted—because it wasn't her.

And finally, how Jared held the power over it.

"You can make it go away. Because it . . ." I was afraid to say the next part. "Because it came from you."

He'd watched me intently the whole time I spoke. Now he gave a slow shake of his head.

"You're unbelievable," he said, standing and looking down at me. "I finally find a way to make it up to her—to show her how much I care about her, to give her what she really wants—and you're trying to make me think it's all in my head?"

"No, not in your head at all," I said. "It's real, but . . . you can control it. It happened because you love her so much—but it doesn't have to be this way. Or go this far."

"So I just shouldn't care so much?"

"It has nothing to do with how much you care," I said. "I know how much you love Laina. It's obvious."

His mouth twisted into an ugly frown, and he turned and walked a few feet away. With a violent kick, he scuffed his shoe across the surface of a rock.

Then he spun around.

"So what am I, then, a murderer?" He grabbed me by the shoulders, and I thought he was going to push me backward over the guardrail. Instinctively, I grasped his arms and pulled us both away from the edge.

We stood there, eye to eye.

"No," I said. "It's not your fault. But you're the only one who can make it stop."

He pushed me away, like my touch was too filthy to be borne, and I caught myself before I fell to the ground.

My temper flared, but I crushed it. Losing control would just make things worse. Jared would know. He would see. And he would get angrier.

"Laina wouldn't want this," I said. "You told me how amazing she was. She wouldn't want people to be getting hurt. And she wouldn't want you and me to have to be soul mates when we can't even get along for an hour at a time."

He sneered at me. "If you would grow up, that wouldn't be a problem."

Don't react, Alexis. "I know it's easier to believe that you're making her happy," I said. "But she would hate this, Jared. She would hate the fact that you're in so much pain."

His face crumpled, and he looked at me. I got a glimpse of him in the half second before he turned away, sobbing.

415

I felt like I'd just seen a kid realize he was lost in a crowded mall.

Jared wasn't evil . . . he was just broken. That was what we'd always had in common.

But I felt like I'd changed. Maybe because of Lydia. Or maybe it was Kasey, or Megan—or even Carter. Somehow, I'd gotten a little less broken. And for Jared's sake, I wanted him to heal, too. To be better.

I took a step toward him and rested my hand on his shoulder. "Jared, if you can let it go . . . If you can stop tormenting yourself with guilt and regret—"

"That means so much, coming from you," he said, jerking away from me. "You, the world's leading expert at getting over things, right? You can't even look your sister in the eye. You can't even stand up straight in a room full of people because you're so worried about what they think of you. I'm not saying I'm perfect, Alexis, but you've got a lot of nerve to tell *me* to get over something."

"I know I've had problems," I said, tears threatening to spill on to my cheeks. "I just don't want anyone else to die. And I truly do want you to be happy, Jared. But it's not going to be with me. Not ever."

I wiped at my eyes and turned away so he couldn't see me crying.

The sun had risen over the ridge to the east of town,

spilling pale light over the winding grids of the neighborhoods in the distance.

Jared's voice came at me from only a couple of feet away—closer than I'd expected, and much softer. "Then what about a compromise?"

His demeanor had changed. He was sweet, soft, understanding Jared again. And though I'd never be totally comfortable around him, I was disarmed.

"What kind of compromise?" I asked.

"The kind where we both get what we want."

I turned toward him and waited.

"You want Laina to stop hurting people. And honestly, Alexis, I want that too. I feel terrible that those girls have died. I don't want anything to happen to your sister."

Then forgive yourself, I wanted to say. *Let Laina go.*

"And I want . . . I want to know that she's happy, wherever she is. That she's at rest. Not worrying about me for all eternity."

I didn't see a compromise. "I don't understand."

He was totally relaxed now, as beautiful in the light as if he'd been placed there by an artist for admirers to gather around and gaze upon. He reached out and took my hands, swinging our arms slightly between us in a childlike gesture.

"We jump," he said.

Wait.

"We *what?*" I said.

"We hold hands, and we don't hesitate. We don't let fear stop us. We leap. A leap of faith. And that way we'll be together forever, and Laina will be happy. She'll leave your sister alone, and she won't hurt anyone else."

I took a step back away from the cliff.

"Jared," I said. "I'm not going to jump."

"Listen to me." Now he was the one who was pleading. "Life is so hard for people like us. And it's never going to get easier. Believe me, Alexis. You will *never* have a day when you wake up and don't think about the people who have died because of you."

I started to turn my face away from his, but he reached up and grabbed my chin, preventing me from moving.

"It's not just Lydia now," he said. "It's Ashleen. And Elliot. And in a few hours, it'll be your sister. And then it will be more of them. Maybe Carter. Maybe Megan. Who knows? Don't you see? It'll never stop."

"Jared, you're hurting me." I tried to pull away.

But he didn't let go. "It won't ever stop, because what she wants is for me to be happy—and I'm never going to be happy."

He finally eased his grip, and I reached up and rubbed my sore jaw.

"You'll never be happy, either," he said quietly. "I can see it when I look in your eyes."

I jerked my eyes away from his gaze.

"Think about it." He rested his head on my shoulder. "There's no other way."

I'd thought there was another way.

I'd thought I could talk to him and change his mind. But I'd failed.

Just like I'd failed when I tried to save Elliot, and when I went out to help Ashleen. And now I would fail my sister. And by failing her, I would break my parents' hearts.

"Look at how beautiful the city is. Look how clean and bright and innocent." His fingers wove through mine, and he raised my hand to his lips and kissed it. "We don't belong there."

I couldn't speak. The English language had deserted me.

"What do you say?"

Now that he'd made up his mind, he was happier than I'd ever seen him. There was a lightness to his spirit that had never been there since we'd known each other— as if Laina's death had been an invisible thousand-pound weight that he carried around, and it was suddenly gone.

Still holding my hand, he hopped the guardrail and stood on the narrow strip of rock on the other side.

"Come on," he said. "We'll be free. We'll be brilliant. We'll be angels."

Somehow, I found myself standing next to him.

The breeze blew in, a seductive blend of cool and warm air.

"This is perfect." Jared lifted his head high and laughed into the wind. "This is perfect!"

His shout echoed through the canyon, and he turned to me. "This is what she deserves."

But—"It's not what *we* deserve," I said. "I don't deserve to die. I don't want to die."

I tried to pull my hand away from his, but we were linked like two pieces of a chain.

"Let go of me," I said. "You can jump if you want, but I'm not going to."

"It doesn't work that way," he said. "It has to be both of us."

I shook my head. My neck was stiff. My body was flooded with the exhaustion of the past ten hours.

"Trust me." He took a half step forward to look over the edge.

No.

I don't trust you.

He was wrong about too many things for me to trust him. And one of the things he was wrong about was that killing ourselves was the only way.

Because if he wouldn't come to terms with Laina . . . If he refused to shut off the faucet . . .

"Does your sister want to die?" he asked. "Does she deserve to die? Because if you don't do this with me, that's what's going to happen. And then they'll lock you up, and Laina will never quit."

But you could make it stop. You could turn off the faucet if you wanted to.

"It's what she wants," he said. "And it's what I want."

"Jared," I said.

He turned to me, a question in his eyes.

Blow up the kitchen.

I yanked my hand out of his grip.

And I pushed him. Hard.

37

HE CRIED OUT AS HE LOST his balance and began to slip backward. I reached behind me and grabbed the guardrail with my left hand—

And somehow Jared got hold of my right one.

He fell, but his hold on me stopped him from plunging into the canyon. The jolt made my left arm, which was hooked over the wide metal bar, feel like it would rip from my body, but I held the railing and didn't let go.

"Lydia!" I called, my voice blasting through the canyon. "Lydia! I need you!"

"What are you doing?" Jared growled. He struggled with his free hand to get a fingerhold on the rocks, and he was kicking his legs and flailing his body, which made it even harder to hang on.

My strength was about to give out. And I knew he would never let go of me . . . so it would be me letting go of the railing.

And we would both die anyway.

But not because I wanted to. Not because I was giving up. Not for nothing.

"Alexis!"

Lydia came into view next to me and immediately dropped to the ground and wrapped her arms around my waist from the other side of the guardrail.

"Let him go!" she said.

"I'm trying!" I said. "I can't!"

Jared was grunting, digging his fingers into my arm, cutting out half-moons of skin with his nails.

"Then let go of the guardrail," Lydia said, her voice vibrating through my body. "Alexis, I won't let you fall."

I looked at Jared, and at the vertical drop below him.

"What are you going to do?" Jared asked, shaking with effort. "Drop me? You think you can live with that? There are search parties down there, Alexis—and they can all see us. . . . You can't even look in a mirror without bursting into tears—you think you can live with being a killer?"

"I guess . . ." I swallowed hard. My jaw was chattering uncontrollably. "I guess I'm going to have to learn to."

And then, with nothing but a ghost to hold me, I let go of the guardrail and began to pry Jared's hand off my arm.

Jared's eyes flashed with a sudden shock of fear and

accusation as he realized what I was doing. "No! You can't do this! I don't want to be alone!"

But I managed to get my thumb under his thumb, and then it was like his hand just peeled off of my arm.

He slipped and seemed to stretch out over the space so that he was lying on his back, staring up into the sky . . . just like Laina.

And down, down, down he went.

38

AT 7:06 A.M. ON MARCH 3, I pushed my ex-boyfriend off a 103-foot cliff.

He landed on the rocks below, dead on impact.

Jared was right. There were search parties down in the canyon, and the people in the search parties could see the whole thing—my parents included.

My name is Alexis Warren. I'm sixteen years old.

And I'm a murderer.

39

I FELT LIKE I WAS EXISTING OUTSIDE OF MY BODY.

At the same time, there were plenty of reminders that I was in the real world: the cuffs on my wrists and ankles. The hard, slightly warped plastic of the chair beneath me. The edge of the table pressing a line in my stomach as I leaned forward, resting my head on my outstretched arms.

My parents were out there somewhere. I'd only gotten to see them for a minute, and all I could focus on was their glazed eyes. They looked at me differently—now that I was a cold-blooded killer. Everyone did. I felt the gazes of the police officers like indelible ink on my skin. I heard their shocked silence like a buzzing in my ears.

Kasey was safe. Carter and Megan were in custody. They were going to be questioned for helping me get away from Harmony Valley.

And Jared was dead.

But that was all I knew.

I hadn't seen Lydia since I fell backward onto the rock, hitting the back of my head on the guardrail and not realizing until I dragged myself down to the parking lot that I was bleeding all over myself.

I was waiting for my lawyer. I wasn't supposed to say anything to anyone without my lawyer. But what could I say?

Finally, the door opened.

Agent Hasan came in. I started to stand, but she held out a hand. "Don't get up."

As if I'd been doing it out of courtesy and not the desire to run away.

She sat down across from me, arms folded on the table. For a long time, we looked at each other.

"You killed Jared Elkins?" she asked.

"They told me not to talk without my lawyer," I said.

"Alexis, you killed Jared Elkins," she said. "He was unarmed. There were two dozen eyewitnesses. So look me in the eye and tell me two things: did you *have* to kill him?"

"Yes." I met her gaze. It was an admission, but what was I going to do, deny what I'd done? Jared was dead. His cold, lifeless body was laid out on a table somewhere. At that moment, his dad was probably being driven to the morgue to identify him. If I thought about it for too long, something inside of me started to feel like a tight-rope walker without a net. But I *had* done it.

And I'd do it again if I had to.

She made a mark on one of her papers. "Second question: can you assure me that it's over?"

"So, you believe me?" I said. "That I wasn't behind any of it?"

"Don't answer a question with a question."

"Yes," I said. "It's over."

She looked down at the table. "For the record, I believe you. And for what it's worth, putting you into Harmony Valley may have been . . . avoidable."

I rolled my eyes. "Apology accepted."

Agent Hasan stared at me for a long time. "You know there's zero evidence tying Jared to those girls' deaths."

"I know," I said. "And I'll bet there's a lot that ties me, right?"

She shifted in her seat. Then she leaned forward, resting her elbows on the table, which made her shoulders shrug up near her ears. She gave me a long look. "Yeah. There's a lot."

"It was self-defense. I have to find a way to make people believe me."

"You're not going to find a way, Alexis. You're the one with probable cause. He's literally an altar boy with a spotless record. So unless you can come up with a good reason for being at the scene of Ashleen's and Elliot's deaths—"

"I can see ghosts in photographs," I said.

The room was silent. Agent Hasan's expression betrayed more interest than she would have wanted it to. "Really."

"You couldn't find this ghost because it wasn't a ghost," I said. "It was a poltergeist. I knew how to find it, so I tried to save Ashleen and Elliot. And Jared could have made it stop, but he was never going to. The thing about a poltergeist—"

But she cut me off by holding up her hand. "Keep your secrets, Alexis. That's extraneous information at this point."

Of course. Because as long as there were no mice left in the pantry, she didn't care why they'd been there in the first place.

It wasn't like I could tell all that to a lawyer anyway.

"Purely out of curiosity," she said, looking almost amused, "why are you telling me all of this now, and not a week ago?"

Our eyes met. "I don't have anything to lose."

She shrugged, like that was as good a reason as any. "I've helped you a lot over the years, Alexis."

"Not because you wanted to." My voice was robotic.

I couldn't help but speak the absolute truth. And why not? What could she do to me? "Because it was your job to cover things up. To *take care* of them."

She sat back, adjusting herself in the chair as if my statement had been a jacket that didn't fit her right.

"What would you have done to me if you'd known?" I asked. "A week ago?"

"What would I have done?" Now she leaned forward so our faces were only a foot apart. "Probably the same thing I'm going to do now."

I held my breath.

"Offer you a job," she said.

I was so surprised that I actually laughed, though it came out sounding like someone had punched an unsuspecting cow. "Yeah, well . . . I'm about to go on trial for murder, so . . ."

"Now, come on. You know that I can take care of little problems like that."

Yeah, I knew it.

And she really meant it. She was willing to help me. "But . . . why?" I asked.

She shrugged, looking a little helpless. "You're smart. You're dedicated. You're relatively fearless. And God knows you're lucky as hell. So you might actually be useful."

I sat up. "Useful?"

"Useful. Meaning *of use*. An extra pair of hands . . . and eyes."

"Um," I said. "I don't think so."

"You're saying no, and I know you mean it," she said. "But do me a favor before you completely write me off: go back to school."

I stared up at her.

"Yeah, I said no third chances, but why not. Just make a deal with me. I'll get this charge lifted. I'll get everything explained away. I'll get a gun planted on the scene and Jared's fingerprints all over it. You'll be cleared for self-defense."

It certainly sounded too good to be true. "And what's my part of the deal?"

"Go back to your life. Try to be normal, now that everyone you know has seen you kill another human being."

"That's all?"

"That's plenty—and if you don't believe me now, you're going to very soon." As she spoke, she reached into her pocket and pulled out a key, first unfastening my wrists and then giving me the key so I could bend over and free my ankles. "I've met people like you, Alexis. They spend years trying not to feel like a freak transported in from another dimension. It *never* works. No one will ever look at you the same way again. And on top of that, you're tainted. Psychically speaking, you're a magnet. You're going to spend your whole life wondering what's coming. What spirit is going to be drawn to you next. Who's going to get hurt if you don't watch yourself."

I thought about Aralt and Laina. How they'd just seemed to sort of find me.

My resolve was beginning to weaken.

"Or . . . come with me. Be around people who understand you. Learn the ropes. Try your best to keep people safe from themselves."

I stared at the table, which was carved up with initials.

I was remembering my parents' faces as they watched me get loaded into a police car, handcuffed.

Then I imagined seeing that look in the eyes of every single person at school. All of them staring as I walked down the hall. Never having a moment when someone wasn't looking at me and thinking, *Killer.*

"If I went . . ." I said. "What about school?"

Agent Hasan started to answer.

"Oh, *please.*"

The voice came from behind me.

Lydia circled the room and stood next to Agent Hasan. "You're not seriously considering this, are you? News flash, Alexis: she doesn't help people—she locks them up. If you want to help people, you're just going to have to keep monkeying your own way through it. But God, that's better than being a nameless drone in a suit."

Agent Hasan finished her spiel. I hadn't heard a word of it.

Lydia came up beside me. "Do you know what she's really saying? She's saying come with her because you should be scared."

"But I *am* scared," I said.

Agent Hasan smiled, thinking my reply was for her.

"Yeah," Lydia said. "But that doesn't mean you run away and hide. I mean, think about it—has she ever actually helped you? So she's incredibly gifted at sweeping things under the rug. Is that what you want to be part of?"

I stared down at my hands.

"You know what?" Lydia said. "You have to make this decision for yourself." And she disappeared.

Agent Hasan was waiting for me to speak.

"I . . . I don't think I can go with you," I said. "I have to stay here. I have to at least try."

"Oh, sure. Good luck with that," Agent Hasan said, shaking her head and starting toward the door. "Tell you what—give it two weeks, then give me a call."

I looked around. "Do I just wait here, or . . . ?"

"Come with me," she said, gesturing to the hallway.

"You're free to go. You'll get a call from a man named Neilson. Just do exactly as he says and everything will be taken care of."

"Um . . . thank you." I almost said *for everything,* but I realized how untrue that was. "For your help today."

"Don't thank me now." As I walked past her, she patted me on the shoulder. "Thank me in two weeks. Have fun out there."

40

WE'D WAITED IN THE CAR until the last possible minute.

"Are you ready?"

I stared at the front of the school. "No."

Carter reached over and took my hand. "It's going to be okay, Lex."

"I don't know about that."

I stared into his eyes, as blue as a tropical sea. A tropical sea a million miles away. One I passionately wished I could be beamed to. Actually, at that moment I'd take pretty much anywhere but Surrey High.

"You're brave," he said. "And you're strong. You can do this."

"Sure, if you say so," I said, gazing at the doors.

The two-minute warning bell rang.

"I guess I have to go to my locker," I said. "See you at lunch?"

And suddenly I was alone, walking down the school

hallway, feeling like a famous actress making an entrance with a spotlight shining on me. Only the glances being shot at me weren't the kind of looks movie stars get.

I reached my locker.

About forty different people had scrawled MURDERER across the door.

You're brave. You're strong. You can do this.

I tore my gaze from the graffiti, pulled out my books, and went to first period. The teacher looked up at me, then went back to taking attendance. I was late, but he didn't say anything about it.

I sat in my normal desk. The four desks immediately surrounding it were empty.

When I got to second period, my library study hall, a security guard was sitting on the couch.

"I'm sorry, Alexis," Miss Nagesh, the librarian, said, fidgeting nervously. "You're not allowed to be in here unsupervised. And I'm afraid I don't have time to sit with you. So you're going to have to spend second period in the main office from now on."

I nodded and let myself be escorted across campus. In the main office, I sat at the in-school suspension desk in the corner and tried not to feel the eyes on me. Which was kind of like a dartboard ignoring the darts.

And so on.

Between third and fourth period I stopped by the

yearbook office. Fourth period was the yearbook elective class, so the *Wingspan* staff—most of whom were people I'd been eating lunch with for a month—were sitting at their desks.

Mr. Janicke stood up when I came in. "Oh! Alexis—it's, uh, nice to see you. I guess this is as good a time as any to, uh, talk. I hope you won't be too upset, but some members of the yearbook staff would be more comfortable if . . ."

"If I quit, right?" I said.

He nodded.

"Well, that's why I was coming by," I lied. "I was just going to drop off this memory card and tell you I decided to resign. So . . . good luck."

"Thanks," he said. "And we're still going to do the Lydia Small memorial for you. I think it's what Elliot would have wanted."

"Sure," I said. "Thanks."

By lunchtime, there was hardly a visible patch of paint on my locker. I even saw a couple of kids writing on it as I approached.

But you can imagine how fast they ran when they saw me coming.

Somebody had written BODY COUNT: 4.

And somebody else had written AND COUNTING.

Lydia, Ashleen, Elliot, and Jared. No matter what the official stories were, nobody seemed to believe anything except that I'd murdered them one by one, in cold blood.

At least Kendra had finally woken up. And she didn't remember anything about our conversation in the woods. So my body count wasn't five.

See? You can be a murderer AND an optimist.

I changed my morning books for my afternoon books and reached into my bag to grab the paperback I'd finished reading in English. But as my hand groped for the book, my fingers hit something small and hard.

I froze, then dug around until I found the hole in the seam, which I'd been too busy to repair. Something was stuck between the outer layer of fabric and the inner lining. I fished it out and stared in disbelief at the object in my hand: a small glass woodpecker attached to a thin gold necklace. I shut my locker door and reached up to fasten the chain around my neck.

Then I went to lunch.

I stepped into the cafeteria just as the bell rang.

And I swear on Lydia Small's grave, every eye in the room turned to me.

I figured sitting at the yearbook table was out. But I guess I'd thought that maybe my sister's friends might make room for me. Or the Doom Squad, maybe? They claimed to like scary people.

But everywhere I looked, tables were weirdly full.

Or not full . . .

They just didn't have any extra seats. Empty chairs were piled high with bags and coats.

Making it clear that I wasn't invited.

Back to my old seat at the Janitor's Table, then— except the whole table was gone.

I took one last look around the room of three hundred silent high school students, and something inside me threatened to break.

Why had I thought I could come back here?

I heard Agent Hasan's words in my head: *Good luck with that.*

And suddenly I didn't think I'd need two weeks to give her my answer, but I knew she'd make me suffer through two weeks of it anyway. Make me sink as low as I could go so I'd never be tempted to doubt her again.

But my miserable reverie and the quiet of the room were broken by the squeal of chair legs on linoleum.

And on the far side of the cafeteria, my sister stood up. A second later, Keaton stood up. And Mimi.

They started walking toward me.

From the other side of the room came the muffled

sounds of an argument, and then the words, "Then I *quit*!"

And Marley stood up from the yearbook table. Then Chad.

They walked toward me, too.

Kasey reached me first. "So I guess we need a new table."

"Um . . ." I braced myself to make sure my voice would be steady before I spoke. "I don't see one in here."

"It's totally warm enough," Marley said. "We'll sit outside."

"Did you really just quit yearbook?" I asked. "Both of you?"

She nodded.

"They'll never make it to print without you guys."

Those were tough words for a lifelong overachiever to hear. Marley winced a little, but she forced herself to smile. "I don't care. Elliot would have wanted it this way. She would have told them all to go to hell."

As we walked out to the courtyard, Lydia appeared next to me. "Five friends? That's five more than you had freshman year."

I laughed.

"What's so funny?" Kasey asked, settling on a picnic table.

"Nothing," I said.

"Lex!" Across the courtyard, Carter was sprinting toward us, dodging the kids who sat on the ground.

I set my lunch box on the table and headed to intercept Carter. I would have run, but I didn't want to cause mass hysteria.

When I reached him, he wrapped his arms around me. "I'm sorry. I got stuck talking to my teacher. I didn't know. I didn't mean to leave you alone."

"It's okay," I said. "I'm not alone, actually."

Carter looked over my shoulder and saw the table full of people. Then he pulled me into a hug.

I closed my eyes and thought, *Maybe they'll never like me. Maybe I'll always be an outcast.*

Life might be pretty crazy from now on.

But maybe crazy was my new normal.

"You all right?" Carter asked, lifting my hand and kissing it.

I raised my chin and stood up straight.

I've been bad.

I've been good.

Weak and strong.

Brave and afraid.

A hero and a killer.

But the one thing I've never done is run from my problems. And Agent Hasan wasn't going to scare me into running now.

I reached up and touched the tiny curl of hair that was growing over Carter's ear. "I think so," I said. "I mean, I will be."

And I would, even if it took a year, five years, ten years—I would be all right.

I knew it in my gut.